PRA

FOR MY SISTER

"A beautifully told story that will break your heart, open your soul, and ignite a fire within to become part of the solution. Share it far and wide with all of your sisters."

—Arielle Ford, International Best-Selling Author of *The Soulmate Secret*

"There is a timeless longing you feel that makes you want to keep turning the pages. Puja Shah delivers this reality in a way that is mournful, yet gentle and kind."

—Christina Rasmussen, Best-Selling Author of *Second Firsts*

"Puja Shah's riveting words will grasp you from the first page, leaving you feeling every emotion along the way. This is a book people won't stop talking about."

—Jyoti Chand, Influencer and Author of *Fitting Indian*

"Puja has created a world full of vibrant and rich characters who exemplify the human spirit. Her graceful poetry is seamlessly intertwined to not only be hopeful, but cheer for everyone in this book."

—Sheetal Sheth, Award-winning Actress and Author of *Always Anjali*

"Puja Shah's exquisite debut novel is a thoughtfully researched and captivating story illuminating the unbreakable bonds of sisterhood."

—Dr. Rashmi Bismark, Author of *Finding Om*

"*For My Sister* is at once both a hopeful tale of sisterhood, love, and resilience and also a heart-wrenching cautionary tale."

—Huda Al-Marashi, Author of *First Comes Marriage*

"A masterfully written book that awakens every emotion and a much-needed narrative. . . . *For My Sister* is easily stacked with some of the best books I've read."

—Dianne C. Braley, Author of *The Silence in the Sound*

"*For My Sister* is a gripping and deeply moving story. . . . This page-turner is full of insight, inspiration, heartbreak, and hope."

—Tejal V. Patel, Author of *Meditation for Kids*

"Puja Shah's honest and contemplative story embraces that which is wonderful about India, even as it cries out for social transformation. Rich in the texture of its use of language, Puja Shah's first novel is a work of marvelous beauty."

—Marsha J. Tyson Darling, PhD, Renowned Professor

"Bravo! . . . Puja Shah is precisely the fiction writer the literary world and global readers need to finally begin understanding the plight of women and girls across the globe."

—Sasha K. Taylor, Child Marriage Survivor

"Puja is a masterful storyteller. *For My Sister* is a story of hope and empowerment. This novel is an important read for all."

—Susie Walton, Author of *Key To Personal Freedom*

"*For My Sister* is an engrossing tale of twin sisters. . . . Their story will pull you in and not let go."

—Carla Damron, Author of *The Orchid Tattoo* and *The Stone Necklace*

"*For My Sister* is a beautiful and profound story of hope that vividly captures the strength of the human spirit."

—Shetal Shah, Author of *Shakti Girls*

"I was totally engrossed. . . . I highly recommend *For My Sister*—the interplay of tension and emotion will keep you reading until the final page."

—Professor Winona Howe, Author of *Sita and The Prince of Tigers*

"Puja Shah's vibrant prose, intriguing narrative and thoughtful storytelling in *For My Sister* makes for an engaging and beautifully written novel."

—Penny Haw, Author of *The Invincible Miss Cust* and *The Wilderness Between Us*

"Powerful storytelling, it's a heartbreaking story that is still able to evoke hope as it shares the beauty and struggle of perseverance and resilience."

—Sonee Singh, Author of *Lonely Dove* and *The Soul Seeker Collection*

"An incredibly intense and riveting read."

—Amy Maranville, Author of *Padmini Is Powerful*

"*For My Sister* is an important book, bringing forth a social issue and message for change that is deep within Puja Shah's beautiful prose. A must-read!"

—Jill McManigal, Co-Founder and Executive Director of Kids for Peace Global nonprofit

"Through a compelling narrative about fictional sisters Asya and Amla, author Puja Shah brings to light the all too real and common, evil of human trafficking...the courage, and love shown by the sisters in this story, and those who helped them to escape, is present in so many real survivors, and those who, as we speak, are suffering in human slavery."

—Alisa Gbiorczyk, Head of Global Operations, DeliverFund nonprofit

"Even as you read this very engaging novel today, every thirty seconds another child becomes a victim of human trafficking across the globe."

—Mangneo Lhungdim, Executive Director of NGO Oasis India

For My Sister

by Puja Shah

ISBN 978-1-64663-796-6

Published by

3705 Shore Drive
Virginia Beach, VA 23455
800-435-4811
www.koehlerbooks.com

Dearest Mom ♡
In honor of you and how
you give, plus the example you
are of, growing into your
esteem & the stand
you are
for education
I donated
$250 in
your name
and honor
for
"just like
my child"
This
book
tells
the story
of the
change
needing
to happen
and this
organization
is doing just
that.
Love you, J✓

PUJA SHAH

FOR
MY
SISTER

A NOVEL

♡

Poya S

VIRGINIA BEACH
CAPE CHARLES

"Never stop writing."
—Late Krishna Shah, Dada

TABLE OF CONTENTS

PART 1

AMLA

MARCH 2003

CHAPTER 1

Our tribulations began when Mummy began to lose weight. Suddenly she had to wrap her sari twice more than normal, and her petticoat hung low since it did not fit her small waist anymore.

Nani asked Mummy if she was eating—if there was enough food. "Are Asya and Amla getting enough, too?" she whispered in the kitchen while I helped Mummy knead the roti dough for that evening's dinner. "They are fifteen and still so skinny."

"Yes, of course, I am just feeling more tired lately. I don't know. Maybe it's an infection. But please do not worry; we use the well now and boil the water. I do not have a fever. It will pass . . ."

Nani looked uneasy as she helped Mummy carry her pots to the stove.

We had heard of many neighbors getting a stomach infection that summer. Mostly it was the families who brought water from the river, where the new American company let their factory's pipes empty. They said the waste was healthy—that it was leftover drugs for American families, helping them to have healthy hearts and to fight their infections.

Puppa didn't believe it. At breakfast one morning, when we were eating roti and mango pickle, he said the Americans were so plump, how could they need anything else to be healthier? Mummy asked him if he had ever seen an American.

"What kind of question is that?" he had shouted at her, throwing his thali in her face.

Luckily, he missed, and the plate of food landed on the floor. We hated when he was angry. While Asya and I cleaned it up, I asked him again, for Mummy: "But *have* you, Puppa?"

And for a minute he looked at me like he would throw the rest of his breakfast, but he kept his eyes on his cup. "No, but I have heard that they are very healthy, not scrawny like you and your sister." He tore the roti that remained in his hand, dipping it into his cup of steaming chai. I looked at my sister, who raised her eyebrows as if to say, "That's enough." To me, these were the small wins I held inside. It felt better than staying silent.

I knew it was not this way for Asya. She preferred to stay out of trouble. While we looked the same, my sister and I, we were quite different. Everyone always confused us, even with the brown birthmark on her forearm and the small mole next to my ear, which my hair always covered.

When we were born in our small village in Madhya Pradesh, our nani, who helped the nurse birth us, told Mummy, "Two girls! His family will curse you. Give them names with meanings so they can carry their heads high."

When Puppa came into the room, Nani began to fold the blankets she'd placed around each of us so Puppa could hold us, but he said, "I do not wish to hold them." Asya turned her head to Puppa, and I put my hand on Mummy's heart, and he walked out, unable to scold our mother in our presence.

Mummy said she was at her childhood home, lying on the hemp cot, holding us, one in each arm, as she recovered from the delivery. The birthing nurse was a Dalit who would not normally look Mummy in the eyes, yet when she saw our mother's tears, she held a wet towel to Mummy's forehead.

That is how we got our names. Amla means "pure love," and Asya is "strength and grace." These were the qualities Mummy saw in us early on—Asya's kind heart, even in the face of such disdain from Puppa, and my compassion when I held my hand up to my mother's heart, as if to soothe her, even though I, too, was being rejected. Mummy said we were her *devis*, her angels from Rama.

Everyone in the village looked at Mummy with pity when they heard the news of her twin girls. She walked in the village openly, often wearing both of us in a wrapped cotton cloth around her small torso. They were surprised when she would smile at us, cooing at our almost white faces.

We inherited our golden, tawny skin from our nana, along with our mother's jet-black hair and almond-shaped hazel eyes. Mummy also said he passed his strong voice to me, while Asya had his quiet understanding.

Mummy later told me that she was sure everyone could hear my strong voice when I cried. "Beyond the walls of our small village, into the mountains and all the way up to the skies," she would say, holding out her hands dramatically. But I always quiet down when I was placed next to Asya.

It did not take long for Puppa and his parents to find love for us, despite the double burden we had brought on our family. Our nani would walk from her home nearby to rub sesame oil on our skin to keep it from darkening. Dadi would tell Nani to use coconut oil instead, and the bickering would start.

Mummy said she did not mind them fighting over what they thought was best for us. She was grateful for it—for the love we brought into her home, and for the ability to see her own mother every day. There was also the matter of our redirecting Dadi's attention so that her critical eye didn't wander to Mummy's *daal*, how she prepared rice pudding, or how she folded towels. She had not planned on becoming a mother at age nineteen.

Our grandfather had not raised our mother for housework. Nana had wanted her to be a teacher, and planned to send her to college. But he passed away when Mummy was only seventeen, so Mummy's journey was over far too soon; they could no longer afford her schooling. Even though she truly wanted her daughter to have a higher education, Nani didn't think it was practical; they would never be able to afford it. She insisted it would be better for Mummy to get married.

Suitors came from neighboring villages when they heard of how beautiful she was, but only Puppa's family promised they would allow Mummy to finish her schooling after marriage. So, despite their low income, despite Puppa's crooked teeth and large nose, she agreed to marry him. It was her only chance of becoming a teacher.

When I was ten years old, I asked Mummy, "Why didn't you finish your dream? Was it because we were born? Was it because Puppa lied?"

Mummy's eyes became wet with tears, and Asya pinched me. She hugged Mummy and told her that when we were older we would make sure she finished her schooling and assured her that she could even teach our kids in school—her future grandchildren.

I bit my lip as I listened to my sister's assurances and wondered if we would be able to fulfill them in a world where girls were lied to. How many lies had Mummy heard in her life?

CHAPTER 2

I stood by the water well with Chotu. We had just finished welcoming spring with Holi earlier that week. I kept thinking about how we had smeared colors on each other's cheeks. I saw Asya running towards us, and I was annoyed. She always tried to stop us from talking. "Boys just want one thing, Amla," she would chide me. "Remember what Mummy told us? We are the fairest girls in the village. We have to be careful."

When we started bleeding every month, Mummy gave us a lecture on boys. Our breasts were forming, and she told us that boys would notice us more. It made Asya more cautious, but it had the opposite effect on me; I was more curious about boys than ever. I became aware of what I found attractive, the way Chotu smiled or winked when he made a joke. What did boys notice about me?

It seemed to me that lately, Asya never wanted to have fun, even though I knew how she felt about Sandeep bhai. "Be present," Sandeep bhai said during surya namaskar, our sun-salutation exercises. I caught Asya watching him as he passed by our row when we bowed to the earth, then stretched back up to touch the sky.

I asked her one day while we walked home, "Why do you always look at Sandeep bhai like that?"

"Like what?" She kicked a Thums Up can on the road.

"Like he is Shah Rukh Khan." When she tried to deny it, I just rolled my eyes at her. "Asya, when will you realize, I always feel what you feel. I just know."

She told me how she really felt, and this time I listened: She got warm when he spoke to her. She liked his wide smile and how his hair curled at the ends. He had recently graduated with a secondary-school teaching degree, but after working as a bus boy for extra money at a yoga ashram in Mumbai that was known to be visited by movie stars, he returned home and chose to teach yoga like his own great-grandfather had done instead. Yoga had not been taught at our school before, but his family knew the headmaster, who agreed to allow it.

When Asya got to the well, out of breath, I felt her fear. She didn't have to say anything. Something was wrong, I knew.

"Asya?"

Her jaw tightened. That was how she stayed strong. She told me we needed water fast.

Chotu asked, "What happened?"

Asya did not look at Chotu. She explained that she and Nani had been gathering the coriander leaves from the garden when they heard the clay pot in the kitchen hit the ground. Mummy was on the floor. She was vomiting fluid and blood. It was all around her head as she lay there throwing up, holding her stomach and heaving as Nani ran to Mummy and screamed at Asya to get water.

Asya's eyes were wet, and Chotu lifted the bucket from the well faster than I had ever seen him do, handing it to me before Asya took it from my paralyzed arms.

"Amla, hurry!"

She ran towards the house, her white linen dupatta swaying behind her and her silky hair pulling away from her long braid, her feet hitting the ground hard, with a grace I knew I could not follow.

"I'm scared," I said to Chotu, wanting to fall into his arms. Chotu put his hand on my shoulder, squeezed it, and told me to go. I expected to see him right behind me as I ran to Mummy. When I turned my head, he was getting smaller in the distance. I turned my head away from him and rushed forward.

My heart beating fast, my head started spinning at seeing Mummy like that—just how Asya had described her, in an expanding pool of blood. It had already been almost half an hour since she had fallen.

With us crouched beside her, Nani was putting the towel on her forehead when Puppa walked in.

He looked pale at how sick Mummy looked, like she had lost the light inside of her. He kissed Mummy on the head and stroked her hair. "Jaya, please, please . . ."

Asya went to him and took his hand as I held back my tears and wrung the cloth in the hot-water pot for Nani. What was happening to Mummy? The fear rose from my stomach, enveloped my heart, and rushed out as hot tears. It felt like when I was a little girl clutching Asya's hand as we rushed through legs at the market. I was always afraid that if I didn't hold tight enough to Asya, who was holding on to Mummy, I would lose sight of Mummy's sari and lose her forever.

I tried to memorize the details of our family in that room, pretending it was a photograph: Puppa's eyes on Mummy, the stack of Mummy's folded petticoats on the chair, the sun beaming into the room with air particles floating about and highlighting Asya's hair. I wanted it all to stand still.

Puppa called his parents, and they arrived faster than they had when Asya and I were born, or so Nani said under her breath. They brought Dr. Pathak with them, and he told us he would need to bring Mummy to the city hospital for tests, that this was serious.

"Asya, Amla, pack her clothes," Nani said. I looked over to Mummy's petticoats, thinking of what to bring to the hospital, but Asya had already started packing. Dada pulled Puppa aside, telling him to stay strong for his family and stop crying.

Puppa shook his head. He took deep breaths and pinched his nose to stop the tears.

Dadi was telling Asya it would be all right, that Mummy was going to get better. *Is she?* I wondered. I whispered a prayer of protection, pouring the Sanskrit sounds out into the sunbeam before me.

Even though he wasn't talking to me, I took in Dada's words and swallowed the tears trying to creep up my throat again. I looked over at Asya, who looked scared but tightened her jaw. I had to be strong for my mummy too.

CHAPTER 3

At first, Nani came to help with the housework every morning after Mummy left since Dadi told Puppa that her weak knees made it hard for her to do it all. After breakfast, Nani would wash the dishes and sweep the floor. The morning she spilled chai on Puppa's new trousers, Dadi started screaming at her, and Asya and I looked at each other. I didn't want Nani to leave; she reminded me of Mummy—the way she hummed while grating ginger for the chai, the way she paused each time to pick the incense scent during her morning prayer. I was afraid of what it would be like without Nani. Like we would lose more of Mummy than we already had.

Dadi told Nani that she was causing too much trouble and wasn't helping at all. Asya and I were standing at the doorway, gathering our things for school. The way Dadi carried on, it was as if she had forgotten we were even there. "If it wasn't for Jaya being sick, look at our family, we would not be struggling. My poor son has to work even harder to keep up with these hospital fees." I saw anger in Dadi's eyes—the type of anger that came from fear. She was just as scared as we all were.

Yet it wasn't Nani's fault that she had spilled the chai. Her arthritis was getting worse. Puppa bought medicine for Dadi, but no one did that for Nani, and still she never complained about anything, even when her hands shook.

Nani looked at Dadi and then at us before saying, "We will speak when Asya and Amla are at school. Let's go, girls. You must not be late."

Asya pulled my hand to move behind the front door gate where they could no longer see us, but we could still listen in from the broken window. We wanted to hear what else Dadi said. I wondered if maybe they would talk more about why Puppa never let Mummy go back to study.

"And with you always here, with your daughter always doting on these girls, how will we get them married? How will they ever know how to do anything?"

What did she mean? We did so much, and wasn't it for our own livelihood to know how to cook? Now I started to understand Dadi's desire was to prep us to be good wives, for our future husbands' livelihood.

Nani defended us, like Mummy would have, and told Dadi we knew plenty. That Mummy made us help with the dinner every night, and that we did the ironing and laundry every weekend. "They are studying so they can go to the city and have real jobs. Amla has told me she loved learning about Indira Gandhi. Times are changing."

Nani was right. I had shared my thoughts with her after we read about Indira as the first female prime minister of India. Years later, no woman had followed her. Nani had mentioned Prime Minister Gandhi was not popular during the Emergency, and that even Nana had been forced to have a surgery. "But you, Amla, I know you will be a wonderful prime minister." I wondered what she meant about Nana, but I never asked.

I looked over at Asya, who looked worried. "Asya, don't worry. Nani will let her know who's right." I winked at her, but Asya's expression didn't change.

"And what will studying do? Did it do anything for your daughter?" Dadi snapped back.

I felt heat rise within me. Mummy was smarter than all the other students' mothers, who did not even know how to read or sign their own names on homework assignments for their children.

"No, it did not help her," Nani said softly. "But it will help these girls. They are smart. We must let them study."

I heard Puppa flutter the paper in the kitchen, but he stayed silent. Why didn't he defend us? His wife? Didn't he tell her he loved her when she left for the hospital? Where was that love? Mummy always said men were cowards in front of their mothers. Was that what was happening now?

"With these hospital fees, who can afford school fees for these girls? There are two of them, remember? If anything, we could only send one to college. Who will tell them this? How can we choose which one?"

Nani didn't answer. I decided right then and there that I would never let that happen; we could never be apart. Yet I still felt scared. So much of our lives were not in our control. Asya and I stared at each other as if we had already been separated. She hugged me hard as I tried not to think of the day we would be apart.

When we got to school, we rushed off to our classrooms. For a second, I thought to confess my theft to Asya, but we didn't have time. We were already late. Other children were rushing too. It was the beginning of April, and the heat that came before the monsoon holidays had started to settle into the village earlier than usual.

I felt a pang of guilt as I opened my rucksack and took out Asya's ruler along with my books. I had lost mine when I snuck out to meet Chotu by the field behind our school while Mummy was shopping. We did our homework first, but when he started kissing my shoulder, time escaped us. I had to run home and probably dropped it in my haste to gather my belongings. When I went back to look for it, it was nowhere to be found. So when Asya wasn't looking, I grabbed hers. I needed it; our class always did math review before hers anyway. I'd get it back to her in time. I could have asked her, but I knew she would look at me in disappointment, like I was messing up once again.

When it was time for geometry readings, I took out Asya's ruler, its edges clean and shiny—the way Asya always kept her things. She had wrapped hers in a small cotton cloth, keeping the numbers bright, unlike mine that had begun to dull.

I finished my worksheet quickly and asked our teacher, Mistress Urvi, to let me use the bathroom. She said no and told me to wait. I folded my legs together, pretending I couldn't wait another minute. Still she made me wait.

By the time Mistress let me go, Asya's class was well into their math time. Kicking myself for doing this to my sister, I ran over to her classroom fast and peered in. The students there were also working on their worksheets. I saw Asya placing her thumb on the paper. I recognized the gesture. Mummy had shown us how to measure an inch by holding our thumbs and index fingers a certain length apart. She had also shown us how to calculate the difference to centimeters, even though we would never learn that in school. Mummy said it was in case we ever went to the US, like a few of the villagers who went on to Mumbai for university had done.

I knocked and cleared my throat before I spoke. Asya's teacher was far stricter than my own and always looked at you like you were smaller than you were.

"Amla, how can we help you?"

"I have my sister's ruler; may I give it to her?"

"And why do you have her ruler? Your mother was told to purchase two rulers."

The day we purchased them at the market, Mummy had brought the price down to half when she told the shopkeeper that she had two of us attending at the same time, unlike the other mothers who could buy one that could be passed down to all the younger siblings.

Mummy was wearing her peacock-colored salwar kameez, the one with the beautiful flowing scarf. Her eyes always looked green when she wore it, and with her wide smile, I knew he would not say no to her. He handed her the wooden rulers, telling her he would make an exception.

I should have told Asya I broke mine. That would have been the right thing to do. But I knew it would end up getting back to Mummy, who would tell Puppa, and I would be scolded . . . or maybe even worse.

Asya raised her hand as Mistress Sheela raised her eyebrows. "Yes, Asya?"

"Mistress Sheela, I let Amla borrow mine. It is my fault. I forgot to retrieve it from her, and she must have thought it was hers." Asya let her eyes meet mine before they fell to her feet. Her disappointment made my heart beat faster from shame.

"There is punishment for failing to be prepared, Asya. You understand this?"

"Yes, Mistress."

I stood holding the ruler and feeling defeated. It was a worse feeling than when I had eaten both halves of the Western chocolates Mummy saved for Asya and me on our fifth birthday. That morning, Mummy had placed a Cadbury bar on the table, triumphantly, the purple wrapper and gold foil gleaming like treasure. Our neighbor had gone to Mumbai for a wedding months prior, and Mummy had arranged for her to bring the chocolate back for us. It must have taken Mummy saving money from her trips to the market, probably negotiating the okra price and skipping cashews that week, to give Pushpa auntie the money to purchase the chocolate.

Mummy said she would cut the chocolate bar in half that evening after dinner, for each of us. That afternoon, as we waited for Mummy to prepare our special dinner, I decided to climb the tree near our house. I could hear Asya below me, screaming at me to come down, that it wasn't safe, and sure enough, I fell. My elbow took the worst of it. That evening, we never celebrated with the chocolates. Between the doctor, my bandages, and all the prayers and gratitude that I was okay, we went to bed later than usual. Mummy handed us the chocolate halves as she kissed us each good night, telling us to wait until morning so we could rest. When she left the room, we each took small bites and placed our chocolates next to our pillows.

The next morning I was still in pain, so Mummy kept me home with her. I was jealous that Asya would be at school with our friends. I felt so sorry for myself that after Asya left for school, I ate both pieces. I felt horrible, but when Asya got home, she didn't even complain. She hugged me and told me I had hardly missed anything that day.

"Alright, Amla. Hand your sister the ruler. She will have ten points deducted from her marks today."

I walked over and gave my sister her ruler. She kept her eyes down, taking it without looking at me. I squeezed her hand, trying to tell her I was sorry. I was relieved when she squeezed back. She gently let go and mouthed, "It's okay."

CHAPTER 4

In the weeks following Mummy's hospitalization, lots of things changed. Nani did not come to the house as often, and Dadi gave us chores "to teach us to be responsible," which meant we were alone most of the time. Puppa got a second job as a train station guard to pay for Mummy's doctor fees and didn't get off work until the middle of the night. It gave me more freedom to sneak out and see Chotu. He had found a deserted shack by an old farm near the school. Even if we just lay together, it felt better being with him than at home, like I was escaping the heaviness of uncertainty I felt every day Mummy was gone.

One night after being with Chotu, I walked in to see Asya doing her Sanskrit homework on her bed.

"Where were you?" she asked.

I didn't bother lying; she already knew where I had been. "Asya, I'm home now. Don't worry." Her eyes followed me as I walked over to my knapsack and pulled out my homework and sat next to her.

"No, you can't copy anything." She covered her sheet so I could not see. Why did she automatically assume I was up to no good?

"I'm not copying. There's just more light on your side."

"If you changed the kerosene in your lamp once in a while, you'd have light too."

Why was Asya so angry? Because I had left her alone most of the evening after dinner? I looked around and realized she had cleaned up the kitchen all on her own. I touched her hand, but she pulled away.

"I'm sorry, Didi," I said. "I'll make the chapati tomorrow morning so you don't have to."

Her eyes became softer, and her shoulders came away from her ears as she shifted in her seat.

"You run around hiding behind buildings with Chotu all night and think I am supposed to just say it's okay? Amla, you'll never grow up. And do you think Chotu wants to marry you? Rachna told me he is going to be promised to his father's best friend's daughter, who is rich and smart and will study to be a doctor in Jaipur."

I pressed my lips together and grabbed her homework sheets.

"Hey!" She lunged for my arm, but I swung around and tore the worksheets in half.

"What do you know? You don't know what it's like to be in love! You sit there dreaming about your yoga teacher, and guess what, Asya? He will never love you. He doesn't even know your name!"

She pushed me hard, and we were on top of one another until I pulled her hair and threw the steel bathing bucket across the room.

"I hate you!"

Asya let me go. The kerosene lamp flickered above her as she held the crumpled homework in her hands. She didn't even look up at me when I ran out of the house.

My head was spinning and heart pounding after our fight. It was the first time I had ever told Asya I hated her. I didn't, of course, but what she said really hurt. And really, what did she know about love? What did she know about Chotu and me? She thought it was all about him wanting to kiss me, when we actually shared moments and dreams with each other. When Chotu had a fight with his father, he cried to me and said he had never talked about his feelings like that with anyone. Mostly, I knew Asya was jealous of me being close to anyone else. Even at school she was like that. Just because we were sisters didn't mean she owned me.

I didn't know where to go, but Chotu had said he would be fixing his scooter that night, so I hoped he would still be outside. I heard voices as I walked around the well, approaching his family's compound. Chotu's family lived in a nicer area than our own. The homes had small front gates and an outdoor space that fit not only a scooter but a parked car as well. His father was a bank clerk in a neighboring town and wore Western button-up shirts to work.

Chotu was outside tightening a bolt on his scooter, and I started towards him eagerly but stopped at the sound of his voice.

"Of course, yaar. She's easy. I'll have her panties off by next week."

My face burned. I heard his friend laughing, maybe Jintan. My heart sank deep within me as he continued.

"Just today, I was saying, 'Oh, Amla, your eyes are so beautiful.' I'm like a natural Akshay Kumar. I love those little tan nipples of hers, that's for sure."

Jintan stepped into the light. "How big are her nipples?" he asked. "Half a rupee size, or bigger?"

I turned away, ashamed at myself for thinking he'd meant it when he kissed my eyelids, telling me he loved my nose and small ears . . . touching my stomach, saying it felt right.

I contemplated leaving, but I marched up to them instead. What would they say to my face? Jintan saw me first and nudged Chotu, whose mouth dropped.

"A-amla," he stammered.

"Answer him, Chotu. Half a rupee size or bigger?"

Jintan murmured a goodbye as he hurried off.

"Amla, you know I would never answer him. I care about us—"

"Us? There's no us now, Chotu." I walked away with my head held high, then started sprinting when I was out of sight.

By the time I returned home, I was out of breath after swallowing tears the whole time. I sat against our dwelling wall with nowhere to go. Asya was probably still upset, and I missed Mummy. I cried without holding back, burying my face between my legs. I felt horrible for saying I hated Asya. Would she forgive me? Why hadn't I listened to her about Chotu?

The door opened, and I heard my sister's voice as if I had called her there. "Amla?"

I let the warmth of her hands, something I knew before even entering the world, comfort me. I let myself fall into her as my sister held me close—without judgment.

CHAPTER 5

Two months after Mummy was admitted to the hospital, when Dada called Dr. Desai from the SDT shop near Dadi and Dada's home, the doctor told him we should come to see her. The cancer was getting worse, and they needed to operate immediately. Dada told the doctor we would come. They didn't mention that Puppa was still saving for the operation fees.

Puppa said we would take the truck with the goods going on the Mumbai route, which would drop us at the bus transfer, and then catch another, bigger bus to Mumbai.

"Will Nani be coming?"

I wondered how we would all fit, how Nani would be able to travel with her arthritis, what would happen if Dadi came also.

"No, just the three of us. It is all we can afford for now, and Nani has said she cannot take the bus that long, so she will see Mummy when she comes home."

"When she's all better," I said matter-of-factly. I did not understand the commotion about this *cancer*, but I did know that Mummy was strong. She always got better before any of us. People were always amazed that her tiny body had carried both of us.

"Yes, beti." Puppa's eyes were tired. As he looked out the window, I wondered if he was still crying at night. Puppa had become softer without Mummy around. There was no more shouting, no more throwing things. He cried more than he yelled now. I suppose it was better.

I was excited about the idea of taking a trip and seeing Mummy. I missed her voice the most. The comfort in her singing, the way I listened for her in the morning to wake me.

I looked at Asya, but she was staring down at her hands and looked worried. "Is the operation scary, Puppa?"

Puppa glanced at Asya and shook his head. "No, beti. Dr. Desai just wants to talk to us about it. Let's go see on Sunday together."

I finished giving Puppa his chai and went to my cot, burying my face in my pillow. After what happened with Chotu, Asya had let me sleep in her cot for the whole week. I had moments where I remembered our conversation, unable to think about seeing him again. What would I tell Mummy? She always knew when something was off with me.

Asya came in to sit beside me and touched my back.

"Mummy will know something is wrong, and I will have to tell her, Asya. How can I face her? She will be so disappointed in me."

The fact that we had kissed and that he had touched my breasts was embarrassing. No one in the village even thought of doing such things before marriage.

"Amla, it's okay. Mummy won't judge you. You don't need to tell her anything. Just be the Amla she loves. She probably misses that."

I did miss running behind Mummy to scare her while she was cooking, or grabbing the cauliflower and eating bits of it without asking while she was cutting pieces. It always made her laugh the whole time.

"I love you, Asya," I said as I threw the pillow at her. When she giggled, I knew I had my sister back.

"Are you worried about Mummy's surgery?" I took the moment to let her open up to me, thinking of how she looked with Puppa. As excited as I was to see Mummy again, I was worried, too, and hadn't felt able to talk to Asya about it. There was so much fear in the air at home these days that it was impossible not to get caught up in it.

"I don't understand what it means when they say it is spreading. Where and why? No one is telling us anything, and it seems like even Puppa doesn't understand it. That's what scares me even more."

I nodded in agreement. I didn't have any answers, but I held my sister's hand. There was a quiet strength between us when we were together.

• • •

The trip to Mumbai would be the biggest adventure of our lives. We had never left the village, and Puppa could see how excited we were. We sensed that he was also excited, since he let us buy Maaza mango juice from the bus stand and smiled when we talked of Mummy. It was a nice distraction from my heartache at losing Chotu.

"Your mummy will be very happy to see you both," he said after we boarded the bus. Asya and I shared a seat, as Puppa had paid for only one ticket between us. Asya's concerns gnawed at my mind, but I still felt hopeful for Mummy and believed that if she just saw us, she would feel better and maybe gain strength to stop this cancer spreading in her body.

The journey was long, and Puppa had told us not to pack many clothes so we wouldn't have to pay a luggage fee. We would be staying with his best friend from his old job, who lived close to Mummy's hospital and had girls our age whose clothes we could borrow. I didn't mind borrowing clothes; it was fun to wear different things than my own. But when we were leaving, I saw Asya had tied an extra dupatta around her waist, saying she wanted something of her own to bring.

Mummy always told us how very alike Asya and I were—in how we smiled or what we found humorous. Yet the ways we were different seemed to surface more without Mummy's voice to remind me. It was suddenly clearer to me how hard it was to come into my own self when everyone was always comparing me to how well Asya did something or listened. I knew Asya could sense this, our constant threat to one another as we tried to root our own identities into the world. It was an unspoken way of life for us. I looked over at her and saw her gazing out the window. The silence of our bus ride invited these thoughts to my mind. Did she ever think about this too? Would this ever change?

I watched the empty fields pass by, the dirt roads filling the air around us with a haze, each minute taking us closer to Mummy.

When we arrived in Mumbai, it was already dark. Everyone rushed off the bus, and it felt like being inside a swarm of mosquitoes from the monsoons. Puppa kept us close and told us to hold each other's hands, hold his shirt, as we tried to get through the hundreds of people at the station.

From the corner of my eye, I saw the men Puppa had warned us about before our journey. We were far away from our village where we called the men our uncles and everyone knew our father, and his father, and our mother's father and our grandmothers. These men held alcohol bottles in brown bags, and their eyes searched my sister and me, sending a chill down my spine. Leery, I squeezed Asya's hand tighter, thinking of Babu bhai at the chaiwala stand and Nilang uncle from the post office, whose eyes would never search us this way. I wondered, *Is this where Mummy was sent to be better?* Asya walked faster, pulling me and hugging Puppa's arm. We needed to get to Mummy as fast as we could.

CHAPTER 6

Our new cousins annoyed me. They were not our real cousins like Saranga, our father's sister's daughter at whose wedding we danced in the streets all night. These cousins were the children of Puppa's good friend Guhan uncle; Asya and I tried not to laugh when we saw the cheap wig he kept pinned to his head.

Guhan uncle and Puppa had worked as cleaners for Air India together ten years ago. When Air India had layoffs, Puppa went back to the village and got work at the railway station. Guhan advanced departments, though, and they offered him a job in their London office, where he worked for several years. The family had returned to Mumbai just last month, after what Guhan uncle called "a minor disagreement" with his boss.

His daughters were not twins like us but were close enough in age to seem like twins. The girls kept asking Asya and me if we had ever seen movies or if we knew what Cadbury chocolates were, as if we were coming from another country.

"We do not live so far from Mumbai, you know," I told them. And they would smile at each other and ask us more: "Do you have electricity in your village? I heard you have to get your water from a well outside and even go to the bathroom in a hole outside? Do you know what a toilet is? Have you ever had Maggi noodles?" Whenever we betrayed our ignorance, they would react incredulously. "You *really* never had Maggi noodles?"

I wanted to ask them if they have ever watched a guru who was over 100 years old sit on a hill for thirty days straight, all during Sravana month, fasting and praying and never even moving an eyebrow—or eyelash, for that matter. Once, when we were in primary school, Chotu and I walked right up to Baba's face and saw an eyelash sitting on his cheek, and he didn't even move. Mummy saw me and ran over and told us not to bother him, but the next day, on the way to school, I checked and the eyelash was still there. He never even touched it.

I wondered about what Baba thought about before he meditated— before he sat still to let the thoughts fall into the silence. I had felt this silence inside of me during yoga. The first time I followed my breath the way Sandeep bhai told us to, I felt it move from my chest into my belly. I felt the way my shoulders fell from my ears, and I just listened. I stopped thinking about Chotu's dimple and about the roti in my lunch box. First I let in the sounds of my classmates shifting their seats on the ground, then the hum of the air around me. It took me to my breath, the sound of it entering and exiting my body, filling and collapsing my lungs at each cycle, and I got lost in that silence.

When I told Asya about it, she said there was too much to think about. What silence? It was my secret silence. Baba knew the secret too. He escaped into the silence and away from the places that weighed heavily on our hearts. I did it at night sometimes, when Asya was asleep. I'd let my breath carry me into the night sky. These city girls were only used to loud street noises and cars everywhere with no trees except fancy bushes in front of their house. I wanted to ask them if they had ever seen lotus flowers bloom across the whole lake right after the monsoon, filling it so it looked like you could jump from one to the other without ever getting wet but was too beautiful to ever want to touch.

I started to speak, but Asya, with all her grace, answered for me.

"No, we haven't tried those and don't know much about this place, as I am sure you would never know about our village. We hope you can see it all one day. It's beautiful."

Asya looked at me and smiled. I knew she thought she had rescued us, and usually I would have agreed, but I felt upset that she had held me back. What if instead of just telling them it was beautiful, what I shared could help them see the beauty? But I smiled back at my sister and let it go, like my breath.

CHAPTER 7

The hospital had long corridors that smelled horrible. It was an odor like nothing I had ever smelled before. More sour than unripe mangos, and it felt thick to my nostrils. Asya held my hand, and Puppa tried to find the right desk. His reading was not always the best, and with so many things written in English, it got confusing. We tried to ask people for help as we searched for Mummy, but everyone was so busy that they hardly answered or stopped to help. I found myself sweating, anticipating seeing Mummy.

We found the cancer unit, and the nurse who sat on the other side of the glass window told Puppa to wait, that the doctor would come speak to him and bring him to Mummy when he was available.

"How long will he be?"

I was surprised at how timid Puppa was in front of this woman. Normally, he would stand proud, sometimes even look down when he spoke to women, the way he did to the Dalit women who cleaned the village's washbasins. I was equally surprised when the woman did not look up at Puppa, just answered as if we were taking up her time, after we had traveled so many miles to see our mummy, who we hadn't seen in months.

"When he is ready, sir, he will come get you."

We sat on the cold metal chairs, and Puppa grew fidgety, looking around, telling us we would see Mummy soon. Asya touched Puppa's shoulder when he sat, and he took her hand, holding it as I reached for Asya's other hand for comfort. After a few moments of sitting anxiously, I remembered seeing a small white cart with KOOL KULFI written in green-and-orange letters when we passed the corridor near the hospital cafeteria. I asked Puppa for some money to get something to eat from the cafeteria. I thought he might scold me, but he agreed, reaching into his pocket and pulling out a crumpled note. Asya looked confused and got up to come, but I nudged her to stay with Puppa. "I'll be fine. Don't worry. I'll bring us something." She had a flicker of worry in her eyes, and I squeezed her hand to reassure her.

I found the cart, and behind it was a bald man reading the paper on a stool. I wanted to get three, but Puppa only gave me enough for two. "*Do kesar pista kulfi.*" I felt grown up ordering it on my own. He handed me the cold desserts, each wrapped in a circular paper cone, and I ran back so they wouldn't melt too much. Slightly out of breath from running, I approached Asya and Puppa. "One for you, Puppa. Asya and I will share. Ice cream fixes everything."

Puppa had said that to us on our sixth birthday when he took us to get new bangles and Asya and I both had fallen exiting the rickshaw. He kissed our scrapes and took us to get ice cream right away.

Now Puppa smiled and handed me his kulfi and said he would just need a bite. When we were done, we waited. Without the distraction of our sweet treat, my fear returned. Was Mummy okay? When could we take her home?

I am not sure how long I slept, resting on Asya's head as she slept on my shoulder, knees colliding as we sat cross-legged on the chairs. We only woke up when Puppa called to us.

"Let's go, beti. Amla, Asya, *aa jao.*" I opened my eyes to see Puppa reaching his hand for us. There was a blur of a short, stout doctor behind him.

The doctor led the way down a long hallway painted green. He waddled as he walked, and although shorter than Puppa by inches, he was wider, and his round belly stuck out from his unbuttoned white coat. He glanced over his shoulder at us, and seemed to think we were too far away to hear him because he turned to Puppa and said, "If we do not operate, there is nothing we can do. I'm so sorry."

I spoke up. "But the medicines, Puppa, we can afford that for now, right? Will they help, Doctor?"

The doctor looked at me, and then turned back to Puppa. "The medicine is just keeping her from feeling the pain, and even so does not work so well. We need to stop it from spreading, and removing the whole ovary is the best option. If we do not do that, I am afraid she will not have much time before . . ."

Asya touched my arm, as if to keep me from asking more. But Puppa stopped walking and grabbed hold of the doctor's arm. "Doctor Sahib, we are not wealthy. Please tell me: how much time do we have? I must know so I can save the money."

The doctor looked back at Asya and me now. His expression was empty. "As fast as you can would be best. Now I have other patients to tend to." Then he walked away.

Puppa's head drooped, and I knew what it meant. I felt it in my heart, and as I watched the doctor walk away, holding the clipboard to his chest, I wondered if that was all he would ever know of my mummy: the facts of her disease. Before that clipboard, there was a history of smiles and laughter and vibrancy that I could communicate to him if he just stayed, if he just tried to help us bring her back, but I was already understanding that in Mumbai, no one would help people like us.

CHAPTER 8

Mummy was shivering when we walked into her room. She smiled at us, but she was not the same Mummy we knew. Her eyes were a dull, monotone gray, and as she reached out to hug us, her arms looked so skinny that I thought they might snap. I was shocked to see how different Mummy was.

"My angels," she said, and we hugged her as she cried on our shoulders.

"We will save up for the surgery, and I will be back next week, but you must stay strong." Puppa was speaking low, almost as if to himself.

Mummy told him not to worry—she was always strong. "Now you tell me about school. You both have been good, right?"

After all my worrying, I felt like myself, telling Mummy funny stories of our classmates. Mummy laughed for a moment and then sat back in bed again, her face turning pale and slack.

She touched Asya's arm and held my hand while I spoke. Asya gazed at the veins seeping out of her skin, and Mummy told her to remember her shoulders were still small. Mummy always said that when Asya was worried about a test or chores, telling her she was still her little girl and to stop carrying the weight of the world on her shoulders. Then she asked me to keep smiling. At that, I let my head drop to her chest. I leaned down and kissed her hand. As I tried to fill myself with the scent of my mother, always fragrant with sandalwood soap and her sweet perspiration, I encountered the scent of bleached sheets and Tiger Balm pain ointment instead.

"Tell me, where are you staying here?" Mummy asked.

"Not too far from here . . ." Puppa's voice trailed off.

I looked at Asya, who seemed just as confused as I was. "Mummy, we are staying at Guhan uncle's."

Mummy pursed her lips and looked at Puppa. "Do not do what I think you may do there."

"Jaya, please, do not worry." I waited for Mummy to say more, but she looked too tired. I kept her hand folded in mine, the one I had kissed, as she asked for water. Puppa offered to see if the nurse was outside to bring some.

When he left, I wanted to know more about what Mummy was saying to Puppa. I knew it was probably about his drinking. "Mummy, what did you mean?"

"Hmm?"

"You know, about Puppa not—"

Asya cut me off. "Mummy, do not worry; we will be with Puppa. And we will make sure to come back. We want you home where you belong." She hugged Mummy from the opposite side of the bed, and I glared at her, annoyed, as Puppa reentered with a jug of water. I didn't bother to continue; we didn't need Puppa getting angry.

After Mummy drank the water, we let her rest. I silently prayed to see her again—and well—soon.

When we got back to the apartment, it was already evening. Sweta auntie was setting the table with dinner, so we began to help her right away. Puppa talked to Guhan uncle and updated him on what the doctor said. Puppa asked him if there was a way we could borrow the money and pay him back every week, like a loan.

"My friend, I have my own financial changes occurring with my new job. I wish I could help."

Luckily his daughters were at bharatanatyam practice, so we did not have to talk to them. After we set the table, Auntie fussed with the servant about the lentils while Asya and I went into the main room to watch television, which always seemed to be on in their home. The dance performances on the screen seemed so glamorous, like a world that could never really exist in India, but of course we would never tell the girls we had never seen a television before. The stage was full of lights, and in each passing scene, the performers wore dresses like I had never beheld.

"You know, there is much opportunity here in Mumbai for your girls—for housework or babysitting, even dishwashing."

My ears perked up as Guhan uncle approached us. Puppa followed behind.

"What standard are you in, girls?"

I told him that we were finishing up our ninth standard.

Guhan uncle turned to Puppa, who said with everything going on with Mummy, he was not sure how he would send us to school anymore.

"Let them work now; worry about schooling later."

"I wouldn't want them to come all the way here alone. I cannot leave my work there without finding something here."

"I understand. Maybe look in the village. If there is no work there, do not worry; you are like my brother. I will take care of them until you have enough for Jaya's surgery."

I looked over to see Puppa's reaction, but he was turned away, heading back into the other room. I rose to stand, but Asya pulled my wrist.

"Thank you, yaar. You are a good friend."

I heard the clinking of ice and glass and knew Puppa was taking a drink, something he never did at home but had done here with Guhan uncle every night. If Dadi knew, she would be mad. I recalled Mummy's words at the hospital. The night we had arrived in Mumbai, I smelled Puppa's strong breath when he came to say good night to us.

He almost fell out of the room as he shut the door, which made me miss Mummy's good-night kisses even more.

I sat closer to Asya as we returned our focus to the dancing competition show, letting the beats and rhythm of the music drown out Puppa's changing voice.

The next morning, I was going to let Puppa know I knew he wasn't supposed to drink. But Puppa did not speak to us the whole bus ride back to our village. I tried to distract him and make him smile, imitating Guhan uncle's daughters and laughing at the way they tried to follow along with our dinner prayers. "*Yagna siiiista,*" I said, elongating their funny pronunciation.

Asya gave me a warning look.

"Puppa, don't worry," I said. "Mummy will come home. Remember, like she said, she is always strong."

Puppa looked at me and started to cry. He hung his head towards his lap, the tears rolling down the side of his face and along his neck. He was letting go the way I wanted to. I took his fingers into mine. They were almost double the size of my hand. Asya said, "Puppa, don't cry," but I knew his heart needed to, and I told Asya, "No, let Puppa," and I whispered, "It's okay, it's okay," the way Mummy would rub my back when I was upset about fighting with Asya or a poor exam mark.

He cried the whole way home, without speaking once. I wondered if he was telling me that he felt like he'd failed his family, that he believed more and more that Mummy might not come home, that he did not know what to do if he lost her. I let his tears speak to me, heart to heart, my puppa and I, and I understood that his tears were the truth, the answers to a reality Asya and I did not want to grasp. Would we never see our mummy again?

CHAPTER 9

The week after we returned, Puppa went missing. Asya went to the train station before school on the fifth morning to search for him, and the conductor said he thought he had gone to Mumbai again, but he had not seen Puppa for days. Dadi and Dada found Guhan uncle's phone number and called him from the SDT phone booth, but Guhan said he had not heard from Puppa at all. When Dadi tried calling the hospital, they told her Mummy was still there and asked if Puppa was coming back.

I focused on housework, washing our clothes in the basin early in the morning so they would be dry by the evening for Asya to take in and fold. It gave me direction, a task to do. It kept me from wanting to curl up in a ball and cry.

Dadi and Nani did not fight anymore. They came to our home and cooked, swept the floors, and did dishes in silence, taking turns staying with us there.

With each night that passed without our parents, I began to feel more angry than sad. How could God let Mummy get sick? How could Puppa leave us?

Now instead of crying, all I wanted to do was scream. At night, when the quiet sounds of memories visited me to enter my dreams, I watched the door, awaiting the sound of Puppa's leather work shoes with the worn metal heel that echoed when he walked on our stone floors, or of Mummy's morning humming. I tried to hum to my sister while she lay awake beside me, in an attempt to fill the silence of our new lives.

• • •

After a month passed by, we no longer waited for our parents. Rumors spread in the village that Puppa had gone crazy, committed suicide, or run away to Mumbai where he was a common beggar. For all we knew, he could have been hit or killed by the city's wild traffic. I felt nothing when people spoke to me about our puppa, or about the prayers they held for our mummy. What did they know?

I wanted to believe in something better, but I was numb to it all. I thought of Mummy and her hospital room often, though. I thought of her when Nani came to sing her morning prayers with us, bringing an offering of fresh jasmine flowers that Mummy would have smiled at. I wished for a bed of jasmine flowers for her rather than the cold steel cot she lay on.

Weeks after Puppa vanished, I let go of the idea that he would come home with Mummy in his arms. Dadi had been going to the SDT stand every day, asking if a phone call had come in from the hospital. When Dadi tried calling, she was placed on hold so long that the money ran out.

"Maybe Puppa is with Mummy, the two of them holding hands as he says bye to her."

I saw Asya cringe and bit my lip. Maybe I had said too much. Normally Asya would have corrected me or said something. She was sullen and only made that face instead.

Even Dadi asked me about Asya. "She is not herself anymore, beti. Where has she gone?"

I looked past her when she asked me this. "She's here, Dadi," I said vaguely. I too was worried but was not about to show it to Dadi. Dadi would embrace me when we came home from school, say, "My beti Amlu," clearly favoring me. I'd watch Asya leave the room and go straight to do her homework, wondering if she would try to meet my eyes. She slipped away gracefully each time.

During classes, I hardly paid attention—more than my normal daydreaming. Mistress Sheela pulled me aside. "I can help you with your lessons, beti," she offered. In my heart I wanted to tell her I didn't care about my lessons. That I couldn't stay here anymore. Without Chotu, with Asya withdrawn from me and the uncertainty of our parents' fates, I was suffocating and confused. I wanted her to help me get out of a life I no longer felt connected to, but where could I possibly go? There was no escape. She searched my eyes, but I just dropped my chin to my chest and promised I would try harder. I made sure to walk out of the classroom before the first tear fell.

When I got home, Asya was humming and washing the clothes in the basin. She seemed to be in a better mood, and even her face looked lighter. I threw my knapsack down to run over to her but saw a paper sticking out of her homework folder and noticed Asya's neatly curved letters. I picked up the paper.

Walls cave in
Without her
Mother of my life
And even with
The sister of my heart
I cannot find my way out
Of this

I let her words dance in my mind and looked up at my sister again, who was feeling the same as me. There we were, together yet so far. For the first time ever, I felt alone.

At school, the teachers felt sorry for us. When I forgot to complete my geography worksheet, Mistress Urvi didn't even scold me and told me it was all right to hand it in the next day. I felt relieved and frustrated all at once. I couldn't concentrate on my worksheets, but I wanted to feel normal again. To be scolded and have Mummy to talk to afterwards.

Asya and I weren't sleeping much and missed our surya namaskar sessions twice. It was something Asya would never have done before. Sometimes I heard her turning in her sleep, waking up to her worried heart, which kept me awake too. I lay there at night, wondering if Puppa and Mummy would ever return. The third time we had yoga, I went as Asya slept in. I told her Sandeep bhai had asked about her. She shrugged and told me to tell him she was sick. It was a lie I was willing to tell since she didn't look well anymore from lack of sleep.

I was worried I was losing Asya too.

CHAPTER 10

Not long after I found her poem, Asya told me about a writing contest she was going to enter and handed me a piece of folded notebook paper.

Darkness falls and my old life returns.
Somewhere inside, laughter feels not so distant,
Comfort in my heart returns
As the newness of this day settles in amongst
Old memories.

I felt encouraged by the fact that she was sharing this with me, and more encouraged by the message of the poem. Maybe I would not lose my sister after all.

When we passed the water well that day, I heard Dadi's voice through the window of our complex. I glanced at Asya, who nodded to show she heard it too.

"For what? How can you ask that? If we do not marry them off now, soon we will no longer be able to help them. Who will care for them?"

"But these men are twice their age, such young girls," Nani protested.

"We both were married by then. What good did it do you to wait for your daughter to marry?"

"I will not allow it!"

We had never heard Nani scream, and shivers ran down my spine as a steel plate hit the ground.

"This is my son's home," Dadi answered coldly. "There is no reason for you to come here anymore."

Asya and I reached out at the same time and held hands for the first time in weeks. We waited steps away from our front door, waited for our nani to come out.

My thoughts came to me at lightning speed: *Do we run to her and hug her? Do we run after her?* The answer came as she walked out the door, pale and shaken; I froze for a moment and then ran to her.

She did not look at us but paused when Asya fell to the ground, hugging her feet.

"Nani, no," Asya sobbed.

I watched my sister and held back tears as I started to understand our fate. Nani took my face and pressed it into her neck.

"Stay strong, my devi." Nani kissed us on our foreheads and left, slowly.

As we entered our empty home, Dadi was pacing and looked worried, then scared as she stopped next to the small stool we used for washing clothes in the basin. She walked over and held my shoulders. "*Theek hai*, here are many chores for us to finish. Get washed up."

I went to the kitchen table where Dadi kept her shawl and saw the photo. They looked older, almost twice our age, like Nani said. Their teeth were stained red from the betel nut they probably chewed, just like the men in Mumbai. I gagged thinking about one of them touching me. There was a handwritten note on the other side of the photograph: RAJAT AND ROHAN, BROTHERS, VAISHYA CASTE. DRIVERS. LOOKING FOR GIRLS WHO ARE UNEDUCATED. MUST BE YOUNG AND HEALTHY FOR MANY CHILDREN.

• • •

In the weeks that followed, Dadi came to the house more and more. I never spoke to her about the photograph but could not get the image of the men out of my mind. I couldn't speak freely with Dadi, and I missed Nani, who laughed when we told her stories after school about the boys who chased us.

Dadi talked about boys with some sort of hidden meaning. "So, are there boys that you like in the village?" she once asked, raising her eyebrows.

Asya and I looked at each other. I followed her lead at times.

"We don't really notice them," Asya said.

"What about you, Amla?"

"Oh, I don't know, Dadi. We are too busy reading to notice anyone."

"Are there boys that approach you or talk to you?"

"No," Asya was quick to answer. "Madame would beat us if she found out we were talking to boys on the all-girls side of school like that. Dadi, you know that."

She returned to cooking dinner as we buried our nose in our books like never before—or at least, I never had.

We started leaving earlier than usual for school so we could stop at Nani's house. We would help her carry her vessels to the kitchen to make her chai, or sit with her on her dried-mud floor and eat the pomegranate she peeled for us. It was our secret time with her, and I loved it. Asya was always nervous, like someone would find us there and scold us.

It annoyed me. "So what?" I would say. "If anyone sees us, it's not like we are doing something wrong by coming to hug our nani!"

Nani would hold us then, both of us, together, as we towered over her small frame. Her arms always stopped short on our backs, but it still felt like the strongest embrace in the world.

I told Asya I could not do it. I would not marry one of the brothers. I told her my plan, what I was thinking, how we could go.

"Will it work?"

I sensed her hesitation; my sister was not sure this time.

"Asya," I said grimly, "we have no choice."

We were supposed to be doing our homework sheets so we could help Dadi with dinner afterwards. When we heard her come in, we jumped up, both of our faces filled with guilt.

Dadi was carrying the long barbatti beans we would cut up for dinner in her straw bag. We washed our hands and took them from her.

"Beti, cut them smaller than last time," Dadi said. "We will add potatoes today."

She was in a good mood and humming the same Hindi song Puppa always used to hum to us. We worked fast, and by the time dinner was ready, Dada was there with us, and we ate together in silence.

I missed Mummy in those moments. She always asked us about school or told us about a funny story from the bazaar. She would say, "And Natu is always chasing that monkey who keeps grabbing all the bananas from his stand. There are so many fruit stands in the market, but he always targets Natu!"

Sometimes we'd have to wait for her to finish laughing before she could tell us the rest of a story like that one, sending us into giggles before we even knew the ending.

"Asya, Amla, Dada and I have decided something."

We looked up at Dadi. I glanced at Dada, but he did not stop eating his daal.

"There is no point in keeping this house. It is wasteful. You girls can come live with Dada and me. We will sell the plot and can use the money for"—she paused briefly—"your future."

"Our future?" I repeated. I knew my tone was angry, and Asya tried to kick me under the table, but she was sitting too far away and missed. I still couldn't grasp what Dadi was saying, about us leaving the only home we had ever known.

"Amla, beti, when you girls finish your term, we will need money for your weddings and to gift to your husbands' families, and since there are two of you, we need more than we can afford, and plus—"

"Dadi, we won't marry now. We still have to study! And besides, who? When? You don't even tell us about our own lives!" I shouted.

Dada turned red and raised his eyebrow at me. I was emotional. I had let the heat rise from my heart again.

"Amla, do not raise your voice at your dadi. You will obey her wishes. She is your elder!" Dada snapped. I lowered my head, defeated by Dada's words.

"I want Mummy," my voice cracked. I swallowed a bite of the green beans into the knot of my stomach.

"Asya, beti, do you want more to eat?" Dadi smiled at her and held a serving spoon full of rice over my plate. After my outburst, Asya was clearly her new favorite. Her smile was like poison in my veins.

That night, we stayed up late whispering about my plan. We spoke of what we wished to study, of leaving the village and telling Mummy, how she would protect us even though she was so very sick.

I was unsure if it would work, but it was all we had. And with Asya agreeing, I had the strength to reach out to Chotu again. He was surprised when we approached him, and I wanted to reach out and embrace him, but I stood afar, my hip touching Asya's hand, letting her presence anchor me as I told him what we needed him to do. I had to swallow my pride to speak to him again, but I knew he had a soft heart when it came to Mummy and would help us.

Packing our home into a small rucksack was easier than I'd thought. I only really cared for and wanted the things that reminded me of Mummy and Puppa: Mummy's green dupatta, a few photographs of them, some drawings from our childhood, and some clothes, especially the lehenga suit Asya loved sharing with me for special occasions.

I let my fingers slide over the fabric lovingly. It was orange cotton with bright-blue embroidery, but it was so soft it felt like the fancy silk saris we loved to touch in the bazaar, always hanging above us like wheels of rich rainbows. Asya encouraged me to take a few more things, so I added the American-style blue pens Mummy had brought home for us one day, telling us she bargained with the shopkeeper by saying that she would send all of our classmates' mothers to his shop.

As Asya packed her things, I went into Mummy's drawers and found her gold wedding jewelry. My eyes were focused and my breath was tight as I took the only bit of wealth in the house. I shook handfuls of safety and bobby pins into the original box and then locked it so that if Dadi looked for it, it would feel and sound like it did before: a little heavy with the clink of metal against wood.

I looked into the kitchen. The steel plates and bowls in racks above the stove were illuminated by the light pouring in from the broken window above our sink, and I got teary eyed thinking of setting our dinner table for Mummy. Asya and I would chase each other while we set the plates, darting past Mummy as she washed dishes and scolded us, firmly but always smiling.

"Are you ready?" Asya asked, appearing at my side in the doorway.

We looked at each other, and she pressed my hand with her long fingers, telling me without telling me, "We're in this together."

Dadi had told Asya that morning to come straight over after school. "Your sister is so emotional; you must help her," Asya told me she had said, imitating her confiding voice and how she patted Asya's arm, so pleased with her.

We knew we had until about 5 p.m. since Dadi always went to the bazaar at 4, when the morning vegetables were cheaper and the stalls were quick to unload their boxes.

We slipped out just when Dadi turned towards the market. I warned Asya that if we saw anyone we knew, we would have to act like we got a telegram from Mummy's hospital to go there but also say that we did not know why or what it was about. I had been able to pawn most of the jewelry, with the exception of Mummy's earrings. We had enough for the train tickets with a little extra left over. I had told the shopkeeper it was for our school supplies, and he gave us five extra rupees and told us he would pray for our family.

"What if we see someone and they don't believe us? What if they go to get Dadi?" Asya had worried.

I told Asya that the whole village was so shaken up by our situation that most people didn't want to spend more than a few minutes talking to us. Mostly they would just tell us about the prayers and fasting they would do for us and wait for our thanks before moving on.

"Don't worry, Asya. We have to stay strong, okay?"

When we left our complex to meet Chotu, my sister followed my stride, and I told her not to look back. We avoided the bazaar and walked behind the one-level flats where Chotu had agreed to meet us. Two women were washing their kids with a bucket between them, and their sons splashed water at each other. Seeing them and hearing their laughter reminded me of a childhood innocence I craved, back when everything seemed simple and easy and worries were for adults.

Chotu was there when we arrived. He helped us onto his scooter and sped off to the bus. As we passed our village, I knew that this was what life was about: tiny moments that somehow merged into some greater fate that we had no control of.

When we arrived at the bus station, there was already a crowd of people waiting, more than when we had gone with Puppa. Chotu said he would wait with us until it came. Asya turned her back, pretending to read some signs so Chotu and I could have a moment.

"Don't be scared, but remember not to let that sharp tongue get in your way," Chotu said affectionately.

I laughed. He knew me so well. I contemplated talking about our last confrontation, but as I looked up at his dusty hair and concerned eyes, I didn't say anything. He tucked a strand of my hair behind my ear. His version of an apology. I wondered if his heart felt sorry that he would never marry me because of our caste difference, like Asya had said.

When the bus arrived, Asya turned to me. It was time. Chotu put one hand on my back and another on Asya's shoulder.

I wanted to turn and wrap my hands around his body, tell him to come find me. But I decided it was easier to just move forward. We waved goodbye to Chotu together and walked to the bus, my sister and I arm in arm. We didn't look back.

CHAPTER 11

We arrived in Mumbai at daybreak. Even through the bus window, I could tell that it was not warm yet. The sun was just edging its way into the sky.

People around us stirred as the station approached. The Mumbai station was crowded, with triple the number of people we'd seen at the village stop. As the bus pulled up, the masses pushed forward, anxious to get on. Asya and I stuck close to a family beside us, a father and mother and their two sons. We followed them as we exited, as if we were part of their family. I held Asya's hand tight. She squeezed back, and we shuffled the rucksacks on our backs to one side so we could still hold hands. We had never been alone like this before, and I sucked my breath in and drew on my courage. We would find Mummy and bring her home; that was the hope I protected from the fears that tried to enter my heart.

As we stepped out onto the street, Asya and I stopped short. I had never seen so many cars. It felt different from when we left the bus station in the evening with Puppa last time, at nightfall. Now the street was filled with traffic. Cars honked more than they moved. There were Tata taxis everywhere, not the small gasoline rickshaws we always saw in our village. Street vendors maneuvered in between the moving cars, carrying newspapers and baskets of spiced nut packets to sell; two of them were young boys our age.

We ran up to a rickshaw that had a Krishna decal on its front window. The cab driver was short and round, his belly protruding from his button-down shirt, barely closing in the center. His eyes looked kind, and I recognized the sound of the ghanta bells of the Aarti song playing from his small radio. Once we got into the back seat, I handed him the hospital address and added, "We must go fast. Our father is waiting for us so we can see our mother." I let myself believe what I told the driver to make it more convincing, as he turned and weaved in and out of cars.

He wasn't as nice as he looked. When we arrived, his hand was still out after I paid him. He had sensed we weren't from here, I knew. He said there was an extra flat fee for luggage, five rupees per bag, and I knew he was trying to scam us.

"We didn't have to do that last time with such small bags. My father would have told us so," I said.

"Your father must have forgotten. You must pay now," the driver said.

Had we been with Nani or Dadi, they would have shut the door in his face, telling him he could never scam them. But I was worried he might not let us go if we didn't pay him more. As I handed over the money, my stomach twisted at the injustice of it. I knew our two small rucksacks in our laps were not considered luggage.

We got out of the cab and headed towards the hospital doors. On our way in, we saw a man wearing a bright-pink sari and lipstick. We had heard of the hijra in our village; a student once said they had come to his cousin's wedding and his uncle paid them and gave them dinner to get rid of any bad omens they might cast on his daughter's marriage. But here in Mumbai, this man walked freely, his sari draped over his masculine body—no one staring at him the way people did in our village. I felt something relax inside of me, seeing the hijra openly wear his sari. Could it be the same for girls like Asya and me?

I remembered where to turn when we entered, and when a woman stopped us, I told her we were going to see our mother.

"What is your mother's name, beti?"

She was kinder than the woman Puppa had spoken to last time. I showed her the hospital paper I had taken from Puppa's files, and she looked at Asya and me and told us to wait.

A shorter woman approached us, spoke to the other woman in another dialect, maybe Gujarati, and then asked me in Hindi who we were. "We are her daughters." *We are her devis, her angels from Rama.*

"Your father . . . he was here some time ago." She cleared her throat. Excitement soared through my heart. *Did Puppa come to save Mummy? Did she already have the surgery? But then, why didn't they come back?*

"We didn't have a return number for your grandparents, so we tried to contact your father at the number he left us. His workplace relayed the message to him . . . to notify him that your mother . . . she passed away."

She looked down and didn't meet our eyes; she didn't gape at my screaming or Asya's knees giving out, her collapsing, and my own falling down inside my soul to what felt like nothing. Even knowing this was a possibility, we had still held on to the hope of coming to our mummy's rescue. *Mummy, Mummy, Mummy* is all that rang through my mind.

When Asya fell, I grabbed her as her eyes closed, and she lay on top of my hip.

The woman who delivered the news to us said she was one of the doctors that had cared for Mummy. She looked tired but was still pretty, with a smooth complexion and deep-brown eyes. She gave me an ice pack, and they put Asya on a cot as a nurse dabbed her forehead with a damp cloth.

While we waited for Asya to wake up, the doctor told me everything. She said that Puppa was drunk when he finally came, that they needed to detoxify him so that he was able to recognize Mummy, to claim her body. Mummy was taken to a local cremation ground where people with no families went. I imagined Mummy surrounded by the bodies of criminals and strangers. She said the nurse that tended to her for many months attended her cremation and saw our father there. He was weeping and telling Mummy he would join her soon.

"The nurse said he had a crazy look in his eyes, and she just assumed it was him grieving. We didn't see him again. He said he would return to pay the outstanding balance of her stay, and we assumed he went back to his village to notify the rest of the family."

I listened to her words, watched them roll off her tongue, the sweat and perspiration building at her upper lip.

"He left one day and never came back." That was all I knew, and I ached for my mother, for her ashes that Asya and I were not there to claim. For Nani, who still prayed for her health, and for my weak father, who I felt I might never grieve for his betrayal to us. Did he kill himself? Where was Puppa?

"How will I tell Asya?" I asked the doctor. I couldn't believe Puppa had left Mummy like this.

The doctor touched my shoulder. "Perhaps it is best if you don't tell her everything now. She is clearly too fragile for it."

"Maybe," I murmured. It didn't seem right, but maybe I should keep some of it to myself. Poor Asya. And now our plan had shattered. I needed to think of something new. *Do we just go home?* Dadi and Dada were probably outraged, and would ship us off to our husbands as soon as we got back.

"Oh, she's awake," the doctor said.

I looked over to see Asya watching us, her face blank. I wondered how long she had been that way, how much of the doctor's story she had heard.

CHAPTER 12

"**W**here are the cremation grounds?" Asya asked.

The doctor told us, then paused. "Do you girls have anyone here in Mumbai? Will you be returning to your village?"

Asya and I glanced at each other. Would we return? Even if we couldn't bring our mummy home? "Yes," I said. "We will be going back to the village, but we just want to see the grounds first, where Mummy was taken."

She gave Asya some mango juice, and Asya drank it, then told me to have the rest while the doctor quickly wrote down the address. The woman was left-handed like me, and with interest I watched her curve her letters. Asya was always praised for being the right-handed one, but I was never scolded or forced to become right-handed. Yet still, I felt it was another way Asya was regarded as better. Mummy's doctor had warned our parents that one of us would likely be left-handed. Apparently most twins are usually opposite this way.

As the doctor handed us the slip of paper, she told us to go now so we could get to the train station in time to leave for our village tonight.

"I'm sorry," she told us, and I knew she meant it. Asya and I hugged her, and she fixed her hair and stethoscope afterwards as we walked away.

Asya looked at me and, without saying anything, hugged me, and I put my arms around her, not wanting to let go. I didn't know what each minute held for us anymore. Who was left to trust except each other?

• • •

We got to the cremation grounds as the sun was going down. It was hard to believe the whole day had already passed us by. Hundreds of wooden logs rested against the concrete walls of the crematorium that stood to the side of the city park. Some ashes from a recent cremation remained on the concrete-slab floor. The open area felt like a desolate retreat from the honking chaos of the city.

We stood together before the large oven with wheels where Mummy must have been cremated, a heavy feeling all around us. With all the cars of Mumbai, the air smelled different here, more like smog than dust. I longed for the bullock carts of our village. I would rather smell the dung they left on our roads than the stench of gasoline. Even so, I knew we could not go back to the village. We had wanted to take Mummy home with us; without her, we had nothing worthwhile to return to.

"Ay, what are you two doing?" a sharp voice called, startling us. We turned around and stood closer to one another as a policeman approached.

"Our mother was cremated here." Asya looked down, as if in respect for Mummy. It still felt surreal to me when Asya said it out loud.

"I see, but these grounds close at dark. You must go home. Where do you live?"

We hadn't talked about where we would be going from here yet. I thought of Guhan uncle, how he had said he knew of jobs we could find.

"We are staying at our uncle's house. He lives in Mulund."

Asya looked at me, surprised—either that I remembered where Guhan uncle lived or that I had suggested going there.

"Okay, I can find you a taxi," the officer said.

Asya kept her eyes on me, whispering fiercely as we walked behind the policeman, "Are you mad? Why would we go there, Amla?"

"Where else?" I hissed at her. *I wish she would just listen to me once in a while.*

She glared at me again as she got into the cab, as if to say, "If this goes wrong, it will be your fault." I followed her in.

The truth is, I didn't have a better idea, and it seemed neither did Asya, so I didn't understand why she was so angry with me. "What is your bright idea then?"

Asya didn't even turn her head when she spoke as she kept her arms crossed, stared out the window, and said, "Would it be so horrible if we just went home and talked to Dadi again?"

"Yes, it would be, Asya. Are you crazy? We would still have to get married to those disgusting men, remember?" We had agreed that we hated Guhan uncle and his house, and I wasn't even sure if he would send us back to the village or not, but it was the only option I saw.

My head pounded as the cab raced through the crowded streets. I was hungry; we hadn't eaten since our bus ride, which was hours ago. Luckily, I had written down Guhan uncle's street address when we left the village, just in case they wouldn't let us see Mummy without an adult.

When I told the driver the address, he asked us if we knew Arun Singh, an old friend of his that lived on the same block. We mumbled a response, and he seemed to get the message that we didn't want to talk. He let us look out the window. I watched the world go by, my thoughts merging with those of what felt like a million strangers walking through this unfamiliar city. Our lives had changed in an instant; we had no parents, no safety.

"What if we say we were sent here, Amla? To work?" Asya asked in a low voice.

She was thinking about it now and relaxed her arms, and I liked where she was taking the new plan. We could still study if we had our own money.

"Remember Guhan uncle told Puppa there are many jobs for girls here, to clean or wash dishes, and he offered to help us find them?"

She was right. We would never amount to anything back in the village, and as I watched women in Western-style pants exit buildings, talking on their phones, I knew that here we could start a real life. A young woman sat at an outdoor café, a book in her hand and laughing with friends. The idea of being like her excited me. It was the kind of life Mummy would have wanted us to have.

"Okay, but we have to tell him we cannot be separated. And ask him if we can stay at his house until we save up enough to live somewhere else alone."

"We can even keep saving and go to college one day!" I grinned, imagining us making chai to study for exams and staying up late with friends.

Asya smiled back.

When we arrived, Asya handed the taxi driver the fare, which left us with only a few rupees to spare. We still had Mummy's earrings, but Asya wanted to wait to use them until we needed to. I knew she just wanted to hold on to them as a keepsake, and I was glad. I didn't want to lose that part of Mummy either.

We climbed up the stairs to Guhan uncle's flat. The hallway smelled of dinner: onions and tomatoes frying with masala, making my stomach growl. I was nervous as we stood in front of their apartment door. While Guhan uncle was supposed to be like family, he didn't really feel like it. I listened to their neighbor's baby crying, and we heard the blare of the television set and finally knocked. The younger sister, Chaya, answered, and after taking in our faces, she looked behind us, perhaps looking for our father.

"Who is it, beti?" Sweta auntie called.

I was relieved it was Auntie, not Guhan uncle, who came behind her daughter, surprised to see us there.

"Chaya, open the door and let them in. Are you girls here with your father?"

I looked at Asya, who swallowed hard and told Auntie no. She waited, as we all stood there, until I spoke.

"They are dead," I said in a flat voice. "Our puppa and mummy are dead."

Asya seemed to regain her strength, and she told Auntie we were in Mumbai to find a job. "Guhan uncle said he knew of jobs. We heard him tell Puppa about them last time we were in the city. We didn't have anywhere else to go, so we came here."

There was a flash of fear in Auntie's eyes as we spoke, but then she told us that Guhan uncle was not home yet; he was playing billiards with his coworkers. Her eyes became soft again as she looked at us, and I was embarrassed to hear my stomach growl.

"*Aa jao*, wash up. We were about to eat. You girls must be hungry traveling all this way."

CHAPTER 13

The girls didn't ask us any questions, just looked at us awkwardly as we put on some of their old pajamas.

Auntie had filled the buckets with warm water for us, and since neither of us wanted to be alone, we bathed together like we had done since we were children. Usually we were fast, always getting ready for school or to help with housework, but tonight we took our time, washing the heavy feeling of our journey, of a past we tried to break free from, of an escape on an unknown path. I tried to take comfort in knowing we were on this path together, but all I could picture was the cremation grounds, knowing Mummy was gone forever.

When we were dressed, the girls had set up extra blankets on the bed they shared, putting four pillows across the side horizontally instead of at the top so we could all fit, even if our feet did dangle off the edge. Asya thanked them, and as we got under the covers, we heard the front door slam. Chaya reached out and clutched her older sister's arm, whispering, "Dad's home."

I had heard the Western way of saying "puppa" before and always thought it sounded heavy and cold. This time I felt shivers as I realized how close "Dad" was to the English word *dead*.

Hearing the fear in Chaya's voice, I pulled the covers up over all our heads. I didn't know why she was scared, but pretending to sleep seemed like the best solution, and I was glad to see Chaya and Nisha follow along. I knew Asya would do it; every time Mummy and Puppa fought at night and came to check if we were asleep or not, we would do the same.

The door opened, and all of us tensed, trying to stay as still and quiet as possible. It did not make me feel better to see that Guhan uncle's daughters seemed just as nervous as we were.

"Guhan," we heard Sweta auntie say, "they are sleeping now. We will talk to them in the morning. Poor girls."

We felt their presence in the room. The smell of liquor was strong enough to make its way under the blankets to our noses.

"It is good they came here," Guhan Uncle slurred. "We will find good work for them. They are very pretty girls."

He didn't say anything after that, but I felt him there; even with my eyes closed, hiding, I felt him watching us. The hair on my arms stood up, telling me this was not a safe place, but what choice did we have? We heard a creak as he leaned against the door, shifting his feet, possibly falling.

"Guhan, you need rest," Sweta auntie said. "Let's sleep."

He didn't argue with her, and when I was sure he was gone, I peeked out from under the blanket into the darkness of our new world.

• • •

In the morning, the girls put their uniforms on and got ready for school. They were keener on talking to us, asking us if we would go to their school with them from now on. Their questions seemed friendlier, almost as if they were glad to have us there, or perhaps it was just pity.

"Will you be living here with us?" one asked.

"What standard were you in at your old school?" asked the other. "Did your old school have a big canteen?"

I wanted to answer the questions as a sign of friendship, but my voice seemed stuck in my throat. Something about seeing them getting ready for their school day, still safe in the lives they knew, made me feel sick. I would never be sent off to school by my mummy ever again.

Auntie saved us this time. "Girls, what are you bothering them for? They have just gotten here. Daddy and I will talk to them, and when you come home, they can read with you while you do your homework."

We all followed her into the living room where a young servant set out chai and toast on the coffee table. Chaya ate a banana as her mother packed her bag for school.

Guhan uncle was reading the newspaper on their large sofa. He looked up as we entered the room and gave us a wide smile. "Amla, Asya, beti, sit down here."

He patted the sofa cushions next to him. I followed Asya, who sat on the edge of a red velvet seat.

"I am happy you remembered that we are your family," he said gently. Guhan uncle seemed different now; when he was not drunk, he might actually be kind. Maybe he could be trusted after all.

"Thank you, Uncle," I managed to say.

We had breakfast together, and afterwards Auntie asked Uncle for money for groceries and to pay the servant. As he handed her the money, he made a joke about him being her money servant. She smiled, but there was no humor in her eyes.

The servant took the empty cups from the table. She looked only a year or two older than Asya and me, and I wondered if that was the type of work we would soon be doing every day. It would be better than marrying strange men we didn't know. I suspected this was more important to me than to Asya since I had actually felt what it was to be with someone I cared for. I felt Asya's hesitation, and when I could, I reassured her with visions of us as university girls. Nisha and Chaya said bye to us, and I waved back at them, trying to swallow my jealousy at their normal life. I wouldn't admit it to Asya, but I did miss our small village school in that moment.

The minute Guhan uncle left for work, Auntie began to relax. She hummed as she put her family's laundered clothes away, and asked us if we wanted to join her at the market. She said tonight she would make something special for all of us. We hadn't had a chance to talk to Uncle about finding Asya and me a job, and so I asked Auntie if he would be at dinner. She paused, then laughed nervously and replied, "Who knows with him."

The market was not like the market we were used to. It was a shop building, with RELIANCE FRESH BAZAAR written over the entrance in large white lettering. No vendors loudly letting passersby know about their daily vegetables and fruits, no flower stand owner asking us to smell his magnolias, no copperwala or chappalwala laying their goods out on shiny waxed tarps, no fragrant scents of cardamom, chili, turmeric, and cinnamon among spice tables.

Here there were labeled shelves with packaged goods and large bins full of vegetables that people placed in plastic bags. Spices were neatly folded and pressed into boxes instead of arrayed in large steel bowls. People packed their plastic baskets with groceries and brought them to lines of registers in the front. I wondered how anyone made connections in this market. How did the vendors find time to hear about a customer's sister's wedding or a husband's head cold? How did the customers get a discount because the shopkeeper knew they would be back in three days for rice or ginger root?

Auntie was busy crossing off things from her list, something Mummy never did. Mummy never even made a list. She just bought what was fresh that morning; sometimes it was eggplant and other times squash. My chest ached as I realized I would never walk beside her through the market again, hearing vendors call out her name. I might never be in our village market again at all.

When Auntie was all done paying, we carried our plastic bags together to the bus. Auntie asked, "Did you like the store, girls?"

Asya was polite and told her it was very nice.

"It was different," I answered honestly. It was all so very different.

CHAPTER 14

When we got back to the flat, Asya and I had no chores to do. We were used to having to quickly cut up the vegetables, prepare the rice, knead the roti dough. But Auntie had the servant come in to begin preparing dinner. I could tell Asya wanted to keep busy, and I almost asked the servant if we could help until I watched how gracefully and efficiently her hands moved. I found myself watching the steps of her routine as I wondered, *Would I be able to do this? All alone in a stranger's kitchen?*

In my mind, I went through the steps of making subzi with her: letting the mustard seeds crackle, adding in the garam masala to coat the vegetables—seeing if I could remember every part of it from just my memories of watching Dadi or Mummy.

Auntie came out of the girls' room with two books. "Since you did not go to school today, here; read three stories from these books."

My heart leapt, and I had to stop myself from grabbing them out of her hands. While I wasn't fond of school the way Asya was, I had been craving knowledge, and the escapism of a good story would be a huge respite from worrying about our future.

The books contained stories from the Ramayana. Asya took hers and sat at the couch, and I sat beside her with the other book. I loved daydreaming about the palace where Rama, Bharat, Shatrughan, and Laxman grew up with gold-lined curtains and beautiful gardens.

As I read about Rama leaving for the forest for exile, and his youngest brother, Laxman, saying he wanted to leave all his luxuries behind to live beside Rama for fourteen years, I thought of Asya. If she and I were princesses, and if she got sent to the forest, would I follow her? I knew the answer was yes, of course; even picturing her walking away without running after her made me feel horrible. But I wondered if it was simply because we were always Amla and Asya, Asya and Amla. Did I really truly love my sister, or was I conditioned to love her and, as my duty, to watch over her, to stay by her side as everyone told me?

I felt guilty for letting thoughts of anything but loving her run through my mind, especially when I looked over as she pointed at Auntie sitting in front of the TV, clutching her sari to her chin in suspense. Knowing it would make me laugh, Asya made a cuckoo sign at the side of her forehead.

I continued reading. When Rama refused to return until his exile period was up, his brother Bharat placed Rama's slippers at the throne and ruled Ayodhya in the name of Rama. It was his duty to his brother. I realized that what tied Asya and me together was deeper than a sense of duty, though—perhaps even deeper than the love Laxman felt for Rama. Asya and I somehow never lost that connection we forged in our mummy's tummy. It was rooted deep in what I remember Sandeep bhai in yoga calling our muladhara chakra, flowing through the *nadi* to our collective mind. Sandeep bhai was often ridiculed for the way he spoke in yoga. Rather than focusing on the strict asana, he asked us questions.

He pointed to the bottom of his spine and said, "This is where your roots are. What first comes to your mind?" Some of the girls giggled, but I'll never forget in that moment, as we meditated in a deep prana, how vividly my sister's face came to me, from a memory of when we fell asleep as children and I had woken up before her, our noses touching in perfect symmetry.

I didn't mention my prana experience to her, but I remember reading my sister's poem after she left yoga class that day, long before she started letting me read her poems.

What I know
Is our heartbeat
Chakras
Memories that feel older than what I remember

I looked over at my sister now and wondered if she was still confused about the village. After the market, she had said if Guhan uncle didn't find jobs for us, we could just go back. I hadn't agreed with her and simply stayed silent. Now as she looked up at me and smiled, I swallowed the weight of my decision to never return.

• • •

When the girls came home from school, I felt like I was watching a scene from a show about a perfect middle-class Indian family. Auntie got up from her TV show and helped them remove their bags and sort through their folders. They put their matching blue cardigan sweaters on the sofa and ran to the kitchen, saying they were hungry, as Auntie prepared their worksheets on the coffee table. They brought cookies out of the kitchen, the Parle-G glucose kind, and handed a few to Asya and me, then walked around the living room, eating their cookies and chasing Auntie as she told them to sit and do their homework.

Asya was teary eyed like I was, so I walked over to sit beside my sister in the living room of a home that was not ours, watching the family that was not ours, missing our mother and Nani and even Dadi, and knowing we only had each other now. I rested my hand on her lap; I had to stay strong for us in this decision. I didn't want her to cave and tell Auntie she wanted to go back.

Auntie looked over at us almost apologetically, and asked us if we had finished our reading. We took the books into our laps again as the girls settled down and did their homework. Someone turned the TV off, and the room fell into silence as we all studied, and I let myself feel like I was just a schoolgirl again.

A short while later, Auntie told the servant to make paneer tikka masala with Panjabi-style naan and pulao for dinner. As she cooked, the spices wafted through the air. Guhan uncle came home, and we sat and spooned the delicious food onto our plates. I decided to savor every bite. I pushed all other thoughts out of my mind and let the paneer melt in my mouth, watching my rice soak up the creamy sauce.

Asya and I seemed to have the same idea. We ate almost four naan each. Every time we finished what was on the table, the servant, whose name I learned was Dhruva, would bring out fresh, steaming bread.

Guhan uncle sat at the end of the table, eating with the same enthusiasm. I was relieved to see that he wasn't drinking, but my stomach still roiled as a paneer cube fell on his shirt, staining it orange. He wiped it off with a napkin Dhruva ran to get him.

"So, Asya and Amla, Auntie tells me you are interested in finding work, is this right?" he asked as the meal wound down. Dhruva started clearing plates quietly, keeping her eyes down and on her work.

Asya looked at me, so I answered Guhan uncle. "Yes, we are hoping to find a job so we can save for a flat and for our studies."

"Hmm," he said, scratching his chin. "How old are you both?"

"We will be sixteen years old soon," I said before glancing at my sister. I wondered if she realized our birthday was in a week; I had forgotten until just now.

Guhan uncle slapped Dhruva's hand as she tried to take his plate. She stepped back immediately and whispered an apology. He took another bite of his dinner without replying. As he chewed, he asked us about Dadi and Dada.

"Do they know you are here? That you will be working?"

I didn't answer, and I hoped Asya wouldn't say anything. We couldn't tell him we ran away from being promised to men or else he probably wouldn't help us get a job. Guhan uncle waited awhile, but when neither of us replied, he finally just said, "I know a friend that can help, and you can live there also." He put more food into his mouth and turned to Auntie to say something when I cut him off.

"What type of work is it?" It may have been rude, but I needed to know. Cleaning? Cooking? Caring for children?

He chewed his food slowly before answering.

"It should be like our Dhruva. So you best learn how to make this paneer, eh?" He smiled, revealing a row of teeth stained orange by the masala. I peered at Asya, who was quiet, but I understood her worry. I looked back up at him. "Thank you, Uncle. Asya and I just want to stay together."

For the next few days, Asya and I asked Dhruva to teach us how to make the different dinner dishes she cooked for us. She was very kind and embraced becoming our teacher, telling us we would need to know lots of different recipes since we did not know if the family would be Gujarati, Sikh, Parsi, Marathi, or even Jain, and all their food was different. She told us we shouldn't believe our female employer if she told us she would come and show us how to make things. "These upper-class mothers never step foot in the kitchen," she said.

In addition to cooking lessons, Dhruva gave us pointers on how to get turmeric stains out with lemon juice while doing the laundry, how to fold sheets so they looked crisp, and the best direction to run the jharu broom, with the long grass strands curving away from you.

Many of her lessons were things we already knew, but it felt different when she taught us. Instead of everyday life, it was training for a job. I told her how Dadi had been training us to do the same, learning the house chores for when we got married. Dhruva looked at us and bluntly asked why we did not get married.

"We wanted a better life than just to be married off to old men," I explained. "Can you study on your time off?"

Dhruva smiled at us. She sounded wiser than her seventeen years when she replied, "You will soon learn that you can never escape a woman's work." She swung her dupatta to the side, her words lingering in the dust particles that rose from the floor as she swept.

CHAPTER 15

T hat weekend, we all went to Juhu Beach. Auntie had suggested
it when Uncle said Asya and I would be meeting our potential
employer near there. He said the man wanted to see if we would be a
good match for the family he knew. He said he even wanted to hire
both of us together, and a sense of relief settled within me. I knew that
together we could get the biryani right, and that Asya made thinner
roti than I did, no matter how hard I tried.

Chaya and Nisha wore Western-style dresses with yellow and red
polka dots. They said their father's sister from America had sent them
since they didn't fit their American cousins anymore. Nisha added,
"Everyone in America is fat!" And it reminded me of Puppa when
Mummy asked him how he knew what Americans looked like.

Life with our parents felt like another time, distant and far from
where we were now. I wondered if Puppa had thought of us at all when
he left our lives. When he left Mummy like that. Asya touched my
shoulder as if she knew what I was thinking. She left her hand there,
and I tried to let the anger within me subside.

Guhan uncle was very proud of his beige-colored Tata car. He
instructed us not to rest the bags on the hood while we waited for him

to unlock all the doors, and to be careful with the tiffin lunch Auntie packed, to put it at our feet so nothing would spill on the carpet.

When a cow walked right in front of us, Auntie joked that luckily Uncle could not curse the sacred cow for touching the bumper of his car, or we would have to cover our ears. We all laughed, but when Uncle looked at Auntie sternly, our laughter retreated as fast as it came. It made me grateful that we were not in the village, meeting our future husbands whom we would fear and never share real laughter with. At least in this unknown journey, we would make money for the work we did.

There was something to see in every corner at Juhu Beach. Women adorned their bodies in large pashmina shawls to carry their babies, large families walked together as herds, men sold pinwheels from baskets atop their heads. Chaya said that the actors Amitabh Bhachchan and Amrish Puri had homes with views of the sea and pointed up to the tallest buildings I had ever seen. I couldn't stop listening to the sound of the water hitting the sand, the quiet-yet-loud roar the waves made as they crashed towards the shore.

Auntie said, "Chee, don't put your feet there; it is dirty," but as we walked along the sand, I ignored the debris that swam up on the shores— full of old Maaza juice boxes and faded plastic containers. I loved the way my feet felt in the sand, like I had become one with each grain and ripple of water. We had visited a neighboring village once where I sank my toes into the dirt by the river this way. There was something peaceful about letting my feet sink into the water and sand, about being able to drown out voices around me with just the force of water.

We heard a strange echo; it was something so new that I looked around in shock, and the girls laughed at me.

"No, no, look up," Nisha said. I followed her finger and watched as the planes flew higher and higher, disappearing into the sky like birds on a sunny day. Uncle explained that the airport was nearby.

"Where are they going?" Asya asked in wonderment.

Chaya said, "America!"

At the same time Nisha said, "Africa!"

Asya smiled and said, "China!"

And soon we all were screaming faraway places we had seen on our geography maps and running ahead each time a new place was said, falling into giggles. We didn't realize how far we had gone until we stopped and turned to see Uncle in the distance with Auntie walking in front of him; she was oblivious to him pulling the small flask from his coat pocket and taking a large sip. Suddenly he staggered forward and knocked down a young boy's ice cream. The boy started crying. The boy's father first reacted with surprise, then snarled at Uncle as he walked away. Thankfully, Uncle didn't react.

"I wish he would stop," Nisha said softly.

Chaya looked over at her sister, who turned towards the water. "He'll never stop," she said.

And we all looked out at the water then, into the vast horizon, and tried to forget the disappointment of our fathers.

The sky was colored a soft pink hue when we went to the pav bhaji stand that Guhan Uncle said was his favorite. Auntie had packed us chana masala in the lunch tins, but he said he wanted pav bhaji in a childish voice, trying to tease her. Auntie didn't smile, only walked with him as we followed them to the busy vendor. Secretly, I was happy to have the pav bhaji, something our family never ate since the pav was so rare in our village, reserved for large weddings.

By this time, his words were slightly slurred, and I was worried about the drive home, but Auntie fed him water from her tiffin mug—when he cooperated. The pav bhaji was delicious, and the butter on the fluffy pav melted in my mouth. The bhaji of mashed vegetables was spicy enough to make my eyes water, and the crisp, raw onions on top made it perfect. We sat on a matted area of the sand where a cart may have been before.

Auntie checked her watch. "Guhan, we must go meet your friend soon, the one for the girls and their job."

Guhan uncle looked up suddenly from his food and exclaimed, "Not my girls; they cannot work there."

I felt my face turn red. Auntie raised her voice. "Guhan, for Amla and Asya, remember? What is wrong with you?"

Nisha looked at Asya, who dropped her gaze before saying quietly, "It's okay, Auntie. We can try another time."

"It's not okay. Where is he? We were looking forward to meeting him."

I was still mad at Uncle for what he had said.

Guhan uncle stood abruptly. He grabbed Auntie's arm and hissed, "Okay, let's go."

I could tell it hurt because when she finally freed herself from his grip, she rubbed her arm where he had twisted it. Nisha met my gaze and then glanced away, her eyes full of shame.

We walked down the beach towards an alley. The day grew dimmer as we left the ocean and entered the darkness of the concrete city again. Uncle studied a piece of paper with the address, and then we spotted a short man standing by a rusted door. A motorcycle was parked out front, and a man in a butcher apron wearing a topi was loading a truck with his goods. The stench of raw meat made my stomach clench. Auntie said we did not want to go inside when she saw the waxed paper packages of meat, the red blood seeping through like wet paint.

Rajiv was not Guhan uncle's actual friend but his friend's friend, who received a cut for placing girls in homes that needed help with housework or babysitting.

"Guhan sahib, you will receive half the pay. These girls will get a place to live, and once they simply pay off the fee for finding the job, they of course will get their own pay for work, usually within six months."

He looked down at his watch as Auntie asked, "When can they return to their families for a visit?"

"Oh, whenever they want, of course, as long as their employer families do not need them on those times." As I followed the conversation, I couldn't stop bringing my eyes back to the methodical way the butcher loaded the meat onto his truck.

Guhan uncle was smiling, his eyes glassy; he was still half drunk. Rajiv spoke about us like we were not right in front of him. "But the girls should know that we encourage them not to try to visit their homes for the first year. Usually they are homesick, and it breaks this feeling for them. Where are the girls from?"

I wasn't sure if we were supposed to answer since he had barely glanced at us. Guhan uncle didn't bother answering, so Auntie put her arms on our shoulders and said, "They are from a small village in Madhya Pradesh, but we are their home here."

"We still have our grandparents' home," I said.

"Yes, yes. Very pretty girls, very, very pretty."

Auntie's hands tightened on our shoulders. We looked at Guhan uncle, who was nodding in agreement. I felt my stomach churn again; I hated being looked at that way.

"Okay, Rajiv bhai," she said. "Thank you. We will be in touch with you."

"Yes, yes, remember it is very good pay."

We said goodbye and left him, but even with my back turned, I felt his eyes on us. Auntie never took her hands off our shoulders as we walked on either side of her.

• • •

On the way home, Auntie and Uncle started to fight.

"Why did you need to drink, Guhan? We are at the beach, and we had that meeting. You knew that." She was upset.

He almost drove into a parked motorcycle, and Auntie had to grab the steering wheel, turning it as we swerved back onto the main road. The four of us in the back seat held hands tightly as it happened.

He laughed and told her to loosen up. She hit his hand when he reached for her leg, and he pulled back his hand and slapped her hard. It happened so fast that all I heard was the back of his hand hitting her jaw. Afterwards, her lip started to bleed.

Nisha held Chaya's head in her lap as I looked out the window as if I hadn't seen anything. We heard crying, but it was not Auntie; it was Chaya, who started to cry uncontrollably in Nisha's lap, with fear in her eyes as to what her father would do next.

He looked at Chaya through the rearview mirror, and I saw his tears, but he didn't say anything and kept driving. We sat in silence even as he parked the car. No one opened the doors; he sat in the driver seat with his seat belt on until he finally barked, "Get out."

We scrambled for the door handles, all five of us pouring out of his beloved car. Auntie didn't wait for him as she ran to the building, letting the door slam. The four of us followed her lead, our footsteps echoing in the hallway.

• • •

A few days later at breakfast, Uncle came in and said, "Amla, Asya, you can begin to pack. It is all set. It is your last day before your new h-job."

He had almost said "new home." Auntie looked at him and said, "Yes, that is your new job; this will still be your home."

She asked us to help the girls get their schoolbags ready, and we reluctantly got up. I wanted to ask him if one of them could come with us or if they would set a date to visit, but I wasn't sure if he was in a good enough mood to answer. The four of us stood behind the bedroom door and held our breath until I decided to ask.

I approached the two of them, their eyes set on me.

"Amla?"

"Auntie, Uncle, will you visit us there?"

Sweta auntie's eyes softened. "That man, Guhan, you don't even know him. Shouldn't we see the house first? The family?"

Guhan uncle glanced from Auntie back to me. "Amla, beti, do not worry. Go get ready with the girls."

I walked slowly, catching pieces of Sweta auntie's whispers.

"Did you call their grandparents? They must want to know where the girls are."

I hadn't thought of this, if he would call them. Would they tell him to send us home instead? I heard Uncle shift his feet.

"Sweta, please. I tried to call the grandparents, but they have not answered my SDT calls. It is a simple job. They are perfectly capable of doing it. Look at Dhruva and how happy she is. Besides, we can use the money, you know. They cut my hours at work, and that Rajiv is splitting his pay with me."

"It's not about the money, Guhan. That man doesn't seem right. And your hours were cut because of your drinking, you know that . . ." Her voice trailed off as Uncle's voice grew louder. I was back behind the door with the others.

"Enough! You don't trust me? You ungrateful *kutiya*, who is the one who makes the money here?"

I flinched at the curse word and heard him move the coffee table. I was afraid he was going to hurt her again. The bruise on her face from the car ride was enough.

Chaya ran out, and I went behind her. I felt Asya grab my arm. I knew she was thinking, *This is not your place*, but I went anyway.

"Auntie, we need help to pack the bags," I lied.

Guhan uncle was standing far too close to Sweta auntie, his eyes fixated on her small frame. As we came into the room, he backed off, and Auntie grabbed the two of us.

"Okay, come; let me see."

She kept hold of us as she retreated to our bedroom, our small feet right behind her. Chaya held on to my hand, too, even when we were safe in the bedroom.

Auntie saw right away that we hadn't packed anything. She started grabbing her daughters' folders and papers, stuffing them into their bags with urgency.

When she was done, she reached out for both of us. She held our hands, looked into our eyes. "Listen to me: if something doesn't feel right, you come back here. I will be here, okay? And—" Before she could finish, we heard Guhan uncle walking down the hall, and she let go of us quickly, pretending to finish packing up.

"Okay, time for school, girls!" she said in a too-cheerful voice. Nisha and Chaya took their bags and headed out the door. Where just two weeks ago I had been so jealous of them, now I saw that school was their only escape.

I wondered how much Auntie could do for us if we ever needed help. Asya's jaw tightened, her worried look coming over her face, and I understood: we could only help ourselves, or else we would return to the village. My confusion flooded me. Was Auntie right? We hardly knew the man, but wouldn't a big agency in Mumbai find us a good home?

• • •

For our last night, Auntie convinced Guhan uncle to take us all to the cinema for a film. It was a weeknight, but he probably felt bad about his behavior that morning, so he didn't say no when she showed him the showtimes in the newspaper.

We ate our dinner quickly, and I almost wanted to invite Dhruva to come with us. She had helped us prepare for our new life, the one that would mirror hers, and I felt closer to her than I did with even Chaya and Nisha. But before I could offer, she smiled and told us to tell her all about it when we came home.

It was a Hema Malini film, and even on a weeknight, the whole theater was full. In contrast to our village's one-screen cinema, this one was huge, with three rooms, each with a screen that felt larger than the sky. Multiple movies played every day, instead of the single film that came every few months to ours.

Sitting in that theater and watching the movie was the most peaceful three hours I had experienced in a long time. I didn't mind that the boys behind us kept whistling during the songs, or the loud crunch of the popcorn under my feet. Even the darkness of the room was comforting, the sounds and scenes filling my mind, carrying me to another world, a place where Hema Malini was my mother who didn't die of cancer, where I wasn't scared about living with a family I had never met, in a city I had barely been to; where I had a place in the world, perhaps in a Bollywood-style mansion with my own room and a dadi who braided my hair and reminded me to study; where there was no need for me to have to care and cook for girls that might be my own age; where even when something bad happened, there was always a hero, someone who cared enough to make it all better.

The next day was our sixteenth birthday. We awoke to find that Auntie had baked a cake with pineapples and raisins inside, in honor of our last day with them. Chaya and Nisha gave us birthday cards that they made with their Western glitter markers, which we knew they only used for special projects. We sat at the table for breakfast together as we read the cards. We hadn't had a cake like that since our thirteenth birthday, when Mummy had spent months secretly gathering the ingredients.

Guhan uncle said he would get petrol for the car and come to the front door to drive us. After he left, Auntie kept fussing about our bags and whether we had packed enough. "You can always come back here if you need anything. You can just come back if something is not right."

She seemed so worried about it that I started to worry again. And what did she mean? What wouldn't be right? *Or anyway*, I thought bitterly, *what* else *wouldn't be right?* We had left everything we had ever known, had no family left, and here we were, my sister and I, going to go cook and clean for strangers. Nothing about it felt right except that I was with my sister.

Asya had written me a poem as my birthday gift. "Asya, you are too thoughtful," I said. "I don't have anything for you. If we were home, I would have gotten you a Thums Up!"

It was our tradition to go to the corner store; Babu bhai would be at his chaiwala stand in front of the store, ringing his bell. "Ah, the birthday twins!" he would say, holding his arms wide open in greeting.

He would order the Dalit who cleaned his steel cups to bring a Thums Up from inside the store. I would give Asya most of it since it was her favorite, and watch her smile after a big sip.

I opened the blue tissue paper I had seen in the garbage the day before and saw her neat cursive writing.

Unknown waters
A water well echoes
The story of two girls
That once shared
One heart

CHAPTER 16

U ncle kept glancing at us through the rearview mirror as if we would disappear. I held Asya's hand the whole car ride. It was raining the day we left, the smells of the monsoons starting to rise from the soil. In our village, the monsoon season's arrival was welcomed with festivals and prayers. Everyone prepared their homes with rain shields, using bamboo slivers, plastic sheets, and broom grass that had reminded me of turtle shells when we were children.

In Mumbai, we saw workers atop roofs, cleaning the chajja of the leaves and accumulated dust to prepare for proper drainage. As we drove and the colors of Mumbai blended together, I thought of an oil painting I had once seen. Asya's classmate had visited London with her parents to see her eldest brother, who was in a medical school there. When she got back she couldn't stop talking about her trip. Her brother had taken her to an art exhibition where she had seen walls of paintings. She showed us a postcard of her favorite painting by an artist named Leonid while we were all gathered in the yard, waiting for our teachers to usher us into lines. As she talked about the beautiful floors of the gallery and the way the water fountain looked like a real waterfall, I couldn't stop looking at the postcard. It mesmerized me. The details were meshed into the beauty of vibrant paint colors, merging to form the scene so clearly. Each tree branch, each sidewalk, each car and person on that street scene blended together so naturally.

In the mess of rain and smog and cars and cows, Mumbai was my street scene, and I took in each color, each raindrop as if to capture it as a photograph, as if it would all disappear one day, in the blink of an eye. Just as our old life had.

We were to meet Guhan uncle's friend Rajiv at a paanwala hut on a busy road. The shopkeeper worked fast as customers took shelter from the rain beneath a small plastic tarp he had put over his tin roof. There they waited for their betel nut delicacies as we waited for our new home, a new life where we could earn a living to save for our studies or even send money home to our village for our grandparents, who could hopefully forgive us.

From the car, I watched the shopkeeper fold the paan leaf and slit the stalk. He quickly painted on lime juice, rolling it into a cone too fast to catch how he did it. As he added the red betel nut mukhwas, the gulkand and coconut flakes, and a sprinkle of cardamom with one hand, he used the other to start working on the next leaf.

We waited in the car until we heard Guhan uncle say, "Look, he is here." Through the raindrops on the car window, I saw Rajiv uncle's short and stout frame approaching our car. We got out and ran towards him, taking shelter under the shade of another shopkeeper's cooking hut. Steam rose from the oil of the cook's large pan. The cook spread the smooth white batter on the blackness of his pan, quickly cooking each wide, flat, roti-looking item and wrapping them in newspaper for the hungry street shoppers. My stomach growled as the scent of his coconut chutney filled my nostrils.

"Ah, if you haven't had Anand's dosa, you do not know what you are missing," Rajiv uncle said. He had been watching me. I smiled and looked at Asya.

"Anand, *do sadha dosa*," Rajiv said to the cook.

The man didn't even look up or speak as he made the savory thin dosa and handed them to Rajiv. When the cook glanced up and saw us for the first time, I nodded in gratitude, and he offered us a genuine smile.

The dosa was delicious—the crispness combined with the soft filling and almost tangy flavor. I was surprised by how fast I ate it. I looked up and saw Asya still holding most of her food. She was moving closer to Rajiv uncle and Guhan uncle, who had started some sort of negotiation.

"It's 20,000," Rajiv uncle said.

"They are two; it should be double," Guhan uncle growled.

He seemed awfully invested in how much money we would make; it didn't feel right.

"Why double? I am also paying the travel fees for both of them, remember?"

"Won't they be in Mumbai? What travel fees?" Guhan asked.

"I am just the middleman, Guhan saab," Rajiv replied. "Since we wanted to place the girls together, we had to search quite far to find the right position. We were trying to respect your request."

"Yes, we have to stay together," I said, worrying that Guhan might walk away from the deal.

"If not in Mumbai, where will they go? My wife has asked that we know the location."

"Can Guhan uncle and Sweta auntie visit us?" Asya asked. Rajiv dismissed us with a glance and spoke to Guhan.

"I have not been given an address, but when I arrive at the office I can collect that for you; however, there is little time. The tickets are already purchased, and they must start work immediately or they will lose their chance. Are you still interested?"

Guhan uncle hadn't had a drink before the meeting, and I was grateful for that as he glanced at us, hesitating. For a moment, it seemed as if he was seeing us with the eyes of a father. What was he thinking?

He turned to Rajiv. "Yes, we will still take the position, but we must have 40,000."

When they shook hands, Asya bit into her dosa. As she swallowed, I tried to swallow the nervousness in my throat. I worried about what these amounts meant for us. It all felt so real now that we were standing there and ready to go. And why were we not in Mumbai; where were we going?

Guhan uncle said goodbye to us and handed me a piece of paper with his phone number to call when we arrived. I held it tight as he ran back to his car once the rain let up again.

I dozed off in Rajiv's car, my head on Asya's shoulder. When I woke to the beeping of car horns, I realized we were in a traffic jam. It was no longer raining, but the air was still wet and muggy as people and cows weaved through the streets between the cars and trucks.

"Where are we?" I asked.

Asya was quiet, and Uncle kept his eyes on the road. "Almost there," he replied. "It's always like this near the station."

I wondered what the family would be like. Would the kids be old or young? Were there grandparents there? What kind of food did they eat? Were they vegetarian? "How many people live in the home we are going to?" I asked.

"Oh, it's a big family. My friend will tell you more. You can call her Didi."

Older sister, I thought. It was a comforting term, but it wasn't real information.

"What's her name?" I asked.

Rajiv uncle didn't answer. Instead he rolled down his window and spat out red gutka, almost hitting a woman carrying a stack of folded kurta shirts on her head. She banged on his car as she walked by.

Asya tugged at my shirt. I looked over at her and she mouthed, "Maybe we should go home. I don't want to go." What was she saying? How could we leave now? I shook my head at her. We had already made it this far.

"Asya, this job is an opportunity. We just have to get past this part, okay?"

"Don't touch my car!" Rajiv screamed at the woman. As the anger erupted from his throat, I retreated in my seat and decided to save my questions for Didi.

Asya didn't say anything else, and I felt scared too, but didn't admit it to her.

Why do men always choose anger?

CHAPTER 17

The station was busy when we arrived. I clung to Asya's hand, knowing all the people-watching would distract her; I might lose her in the crowd if I let go. Rajiv uncle stood behind us and pushed us forward. For a moment I searched the train schedule board for Madya Pradesh, or somewhere close to our village. Maybe Asya was right that we should go back home. But how? Weren't we too deep in it now?

I had never seen a board like this, and there were so many places listed—unknown names that made me realize how very far we would be from any type of home.

We found Didi beside the train schedule board. She was tall, taller than Rajiv and possibly even Guhan uncle. Her fair skin and short hair made her look like a movie star except for her long hooked nose. She towered over Rajiv wordlessly and took our free hands in her own. In our other hands, we clutched our small bags filled with the only memories we had of our old life. Photographs, Mummy's earrings, and the green dupatta scarf. Asya had brought her ruler and some sweets Nisha had secretly handed her before we left.

"Rajiv uncle, you aren't coming?" Asya asked Rajiv.

"No," he replied coldly. "Didi will take you to your new home. Stay close to her and listen to her, or else you will not get the job." With that, he turned and walked away, disappearing into the crowd in seconds.

Could we disappear into the crowd too? Where were we, though, and how would we get back to Guhan uncle's flat from here? And if we did return, would he send us back to the village? I thought of the photo of the two men with the stained teeth and decided I had to push through. In any case, I didn't want Asya to worry, and fear was written all over her face.

Moments later, a train rolled into the station beside us. Everyone started inching towards the train cars at the sound of its whistles. Amidst the pushing, somehow we were shoved through the train's doors, Didi still clutching our hands tightly.

We held on to a railing as people forced their way inside behind us. The doors tried to close, but hands blocked them open, and the train lurched forward while people were still climbing on. Soon the train had left the station behind, the doors closing with a dull thump. There was no turning back now.

The women's compartment was packed tight, but we managed to find a corner to sit down. Asya was almost on top of me, and it felt like the people would never stop entering the car. Where would they all go? We packed ourselves so close to each other that it felt like the train car might burst. I could only hope the ride was not long as we chugged along on our journey to the unknown.

I wasn't sure if we would be working for Didi or not. Between the sounds of people talking, crying babies, and the loud wheels screeching on the tracks, I would have had to scream to ask her anything.

The train car quickly grew hot. Finally one of the babies fell asleep, and another mother pulled her sari over her baby's head to feed him milk. I noticed that the baby had just had his head shaved. In our village when a son was born, they often shaved his head during his mundan ceremony, removing the undesirable traits from his past life but leaving a *sikha*, the single tuft on the crown of his head, to protect his memory.

I wondered then how different our lives would have been had Asya and I been born as boys. I thought, *If I were a boy, I would want to be like Sandeep bhai, calm and always smiling.* I thought of my sister, how smart she was even in the choices her heart made, liking a boy like him.

"Asya, if you were a boy, who would you want to be?"

"Huh? What do you mean, Amla?"

"I would choose to be Sandeep bhai; he's so calm and always smiling. Who would you be?"

Her face softened when I said Sandeep bhai's name. I knew that it would. Maybe she would open up.

"Amla, I don't know. We aren't boys. You heard Dhruva. We are girls, and we will never escape women's work. I still don't know if this is a good idea. Maybe we need to think of how we will get back home instead. Like maybe we can act very homesick—"

"You won't even give it a chance; that is so typical of you."

"What!?"

I felt others in the car trying to eavesdrop when she reacted.

"You can go get married to that dirty man. I don't want to."

"I don't either, ugh. Forget it. You never listen. I'm just trying to think things through here."

She turned her back to me. Her hair caught in my lips, and I pushed it away forcefully.

Maybe I didn't listen, but at least I was brave enough to give something new a chance. There was no turning back now.

CHAPTER 18

We were on the train for a long time, longer even than the trip to Mumbai had been. Too long, it seemed to me, but I was afraid to ask this strange Didi where we were going. What if we didn't understand their customs? What if they were not nice? How would Guhan uncle and Sweta auntie know where to find us? I was very unsure that Rajiv uncle had an address for our new employers. I felt for the paper with the phone number in my pocket for reassurance.

I started to feel what Asya had felt: an overwhelming sense of regret that we had agreed to leave Guhan uncle's house. I had not thought things through.

My throat was dry in the heat, and I longed for water. There were people sitting everywhere, in every corner, every crevice or area one could fit. I looked up at the second level, packed with bags, housewares, baskets, and luggage. Some people even sat in between the cars, letting the rattle of the floor keep them awake.

After a time, it began to rain again. The drops made a lovely, calming *shhh* noise against the train windows. An older woman who was squatting across from us started to sing. She looked frail and small, but her voice was powerful. She sang a song of Shiva and Parvati—

for Teej, the union of God Shiva, and for Shakti, feminine strength. In the stories we heard growing up, Parvati had fasted for 108 days, representing purity of heart, mind, and soul. Her goodness was what attracted Shiva to her.

In our village, after prayers, the girls often tied rope swings with woven fabric to trees to enjoy as the older women sang ancient songs like the one this old lady sang. They always seemed to honor divine love. I closed my eyes to remember the last time we had swung amongst the trees. The neighbor's daughters had found heavy rope and an old tire. When it was my turn, I heard their mother and our mother singing. Their voices echoed a belief that a man could love his wife that way . . . even though neither of them had good husbands. I heard hope in their voices as I let the sun touch my eyelids and the air run through my hair. I kicked my feet up and felt like I was touching the sky.

It was the closest I ever felt to letting my heart's wings soar.

The smell of fried dough and spiced potatoes suddenly filled my nostrils. I opened my eyes to see saw a small white canister being passed around. A young boy no older than three reached up and handed it to me from where he sat on the floor beside his mother. I smiled at him and he blushed, burying his face into her legs. Didi was asleep, but Asya and I ate ravenously; we hadn't had anything since the dosa with Rajiv uncle, and I passed the container to the old woman hunched below me. I found it amazing that everyone shared with one another, and being surrounded by so many strangers didn't feel scary after all.

CHAPTER 19

After several hours, a woman started screaming that she felt cockroaches crawling on her back. She had been sitting in the corner on the opposite end of our compartment, next to a young couple and their two sleeping toddlers. Startled by the woman's screams, both boys began to cry.

Their mother soothed them and then helped the other woman flick the roaches off her dupatta. The boys' father offered her a newspaper to spread out underneath her. She thanked them and checked the floor again for any new insects. The boys stopped crying and sniffled themselves to sleep on their parents' shoulders.

"How old are they?" the woman asked pleasantly, probably feeling bad for waking them.

"They are twins, both two years old."

They looked alike, with their floppy hair and long eyelashes. I saw their breathing sync up—one would breathe in as the other breathed out—and wondered if it was like that for all twins. I wondered if they too would one day realize having each other sometimes felt like the best feeling, and sometimes like the worst. Or that having each other was the only feeling at times, everything else dissolving, since it was the truest connection to anyone they'd ever know.

Asya and I fell asleep hugging one another. Despite the heat, I still loved the warmth of my sister's body, the way we always fit perfectly into one another. Mummy sometimes would find us hugging that way when we were small girls, since we used to share a big floor bed, all four of us, before we moved homes. She said that is how she imagined we slept in her stomach, clinging to each other, heartbeat to heartbeat.

I don't know how long we slept, but it felt like we rolled night to day to night to day as the train carried on. The rain was relentless, pouring down over the windows and dripping through holes in the ceiling of the compartment. When the train jerked to a stop, a conductor yelled through the compartment, and we felt Didi hit our shoulders.

"Wake up, wake up; they are letting us off. The tracks ahead are flooded." It was the first time we'd heard her speak, I realized. Even during the night, she had handed us a bottle of drinking water without speaking. Her voice was surprisingly raspy, and since we were so close, I saw her yellow, protruding teeth.

We exited the car onto a station platform facing large cement fields of unfinished buildings. The smog was so thick and rain so heavy that I could barely see past the tracks. We stood on the platform with the rest of the passengers, crowded together in the only covered area to avoid the rain.

Raspy-voiced Didi spoke again. "We must wait now for the next train. I don't know when it will come."

I had to use the restroom, but then Asya let go of my hand and moved her face into the raindrops, closing her eyes and letting the drops fall onto her tongue, hands, hair. It made me smile, and I let the image of her this way seep into my mind, like a photograph I would never forget. I felt better seeing Asya carefree, like maybe it would work out; I was just being anxious about the changes before.

We waited for hours. The dampness on the concrete platform started to feel cold, despite the warm, thick air. When the rain finally settled down, we saw men working the large buckets on the submerged tracks, clearing out whatever water they could.

Someone had urinated near where we sat, and the stench was horrific, but there was nowhere else for us all to go, so I covered my nose in Mummy's green dupatta scarf. It still had hints of her smell. Jasmine talc powder. Roti flour remnants. The odor of the wood basin she washed our clothes in.

I was scared that in time I would forget her smell or the things that felt so real to me still. The way her slender fingers felt in my hair, the three small creases near her eyes that appeared when she smiled, the warmth of her body when we hugged.

Sadness rose in my throat as I thought of Mummy, and as much as I wanted to let it out, I swallowed it all down. Crying now wouldn't help anyone. Instead I waited for our new life as the second train approached the platform.

CHAPTER 20

When we finally arrived, I was too tired to walk. I just let the sway and push of the people carry me out of the train. Didi grasped our skinny arms tightly.

The train station was like a castle, with large red towers and white-trimmed arches. My left foot had fallen asleep in the cramped train, and as we walked, I stomped on it hard to bring life back to my legs.

With the motion, the strap on my sandal broke, and it went flying into the crowd. Didi was already ahead of us, and I was afraid of losing her if I went to search for it, so I walked on, barefoot. The station was clean, but the minute we exited into the street, the ground was filled with debris and broken glass. Asya peered at me, then took off the green dupatta scarf she cherished, quickly wrapping my foot to protect it. Didi stopped and in her raspy voice told us to hurry.

I tried to run on one foot to spare Mummy's scarf as much as I could as we hurried after Didi. I turned around, just once, to take in the beauty of the railway station before we left it behind. Then I limped along again, wondering what our new home would be like and where we were. I imagined that the family had a girl close to our age and we would become friends in between our chores.

When we found a taxi, it was bright yellow and so clean we thought it could not be for us. Then Didi spoke to the driver in a dialect we didn't understand. Asya asked her in Hindi where we were, and she looked at us, then straight out the open door. Why didn't she answer? Where were we? I scanned the street signs, and everything around us was written in another language. I spotted some Hindi and even some of the English letters Chaya and Nisha showed us, but there was another language I could not recognize.

Then the driver started to play an old song on the radio that we did recognize. It was a Madhuri Dixit number Mummy used to sing and move her hips to.

I looked at Asya and sang, "Ding dong ding, ding dong ding dong ding dong. Ding dong dong. *Ek do teen, char paanch che saath aath nau.*"

And suddenly we were singing along, the two of us smiling—both of us, I am sure of it, imagining Mummy making roti in the kitchen, flour on her cheeks, smiling. Didi smiled with her crooked yellow teeth, and the driver turned the radio up louder for us. Asya held my hand as we drove to our new family in a foreign India.

PART 2

ASYA

AUGUST 2003

CHAPTER 21

D idi dropped us in front of an old, low building, handing us over
to two girls only a little older than us. She turned and strode away
without a word—not that we would miss her; she seemed to go out
of her way to avoid connecting with us, sitting in silence the whole
train ride and even when we arrived. I was exhausted and confused.
Who were these girls? I was still wary of the plan Amla was so sure of.
Nothing yet proved this would grant us the freedom we were chasing,
but for the sake of being together, for Amla's sureness, we were there.

Sajana and Janaki, the two girls who met us, ushered us into a
bedroom. It was painted a dull gray, and there was a large mattress on
the floor. Amla and I fell asleep within minutes, too exhausted to ask
any questions.

For the next three days, Janaki brought us rice and daal to eat, and
we didn't leave the room. We assumed this was something like a waiting
home, if that even existed—where families waited for the girls like us
that would cook, clean, and tend to their household chores. Janaki never
said much of anything, just laying out the tray and leaving the room
again. Once, she brought us some roti and sabzi that we devoured. They
reminded me of home, which made me sad for a moment, but I pushed

the feelings away. In some moments, fear of the unknown gripped me, but I tried to make sense of the new place we waited in.

• • •

On the fourth day, Sajana and Janaki bought us matching shiny red dresses. They were Western style, and incredibly beautiful.

After we had changed, Janaki took out a small black bag filled with makeup. "*Bahut achchha*," she said. Amla and I exchanged glances; her Hindi sounded different.

Sajana told us that Janaki was from Gujarat and had to learn Hindi when she had arrived. It made me wonder how long Janaki had been at the waiting house. Was this her job?

I felt comforted by the presence of the two girls. They fussed over our hair and makeup, talking casually about other girls they knew and laughing. According to Janaki and Sajana, they were the girls in charge, and their job was to help the new girls feel settled.

It made sense, and I wondered if they worked for Rajiv uncle or Didi . . . except every time Amla or I asked them questions about the new family we would work for, they did not answer.

Janaki started putting rouge on our cheeks, red lipstick on our lips.

"Are we going to a party?" Amla asked.

The two girls looked at each other and smiled. "Yes, a special party, but it's happening right here, in your room," Sajana said. The way she said that made me wary, but before I could ask for more details, Jayna, the cook, brought in some Thums Up bottles.

"For us?" Amla asked.

Jayna nodded. She gave the girls a strange look and then left the room again. It felt surreal that just a month ago, we had been in our village in the mud-and-bamboo walls of our sweet home. I thought of Nani in that moment, and tears filled my eyes, but I blinked them away.

Janaki took one of the bottles and handed the other one to the two of us to share. I looked at Amla, whose eyes lit up. She loved Thums

Up more than anyone, and we rarely had it back home. Janaki clinked our bottle with her bottleneck.

"Cheers," she said.

We didn't know what this word meant, but we drank our refreshing soda, and I remember thinking, *The newness of this place and the unknown of where we are going may not be as scary as I thought if we have friends.* The soda tasted different as I drank it, but I couldn't pinpoint what it was.

I'm not sure how long after that things started to get blurry. My body grew heavy. My legs were like hot jalebi, and I heard Sajana saying something, but her voice was long and drawn out. I was on the bed, and I thought Amla was too, next to me. My head was spinning, and everything started to feel like a song. The sounds of car horns, Amla's murmur, doors slamming. I kept opening and closing my eyes, and the noises around me felt more and more distant.

Eventually after what seemed like hours, Janaki spoke to us. She was smiling with a toothless grin. I remembered her with teeth; where did they go? Somehow I could understand her perfectly now.

"Madame wants you to meet her friends. They will come here, and you will let them do whatever they want to you. It will feel funny, but just remember it will be quick. Make sure to be happy for them," she said.

Be happy, be happy, be happy. Was I repeating this out loud or in my mind? I couldn't tell, but it made me laugh uncontrollably. Happy? What was that word? What did it mean to a girl who had lost both her parents, and who was in this strange place and feeling these funny things?

The colors of the room I had thought were dull before were bright. Was this being happy? Seeing the brightness amidst gray?

I don't know how much time passed before two men entered. They came towards us slowly and quickly at the same time. They climbed onto the bed.

I heard my sister making a sound. I turned to look at her. Was she crying or laughing? One of the men was lying next to her, or on her; I couldn't figure out which.

The other man touched my shoulders and pushed his body down

over my hips, trying to pull down my underwear. He had a long beard. It was rough and I told him so, but could he hear me?

I thought I was screaming, but I realized it wasn't me; it was Amla, a bloodcurdling piercing scream that froze me.

I spit on his face for her. I'm sure of it. I cleared my throat and hocked up everything I could and just blew it into his hairy face.

Then the man on top of me slapped me, but I couldn't feel the slap because the pain in my private area was so unbearable. It was as if my brain could only send one signal, one message that would help me comprehend what was happening.

After it was over, Madame came into the room. I was still groggy, and my thighs and pelvis ached. I was bent over on the bed when she spoke. "You are all set now. Welcome to your new work. This is what you will be doing. The next time you spit on a customer, I'll beat you. And don't try to escape. We will have you killed."

She walked out and called for Janaki to clean up.

Amla was curled up on a ball, her back to me. I didn't have the energy to fight with her about her stupid idea to come here. I didn't have the energy to console her either. I sat there with so many questions running through my mind, rising above the numb horror of something incomprehensible.

How had we not seen this coming? How we had failed to see that this would be our fate? Did Guhan uncle know? Rajiv uncle? I couldn't imagine the girls and Sweta auntie knowing.

Janaki came to clean up, and we didn't speak to her, just moved aside so she could take the bloody sheets off the bed. I hugged my knees as she told us that the men were Muslim brothers who had wanted virgins. "They are from the cartel, you know, very powerful, so you are lucky. They paid premium price for you both, and that can bring you closer to repaying your debt."

Our debt. The transaction with Rajiv. I started to understand that we were now owned. Stolen and owned by Madame.

The wheels in my mind started turning. I asked Janaki for a notebook to write poetry. Janaki looked at me and whispered, "Don't tell anyone you can read or write. They will not like it."

"No, no, Janaki, my poems are pictures. I draw each line out." I looked at my sister, who was paying attention now, urging her to play along.

"Yes," Amla agreed. "She can show you."

We searched Janaki for a reaction, but she seemed to believe us. "Oh, I want to see. Let me find something for you."

I was relieved. When Janaki left, I turned to my sister and clasped her hand.

"Amla, we need to work fast. We need to spy and figure out how much debt we are in and how much the Muslim men paid to do . . . that to us."

She lowered her face when I said it. I could tell she felt as disgusted as I did thinking about it.

Janaki returned with a small address book. It was empty.

"This is the best I could find. The cook said it would add fifty rupees to your tab."

"Janaki, what would that make our tab in total?"

"Well, let's see. I heard Madame say you were a deal at one hundred thousand rupees, being so fair-skinned and all, and then you can't forget the cartel paid a thousand for you both, which is almost ten times regular. But then there are your dresses, makeup, and food, of course. And now the book, so what are you at? I do not know maths."

Amla's face sank. She looked at me, and I knew we were thinking the same thing. It would take forever to get out.

But I was the responsible one. I needed to get us out of this mess.

• • •

It took three days for the pain down there to fade for both of us. Amla gradually returned to her amiable self. The other girls in the brothel would sit with her, laughing and telling her stories.

A week later, I was writing poetry in the address book Janaki got us. I hid it under the mattress of our bed.

Dark places
Down there
Freedom
Feels
Far

We were to stay in our room upstairs until Madame told us to come out. Janaki said Madame would wait until after our training so we would be ready to go downstairs and meet customers. She also warned me to stay in line. "If you spit again, you both will be burned with cigarettes in places you never knew you could get burned," Janaki whispered.

I shuddered when she said it. When I told Amla, she of course didn't want to hear it. Instead she asked me a thousand questions I couldn't answer. What was downstairs? More brothers for us? More of the drink that made us laugh and feel heavy but could not take away the pain?

I closed my eyes to try to think of happy memories—to lose myself in the time Nani took us to the temple, listening to the chanting as bells rang against the stillness of intention. On our walk home, Nani told us about the Ganga River. How she had gone as a young girl, how surreal it was to feel a vibration when the gentle ripples of water touched her skin. "It's more than words. This chant is a power inside of you," she had said. So I found myself chanting them in my mind sometimes— *Om gan ganapataye namah*—and trying to create shields of protection around us until Madame's bell snapped me back into reality.

Luckily Janaki and Sajana knew Hindi, or we would be lost. The cook in the brothel and the women we heard on the streets spoke a dialect I could not understand.

"It is Bengali," Janaki told us.

Amla became friends with Janaki and Sajana, but I didn't know who to trust anymore.

The night before we were to start working, Amla told our story to the girls. Sajana held her hand when she spoke about Mummy and reached for my knee when I looked down. Sajana was dark like the night sky, and so beautiful. She had sharp features and big eyes, bright like the sun of her name. She told us her story too. She called her parents Appa and Amma. She said when she was only six years old, her grandfather started coming into her room at night. At first he said he wanted to tell her a story. And so he would start telling her and they would laugh. Then he would get into her bed. His cracked and rough feet would meet hers under the covers. Then she felt the big dry hands. One down there and one over her mouth.

"In the morning he would tell me to be quiet and he would give me chocolates. Even though I loved chocolates, I never ate the ones he gave me. He said no one would believe me since he was the head of the house. My appa loved him and even Amma did too. He was funny and made everyone laugh, but I did not laugh at his jokes as the years went on. Everyone found out when I was ten years old. I got very sick with a fever, and Amma said she would stay in my room with me. I thought God had finally answered my prayers. I slept the whole week straight. They thought it was the fever that was breaking, but even after it was far gone, I kept sleeping.

"Amma took me to the doctor. Amma told her they wanted to know why I was sleeping so much, and the doctor took my temperature and checked my lungs. When she pressed at my tummy and at my waist, I jumped up. I was scared she would check me down there because it hurt too much. She looked at me, and Amma was surprised also. Amma told me to be still, as the doctor was checking and they all wanted me to get better. She joked that when I was better, she could go back to her room to sleep. I started crying that I didn't want Amma to go back to her room. The doctor told Amma she needed to check me there to be sure there was no infection. I'll never forget the doctor's face."

Sajana was quiet, and I took her hand. Her voice was soft and delicate, like a bird's song.

"Afterwards the doctor asked, 'Why don't you want your amma to go back to her room, beti?'"

As Sajana spoke, I remembered the doctor who told us of Mummy's death. *Doctors are like angels*, I thought. *They save our lives when they can, and when they can't, they lay us to rest.*

"I told the doctor, looking only at her, as if Amma wasn't standing there. I told her, 'Because Appa's father comes to my room when she's not there.' Amma started saying no, no, but I told the doctor that he touched me down there and it hurt all the time.

"I heard Amma saying something about mistakes, but she was frantic and breathing fast. The doctor called a nurse to help Amma calm down. When Amma started breathing normally, she was stroking my hair. I should have seen what a coward she was."

Sajana paused, and I wasn't sure she would finish her story. But I had learned to wait when someone was sharing his or her heart. So I just listened and she continued.

"The doctor gave me medicine to take for the infection down there. And when we got home, nothing was the same. Appa was not speaking to anyone, and when I eavesdropped on their conversation, he told Amma it was not true. Maybe it was a teacher; maybe I was doing it to myself."

Sajana said the last part through her teeth. The heat in my heart was rising for her.

"Amma tried to protect me and slept in my room every night when we got back. But then after the medicine was done, when the doctor checked me again and things were better, she asked Amma if she wanted to report anything.

"Amma shook her head no, and Appa told her to come back to bed when she tucked me in that night. I looked into her eyes, but she looked down and went back to Appa that night. Before he could come to my room, I took a few things from my cupboard and ran away. I didn't know where I was going, but I kept running. When I got tired I found a tree in the park and slept there. A man found me sleeping and brought me here."

It made sense to me, and her story woke me to the truth I was scared to face and was living too. When a girl lost her mother's protection, that's when men preyed on them. *Oh, Amla, where have you brought us?*

CHAPTER 22

W e spent the heaviest monsoon month of this new place in training. In our village, when the rains stopped, we gathered and rejoiced, letting the sun back into our days, its warmth touching our faces for the new season of dance, flowers, and food. Here we did not see the sun. I only knew the rain had stopped because water no longer trickled in through the cracks in the roof.

Janaki ran training. I wondered how she had acquired such power until I overheard Madame admitting that she liked her the best.

On the first day of training, Sajana told us that Madame's real name was Mina, and she and her brother were orphans. They were left in a field to die as babies, but two fugitive men, gundas, found them and took them in. A member of the men's family was one of the most powerful dons in Mumbai. He ran an underground passport scheme.

Madame's brother wanted to start a business, and the family helped him build their first brothel. He protected Madame and then offered her a position overseeing a new branch in the city so she would never have to entertain men, just find other girls to do it. Madame had found Janaki herself when she and her brother were on vacation in Ahmadabad. They exited a cinema and saw her outside on the street, looking for food in a box of vegetable peels beside a small tiffin cafe.

Madame asked her where her parents were. Janaki didn't know Hindi but said Madame approached and looked into her eyes as Madame's brother spoke to her in the Gujarati he knew, and Janaki told them how she had run away from an orphanage. Madame told Janaki that she understood Janaki would never have anywhere to go, no family that waited for her or who could possibly love her again, and that she related to that.

Janaki said she chose to go with Madame; she was never taken. "I was an orphan for most of my life. I was twelve years old when I ran away because the orphanage owner said I would never get adopted and he would have to send me away anyway. Madame told me she was saving me and giving me purpose."

We listened to the rain as we sat on the ground in the small hallway between the rooms of mattresses. There was no leak there, and the light came in from a high, tiny window that looked like a gateway to the sky. I wished I could just fly out of that opening. After finishing her story about Madame, Janaki told us the house rules and about the things the men were allowed and not allowed to do to us.

If the men did not want to wear a rubber, we could not force them. She showed us how to put a rubber on a banana, and Amla and I laughed nervously, but my stomach felt like turning upside down at the thought of holding a man's penis.

Janaki also gave us new names. "You no longer have your old names when you work."

I asked her if Janaki was her real name, and she said yes but that her name with customers was Kiki. Sajana was Lola.

"From now on you will be Pinki and Minki to your men. If you slip with your name or even one of our names, then Madame will burn you down there."

Janaki showed us how to get ready. "You have to wear a lot of makeup," she said as she rubbed the rouge all over my cheeks and handed me the kohl tin for my inner eyelids. When I looked in the mirror, I felt pretty. Though I would never admit such thoughts to Amla, I liked the way the kohl made my eyes so bold and the rouge made me feel older.

Janaki was always inserting Gujarati into her Hindi, which I had started to get used to.

"Where are we, Janaki, if not in Mumbai?" I asked as she cleaned the makeup brush. Of course I knew we had been on the train for days, but the concept of another city was hard for me to comprehend. All I had known was our village and Mumbai.

"You don't know? We are in India's capital. Kolkata."

I remembered my history lessons, learning of the British and the way they had opened clubs in Kolkata. I remembered the beautiful railway station when we arrived, the red, castle-like towers.

"Kolkata." I whispered it, imagining the poem I would write about the city.

But before I could form the words, Janaki said, "*Chulo*, we are ready. Customers are coming. You are ready to go downstairs."

I closed my eyes for a moment and longed to be transported back to our village with its familiar sounds and faces, away from what awaited me downstairs. My body ached from the pain that I would feel again. My stomach dropped as I squeezed Amla's hand. It was our first night on the job. We were a long way from home in more ways than one.

CHAPTER 23

Karma sucked. I had a regular once a week who always spat on me after he got off of me. The first time, I thought it was an accident. Slip of his red gutka powder or something. The second time I realized it was his way of telling me where I belonged.

Even after almost nine months of being in the brothel, it took every ounce of control in me not to spit back like I had done that first night with the brothers. I really only controlled myself for my sister. Every time I kicked or punched a customer, Madame took it out on both of us. She wasn't burning us down there anymore because she recently quit smoking. There was a commotion about a lung X-ray, and even her brother, who we were not allowed to see, came to visit her. We overheard them talking in her office.

But she did kick me in my stomach, hard and swift like she knew exactly where it would make me feel like throwing up. Then she'd walk over to Amla and give her one too. That hurt me even more, and Madame knew it.

Each time, she said we lost pay and then would add extra interest to our tab for losing time and customers.

So I started to control myself. I had a technique. Whenever I had the urge to do something to a man, I started to breathe like our yoga teacher Sandeep bhai had taught us. I had seen Amla doing it sometimes before she fell asleep. She told me, "Didi, it's like your Shah Rukh Kahn taught us."

Whenever a man was heavy on top of me, I'd close my eyes and breathe and pretend it wasn't happening so the urge to fight back went away. Or I would imagine something else, like I was running and flying a kite on Basant Panchami, laughing at the hundreds of kites that kissed the sky. If I kept my breath steady, I could last until it was over.

But the spit in my face always shocked me. Like waking me from a dream into a nightmare of reality that my prana—my life force, Sandeep bhai had called it—couldn't get me out of.

Days into nights
When I feel the frights
Of touches I didn't call for
Always sore

My poetry started to feel stagnant like the air here. The days lingered on.

I kept track of time by the sound of the lassiwala, his bell coming down the street every morning. Otherwise morning felt like night, night like day. We were busiest when it was dark.

I still kept count of the days, but it was getting us nowhere. Madame would add our meals, even the water we drank, to our tab. I wondered how much we would save if we starved ourselves. I so wished that I hadn't followed Amla's plan, and that we'd never asked Chotu to take us to the train station. We'd still be in our village. Maybe we could have fought our way out of getting married. Any alternative would have been better. But she was so determined, that sister of mine, and I knew if I didn't go, she would run away alone, and that had scared me too.

• • •

One morning after chores, there was a big commotion; I could feel Janaki's excitement, the same energy she had when she first greeted us. It was hard to believe that our first day was a year ago.

I was folding laundry when the new girl came into the room. She introduced herself and spoke softly but looked us straight in the eye. "Bhima," she said in her shy confidence. She didn't know Hindi, but Janaki said her name was soon to be changed. She had slanted eyes, high cheekbones, and flawless olive skin that glowed every time she smiled.

I asked her if she knew why she was here, and Janaki glared at me.

"Of course she knows. What kind of question is that, Asya?"

Janaki went on to talk to her, saying we were fairly new here, and she nodded and smiled, though her eyes showed no understanding of our words. I stared at Bhima before telling her I had arrived hundreds of men ago. I walked away before Janaki could protest.

CHAPTER 24

M adame was in a good mood all day. She was humming, and we
even saw her smile when the cook brought the tea. At 7 p.m.
when we started preparing for our evening, we understood why. We
were putting on makeup when Janaki told us that Madame was to
add another new girl to her brothel. The girl's brothel owed a debt to
Madame's brother, and as Janaki put it, "It is settled now."

I first met Amira when we were waiting outside for men to arrive.
The gundas began whistling, and I saw her emerge from her brothel,
close to ours. Amira was so beautiful that I wondered how a customer
had not fallen in love with her yet.

The night before Amira was to join us, Janaki told me about her
as we got ready for bed. Amira knew she was the most desired on the
street, and was even able to be selective about customers. She had been
in Sonagachi since she was twelve years old. Now, seven years later, she
worked the street to her favor. Her brown hair was silky straight, and
she had hazel-green eyes like a cat.

"Amira will be working with us now, Asya. Isn't that exciting?"

I didn't feel the excitement Janaki felt as I fell asleep.

When Amira came to our chambers the next evening, I could

not stop staring at her. The way she put on her lipstick, looked at the mirror, and squinted as she combed her beautiful thick eyebrows.

She caught me staring at her. "Asya and Amla, right?"

We had only told her our names once, but as sharp as her eyes looked, it seemed her memory was the same.

Amla glanced up from her kohl as I nodded, and Amira smiled. "I heard about you both, the beautiful twins Madame was proud of. I can tell you are not happy here."

She paused as she blotted her lips and adjusted her makeup in the dull mirror. I stood closer to her, behind her as she spoke.

"I know what you're both thinking. That you'll escape somehow. I understand, I really do. I hated it too at first. But then one day I realized that the men . . . they wanted me over anyone else. I saw other girls trying to look like me. So I made it work in my favor. I decided to make myself the best at what I am good at doing."

"And that helped?" I asked. I found it hard to accept what we did here as a way of life.

Amira shrugged. "Well, I don't feel as if I'm working for them anymore. They may own me, but I can ask for whatever I want and charge premiums. I get more of a cut to ask for the clothing I want."

"And that is enough?" Amla asked. She looked intrigued by Amira.

"Look, you're Amla, right?"

Amla nodded and moved closer to her. She had done this with older girls at school. She loved when she got attention, even sharing secrets about Chotu when she should have kept her mouth shut.

Amira smiled, like a fisherman reeling in her catch. "My life outside of this place wouldn't have been any better."

"Ours too. After our mummy passed away, our puppa left, and we were promised to older men for marriage and we wanted to study. Plus, I was in love with a boy and couldn't imagine marrying the man our dadi found for me."

I couldn't believe my ears. Not only was she confiding in Amira, but she didn't want to marry anyone else because of Chotu? After what he had said? Did she really even want to study?

"Well," I said pointedly, "we aren't studying here now."

Amla stared at me, and Amira looked at us both. I knew she could feel the tension between us.

Amla turned back to Amira. "What was your home like, Amira?"

Amira paused and adjusted the pin in her hair. "My family was so poor we lived next to the airport and my brother collected garbage. When he died, I ran away. I only had my mother anyway, who was so depressed that she didn't care I existed anymore." Amira turned and looked me up and down. "You know, you have plenty to work in your favor too. You and your sister are wanted; you just have a bad attitude about it. Start playing the part, and it makes it more bearable."

She held out her red lipstick, and Amla took it from her hand. I watched their eyes meet, and a pang of anger and jealousy rushed through me.

CHAPTER 25

No matter how long I had been trapped in that place, I still hated getting my period in the brothel. We only had a certain number of rags each, so if I ran out before the day was over, I had to use a slightly wet one. I couldn't stand the feeling of more dampness against my already damp situation. We never got a break during that time either, making it even worse.

That month, though, as I washed my rags, I noticed Amla's were still folded in her box of clothes. I was already a bit late. Was Amla finished with hers already, or did she not get it? Pregnancy was something we always feared, especially since there were men who refused condoms. She hadn't told me recently of any stories with customers; she was too busy being starstruck by Amira. My stomach curled with a sour feeling. Ever since Amira arrived, Amla had followed her like a little pet. It made me sick. I commented once about wishing we had never left, then asked Amla if she shared the same regret, thinking we might commiserate together, but instead she said I was just blaming her like I always did. It seemed like she was taking Amira's advice to heart.

I hated hearing their names, *Amla and Amira*, together. They sounded like a matching pair. The way we used to be. I heard their names together for the first time when Sajana asked me whose turn it was to sweep our quarters. Sajana said she would do the small downstairs floor of the kitchen, Madame's area, and the entryway. That was just like her, always taking the easy route. She knew that Jayna had probably swept her kitchen area that morning, so it would be less work for her.

"Amla and Amira washed Madame's clothes this morning," she said on her way out the door. It did sound nice, their names together—maybe even nicer than Asya and Amla. Maybe the two of them were more alike than Amla and I were. It made me even more resentful that I had joined Amla in coming here.

The building was hard to keep clean. It was not large by any means but used to be a home for the workers of the old rich Bengali families who used to own the brothels. Left to deteriorate, it was right in the heart of a well-walked alley off the main road and collected dust easily.

Sajana once told me the story of Sonagachi. In Bengali, *Sonagachi* means "Tree of Gold." According to legend, during the early days of the city, this area was a lair for a notorious Muslim bandit, Sanaullah, who resided with his mother. After he died, his mother claimed to hear him say, "Don't cry, Mother. I have become a Ghazi." His mother built a mosque there that fell into ruins. The shift from legend of Sonagazi to Sonagachi started. History like this made me miss school immensely and made me angrier at Amla. I didn't belong here. I was supposed to be studying history in school. I was a good student.

When we didn't do our share of cleaning, we were penalized with less food. Sometimes I couldn't make myself clean up, even though I knew I had to do it. I watched the rats run through the holes in the wall. Saw their feces accumulate on the floor.

Jayna would confiscate one of my meals in punishment. Sometimes Amla shared her food with me, but lately she was laughing with Amira during mealtimes and didn't seem to notice whether I was fed or not. It didn't matter, though. I stopped caring about food in those moments; how much plain rice and daal could I eat? I longed for the crunch of crisp fresh radishes that Dadi would squirt lemon on. As I sat on the hallway floor where we lined up to eat, I craved the way it felt to suck the juice out of freshly peeled lychees from the rare tree by our school.

In the afternoons after our chores, we usually spent time resting before the dusk brought in the customers. That was when Amla and I used to share secrets and talk, but lately all I heard was Amla giggling behind Amira's curtain. Even my poetry couldn't give me comfort. I would just close my book and let my pencil fall to the ground as I tried to rest.

CHAPTER 26

W e finished brushing our teeth that afternoon after we woke up. Amla talked as I changed my clothes.

"Amira is now running her own business and is searching for a bhabu. She says that her friend Deepa from her old brothel had a customer that fell in love with her, and now Deepa and the man are married. She says if you get a bhabu, he will take care of you and you can live away from this place. I mean, you still have to work and earn money, but it's money just for you and your bhabu—"

"Amla, what are you even saying? You sound crazy. As for Amira, either she is brainwashed or she's trying to brainwash you." Anger rushed through me as I said it.

"Asya, that's your problem. You blame me, but is it helping? There is no such thing as a good choice anymore. So why wouldn't I try to find something just a little bit better? Why wouldn't I try to make things easier for myself? And why wouldn't I try to take *some* control of my life? It doesn't seem so crazy to me. Why are you so negative all the time?" she snapped at me. "If you could just change your attitude a little bit and play the part, things could be better for you."

She sounded just like Amira. I couldn't even respond to her.

"Fine, don't respond," she said finally.

I held my breath for a second. "When did you get your period last?" I asked. "I am almost finished with mine, and I noticed your rags . . ."

I noticed a blemish that had appeared on the side of her nose as she said, "I'm not worried. I had bloating last week and will get it next week I think. I may be on Amira's cycle now as she said hers is next week too. Don't worry. I won't add to your burdens any more than I already have."

I ran to my book.

Cut down the center
Of a curtain
Tree of gold holding
Fates of sisters
Divided

Afterwards, I shut my poetry book and then finished getting ready by myself to block her out.

The next day, I noticed Amla took a rag to use. I was relieved she wasn't pregnant, but I felt a deep loss. Our friendship, sisterhood, was breaking. What was even more horrible was how happy Madame was about it.

Later that week, on Madame's birthday, her brother sent her a box of rose-flavored chocolates. Madame called Amira towards her and handed her two of them. She was proud of how much business Amira brought in and told her to share one with someone she felt deserved it.

Amira had been applying her Fair and Lovely face cream, either something she could afford on her own or that a client brought for her to keep her skin from darkening; she was always receiving gifts. She put the tube down, and we all watched her walk right over to us after taking the chocolates. We were applying rouge and kohl and pretended not to care. Janaki was seething with jealousy towards Amira, as was I, both for our own reasons.

She looked at Amla and smiled and then popped both chocolates into her mouth.

"None of you are up to my caliber yet. Maybe next time."

If one of us had done that, Madame would have beat us with a whip. But all she did was cackle behind us and walk away.

I tried to meet my sister's eyes in the hope that she saw what a monster Amira was, how she was not going to help us get out of here.

But Amla didn't look at me. She kept her eyes focused on Amira chewing her chocolates and smiling, the brown coating her teeth and ruining her perfect smile.

CHAPTER 27

For about a week, Amla had the same distant, dreamy look she'd had when she was sneaking around with Chotu. She was still doing her chores with Amira, so I didn't have much opportunity to ask.

As we bathed one morning, sharing our water basin as usual, I asked, "Who are you in love with?" I asked her straight. There was not much time here where we were alone.

"No one," she said, blushing. "But, Asya, I have a plan. I know someone who can get us out of here."

I was shocked. Whom had she met? And where? We never left the building except to bring in customers. That meant it had to be a customer making these promises. "Amla, you know the stories as well as I do. Who is it?"

"He said he is an American. It was the man with the pale face and golden hair last week, remember?"

Janaki and Sajana warned us about these types of men, that they would slit your throat and sell your organs after luring you out, saying they could save you. And sometimes even if they got you out, the gundas would find and kill you both. I wasn't sure which was better, to be living in here or dead out there, but still, we had to be careful.

"We can't trust anyone here. You have to be smart."

"I am smart," she hissed. "While you keep counting our men in that dumb book of yours, we are never going to pay off our debt, Asya. It's like a never-ending pit, and you know it; no one has ever gotten out. Just from last week's beating from Madame, it cost me forty rupees for the towels to clean myself up and the extra makeup to cover my bruises. And do you know what the American said when he touched my face where the bruise was?"

I nodded; I wanted her to continue.

"He said, 'Who did this to you? A customer?' And he even had this small, tattered red book, and I saw the English characters. And he called Madame '*Motee ladakee.*'" She smiled at this, and I could see how she was reeled in. I giggled at his choice of words for "the big woman" too.

She lowered her voice more. "He didn't even take my clothes off. He said he has a friend who is Indian and can come back to bring me somewhere safe if I wanted that. He even snuck his phone in and took a photo of me when I said yes."

I wanted to believe her, but I couldn't let her get carried away. The way she did with Chotu, with her plan to bring Mummy home—it was too much. When and where would we go next? "Amla, please, I'm just telling you since—"

"You don't think I can get us out of here. You think you are the only one who is smart enough to count and figure out the math and all your thinking."

"That's not true. But you always jump to do things without thinking them through."

"And where has your thinking gotten us, Asya? We are still here, and keeping a tally isn't helping." Her voice was loud now, and I was afraid one of the other girls—or worse, Madame—would walk in. Her eyebrows knit together. Without a word, she grabbed my water cup and threw it before taking her towel, getting out of the bath, and drying herself.

"Keep your voice down," I hissed. "You know we are only here because it was your bright idea to go to Guhan uncle in the first place."

I knew my words were sharp, but Amla needed to snap back into reality. It wasn't all her fault—I had of course come along—but before I could fix it, Amla's eyes filled with painful tears. She turned and ran to her cot.

"Is everything okay?" I was surprised to see Janaki standing at the door. I wondered how much she'd seen.

"Yes, everything is fine." I walked over to my sister, mouthing, "I'm sorry" the way she had done a million times to me. I meant it, but still, I knew in my gut that she wouldn't forgive easily. Because she knew that despite my best efforts to forgive her, I blamed her for all that had happened.

CHAPTER 28

Amla didn't speak to me for days, but since we were so busy, I was
exhausted anyway. The election was going on, and men came to
Sonagachi in herds. Men in uniforms, politicians, hotel workers, and
drivers.

A few nights after my argument with Amla, something terrible
happened. We were in our room laying our clothes out onto our cots
to get ready for the evening when Madame came running up in a panic
to tell us that Amira had been killed.

We had heard Amira starting the evening early, as she often did for
certain clients. Without thinking, I ran to her room. She was lying on
the floor, her eyes rolled back into her head and her tongue hanging
out. There was a pillow on the floor beside her, which he must have
used to suffocate her. My stomach roiled, and I feared I would be sick.
She was just a girl. A girl who was brought here, like me, my sister,
all of us.

Janaki came behind me and pulled me away. Amla was already there,
standing beside the curtain, crying. I walked over and embraced her.

After everything that had happened between us, all the tension and
arguing, even if I didn't like Amira, I felt for Amla. "I am so sorry, Amla."

She sank into me and said, "It's so cruel. Nothing makes sense anymore."

"This prime minister keeps dividing us all. It was probably a Hindu fundamentalist that did it. Their party is rising and using violence. They are angry with the Muslims for the train fire they started that killed so many Hindus. So sad. I swear, this country is falling apart."

I had been borrowing the Hindi newspaper from Jai, the lassiwala, and reading it when no one was watching. Even though I was always a day behind, I loved following the stories and feeling connected to the world.

Amla pulled away.

"Who cares, Asya? None of that mattered. None of it is in our control. That is all about men jostling for power far beyond this room where we are trapped with all this rat shit and dust and men who don't care if we live or die, who didn't care if Amira just died. Are you even sad that she is gone?" she asked.

"Of course I am, Amla." I reached for her, but she was walking away already.

She was mad at me again. We hadn't spoken about the blue-eyed man, nor had he returned again in over a week, so maybe she was also mad that I was right about him. When would she learn?

CHAPTER 29

Dreams of earth
Dirt smell
And grains
That touch my knees

I missed the way my feet felt on the earth. I missed running through the grassy patches of our village where the cows grazed. I missed pulling up the bucket from the water well, inhaling its wet stone-slab smell.

Here, instead, my nose was assaulted by the smells of sex and sweat and gasoline rickshaws. Sometimes I caught a whiff of grated ginger if I walked by the kitchen and Jayna was just preparing Madame's morning tea. Sometimes it even reminded me of what home felt like. It was those smells that made me feel alive; otherwise, like grass that never gets watered, I felt my roots dying.

Plus, I felt disconnected from Amla still. She was mourning Amira. We all were, but it hit her the hardest. The energy of the brothel had shifted. When we ate lunch, Janaki told her, "We miss your funny stories, Amla." Amla smiled but didn't share anything.

I too needed the Amla who kept our days lifted. I was still keeping my count, and when Amla told me to stop counting for her, I knew that something was off. My gut told me she was hiding something from me, but I just couldn't figure it out. Had the American come and seen her again? Or had she truly given up after Amira? If this were our before life, I would have asked her. I would have known or had an idea, but now, I couldn't figure it out.

I felt so disconnected from reality, like we were living some odd version of life that couldn't at all be true. And without my sister, I was broken. The half of me that I could look at and literally see myself in was gone. I couldn't bring myself to whisper to her when we lay in our cots right next to each other to rest during the day, the way we liked, my legs against hers. *At least we still have that*, I thought as I waited there for the evening to start.

• • •

His accent was different. That was the first thing I noticed when he approached Amla on the street that night and said in Hindi, "I want her." He ducked his face under a blue cap, never meeting eyes with any of the girls. I wasn't the only one that wondered. The gunda noticed.

"Okay, NRI, why her?" he asked, using the term for a non-resident Indian to his face.

He was actually nice looking with his small nose and almond eyes. The man looked nervous but said, "I heard she's good."

The gunda smiled and patted his back. "Yes, yes, you will pay a premium for Pinki, but go ahead."

He nodded, and she walked him into the brothel. I knew there was no premium, but they would make an extra rupee on anyone that was new blood. And we still wouldn't see the extra. Amla wasn't counting, but I would add him to the count in my book.

I had a new young client pick me that night too. As I closed the curtain, he said to me, "I don't want to be here. My friends made me do this."

He was younger than the old, crooked men who usually came. Awkwardly, we sat at the edge of the mattress together, knee-to-knee.

Somehow I got the courage to say, "I don't want to be here either." After Amira and my fight with Amla, I didn't want to stay silent anymore.

He looked up at me and nodded as if in agreement. I sat there waiting for him to lift up my dress and get it over with.

But when he stood, he walked to the curtain to leave. And for a brief moment, even if impossible, I hoped that he would be my savior. That he would whisper, "Come with me," and whisk Amla and me away from this place. As the curtain closed, I saw the faces of many men closing the curtain of compassion to women for centuries. I added him to my count anyway.

CHAPTER 30

The next day while we were mending some dresses that had torn, Amla was acting funny. She started chuckling as if in a daydream.

Janaki looked at me, confused. "Oh my, Amla is in love!"

"No, I'm not!" she said. I looked at her and wondered if that was it. I hoped not. We didn't need Madame thinking that Amla was lusting after a customer and watching our every move .

"Don't worry. It's normal. It happens to everyone at least once. Who is it?"

"She's not in love," I said dully. "She had a secret boyfriend in our village and her heart belongs to him."

"Ooh, tell us about him!"

Amla looked me dead in the eye. I knew that she wasn't thinking about Chotu, but she started to describe him. The girls laughed at the time she almost got caught sneaking around with him as I tried to figure out what my sister was hiding.

Janaki lifted the dresses up and said we still needed to sweep both floors.

"Amla and I can sweep up here," I said. "Why don't you start downstairs and we can meet you?" When she was gone, I touched Amla's hand. "What's going on?"

"Nothing. I'm fine."

I waited for my sister, like old times, where she would pour her heart out and tell me if I just sat with her.

"If I tell you, I don't even know if you will believe me."

"Try me."

We did have to sweep, but I needed to be patient with Amla. If I rushed her, she would blow up, and the moment would be gone.

"The man that came the other day, with the different accent? His name is Vishnu." She paused and looked up at me. "I knew there was something about him that was different, much nicer than the men that come here."

She started to whisper. "Him and his friend, the American with blue eyes, they work to save young girls from these places. He said when he comes again, we shouldn't hide. We need to stay where we are. Amla, they'll be here in three days. We have to keep the plan to ourselves though." She was excited now.

My mind raced. I could only wonder, *How do we know to trust these men?* We had trusted Guhan uncle and Rajiv too. We couldn't even trust our own father to save our mother. "Amla, this is . . . I can't believe it."

"I know. We have to make a plan. Let's do it when we rest after chores."

I tried to hide my apprehension. "How do you know, though . . . that he is really going to help?"

Amla looked disappointed. "You want to be right again."

"Wait, what? No, I am just asking a valid question. How can you trust them so easily? Besides, I have been counting, and maybe we can really pay off our debt and show it. No one has probably written it down before the way I am trying to."

Tears flooded Amla's eyes. She was getting emotional. I didn't want that, but there was no turning back now. It seemed lately everything became an argument with my sister.

"Do you know why I am not giving up on this idea, Asya? Because even if you think that it is all my fault that we are here, that I shouldn't have gotten close to Amira, that these men . . . we don't know if they are going to take us somewhere else or really save us. But I would rather try to believe than hole myself up in this disgusting place and fill notebooks of thoughts that no one will ever read. Poetry is nothing. How is that going to keep us alive? And do you honestly think that devil of woman will agree to let us out with your counting? She owns us, Didi."

I was stunned. She had whispered it all fiercely. I should have reached out for her face, touched her tears, or even hugged her. But I was hurt and swung my hair around instead. I closed my eyes as I heard her get up and take the broom into her hand. In her spite she had thrown my poetry out into the air like it was garbage. I was counting for both of us. It was not for nothing, but she didn't believe me. I was confused and didn't know what to believe anymore. I was afraid to follow my sister again.

CHAPTER 31

I wrote poetry despite my sister.

Streets flooded
Laughter and piss
Happy news I dreaded
Feeling amiss

Five days later, the new prime minister was appointed. Painted signs were everywhere as people screamed and shouted from their windows in our gully. It was pure havoc. People were rejoicing and rallying all at once.

We had drunk customers, angry customers, happy customers. It was the craziest I had ever seen Sonagachi.

We weaved in and out of the curtains, from downstairs back up to the mattresses. In between customers, Amla kept trying to grab me. "We need to talk."

I sensed the urgency in her eyes, and it reminded me of the times she was in trouble. She was still thinking about her crazy scheme with the man who had not come on the third night like she had been told.

Even if she thought he was still coming, it was risky with the election and crooked cops out.

I'm not sure why I hardened. I was still hurt from what she had said. I didn't trust her new scheme, and she knew it, but I couldn't believe she still hadn't apologized. So I ignored her. If she wanted to figure out whatever mess she was in, she had to do it herself this time.

"Okay, later; we are busy," I told her as her eyes grew bigger with pleading. A tall, slim, dark-skinned man walked towards my bed as I turned and closed my curtain on her.

• • •

Fuck. I learned the word from a customer that night. He said that in English, that what we did was a fuck. It sounded funny to me when he said it.

With the election, I was up to many fucks that night but didn't care. I was numb, physically and emotionally, from Amla. Nothing mattered.

The guy who had come with his friends and just wanted to talk was back again for the third time. He asked me if I knew any good jokes that would get him in the mood since his friend had dragged him here yet again. This time I asked him if he was gay, and he laughed until he was almost crying.

"No, I am not gay," he said, and he kissed me on the lips to prove it. It caught me off guard, and my heart pounded as if it were my first kiss. No matter how ridiculous that sounded, the feelings were real. He wasn't pushy like other men; the kiss almost felt genuine the way he paused when he released, and I actually wanted him to continue.

"Okay, now the joke," he said and smiled. I told him I didn't know any jokes but that I wrote poems, so he said, "Please, let me hear one." I closed my eyes and told him the first one that came to mind.

Longing for blue
White
Meshed sky
Between curtains
Of trapped voices

"*Shabhash*, you are like Tagore."

I blushed at his compliment. He had a long nose that made him handsome, and his eyes gleamed. He said he'd never cared for this place, and normally he could find an excuse to study, but with the schools closing after the election riots, he was bored. He touched my body, ran his fingers on my stomach, across my breasts over my sari blouse and the birthmark on my arm. He kissed me again, looking at me languidly, but didn't move to penetrate me, and I was thinking he wasn't going to, and then he slowly got up.

"What do you study?"

I never asked my clients many questions, but he made me want to talk more. I wanted to hear his kind voice again.

"I want to be a pilot so I can fly all over the world, but my father, he makes me study Ayurvedic medicine."

When Amla and I were younger, we would study the small world map Mummy had tucked away in the bookshelf, ripped out of one of Puppa's old Air India magazines. Sometimes she would open it up and show us the countries she remembered the names of. Eventually we helped her and told her of others, and she would say, "Okay, take me there one day." So Amla and I would study the whole map and point to a country, then quickly tell each other the first thing we would do in that country with Mummy. Egypt: We will ride the camels to the pyramids. Australia: We will hug a kangaroo.

As I lost myself in my thoughts, he started to leave. "Bye, Tagore," he said. "Don't stop with that poetry. It may be your ticket out of this dump."

I smiled as he walked away. But then an abrupt noise downstairs snapped me back into reality.

I felt the broomstick rattle the floor. The gundas were hitting the ceiling as the signal to hide. We had been told what to do during a raid. I ran towards Amla's mattress to find her but didn't see her.

"Amla!" I screamed.

I saw Vishnu, the one Amla had spoken about, charging, and then saw Amla moving towards him. There were police officers with him. He'd actually come.

I saw Janaki run towards the back box where we were told to hide if there was ever a raid. We were in the small corner upstairs that led down to the exit, and I screamed for Amla as she looked at the American's back, as he looked down the stairs. She was unsure, so I motioned for her to come. I knew she saw me. We didn't speak, but our eyes did. Then, with a cold final look, she turned from me and ran towards the American.

Maybe I shouldn't have been surprised. Things had been strained between us for some time. But her actions shocked me. She didn't even motion for me to go with her. Plus, how could she trust him, a complete stranger, over staying with me? Trusting Rajiv when Guhan uncle left us got us nowhere.

Janaki was rushing into the raid box, and when I glanced back, Amla was no longer in sight. Where was she? I had an urge to run after them, but Janaki pulled me in, and I didn't resist. Amla had her own path. Her own ideas. Maybe that was for the best. I was going to count it all out. I knew we could get out, and she didn't trust me, though I had once foolishly trusted her.

The lights and faces of customers running out were gone like a flash as we shut the door of our box—like a dream on fast forward, the VHS tapes of Bollywood films we sometimes saw at the SDT phone shop at the village.

Janaki clung to me in the metal box. The sounds had been drowned out when we shut the door with a thud, but we still heard pieces of the commotion. My stomach churned with fear, sadness, and anger. Why was Amla so gullible? Janaki said Madame probably hid her with

Bhima somewhere else, not to worry. The box was under the large fan, so it rattled so loud that I could hardly hear her, especially since she also whispered as if someone might hear us. I was sure that no one would hear us even if we had been screaming.

My upper lip started to sweat. The air grew thick with the two of us crammed and squatting inside. I worried about Amla. Janaki must have sensed my growing despair because she reached out and squeezed my hand like Amla did. "As soon as Madame comes, I will unlock the box."

I nodded in the dark, hoping it would not be long. I started to breathe like Sandeep bhai showed us.

"Breathing in . . . and out," he would say melodically.

Suddenly we heard Madame banging on our box to open up. Janaki tugged at the log, and the metal crate door fell to the floor like a dog kennel. We crawled out, and I took a big breath of air.

"Where is she?!" Madame screeched. She pushed me out of the way to look inside the box, as if Amla were hiding in there to scare her.

"I don't know. I thought she was with you. Janaki shoved me in here. I told her to wait for Amla, but we didn't see her, and we worried the police would find us."

Madame grabbed my arm and twisted it. The pain was startling, and I gasped.

"Do you think I am stupid?" she hissed. "You think I don't know you can read and write? Whatever you and your sister are planning ends now. We are sending the gundas out to find her, and when they do, you both won't know what hit you."

She let go of me and leaned back before spitting on me. Her sputum landed on my chest and dripped down between my breasts. It smelled of paan leaves and stained my shirt. As disgusted as I felt, I feared this was only the beginning of the darkness she would send my way. And this time, I didn't have my sister by my side.

CHAPTER 32

There was a commotion after the raid. The others were excited, talking over each other about what they had seen and heard. I was stunned into silence. The absence of my sister felt like a hole in my chest. Was she safe? Would I find out if she was dead?

Madame disappeared into her room where we heard her talking to her brother on the phone. The four of us, Janaki, myself, Sajana, and Bhima, could not hear anything they said. The sounds of the evening outside took over. These were the sounds I had become used to. They were part of my rhythm during my loud, wakeful nights and unnatural sleepy days.

But tonight was different. The brothel was closed, and we were all ordered to sleep. Unable to glean much from Madame's muffled voice, we retreated to our mattresses as ordered. Since we slept during the day, my body was not used to sleeping at night, and I just stared at the ceiling, wide awake. All I could think about was Amla.

I must have dozed off because suddenly I was startled awake by the sound of Madame slamming down the phone with a curse. I heard her pacing. I heard Janaki asking questions and Madame answering, her voice tense and twisted with anger. When Janaki came back to our room, I was too curious to feign disinterest. I whispered her name.

"Janaki, what is going on?"

I half expected Janaki to tell me it was none of my business and to go back to sleep. But she didn't. Instead she looked at me with an expression of true worry.

She said that Madame's brother had to report the incident to his business partner, the don, after the police came, and now the don was getting on a flight. He would be here before dawn. Madame's brother was angry with her. This was the first time anyone had ever escaped during a raid.

"What do you think the don will do?" I asked.

Janaki shook her head. "Whatever it is, it won't be good," she replied.

• • •

Early the next morning, I woke to the sound of footsteps coming down the hall. The sun had hardly touched the sky. Our scanty curtains hadn't let any light in yet. The footsteps were brisk and full of fury. After last night, I knew Madame was angry. And when she was angry, we got hurt.

I assumed Madame would have her whip, so I turned over to pretend I was sleeping on my stomach. The lashings would be easier to bear on my back. Her footsteps stopped by my mattress. I squeezed my eyes shut, bracing for the bite of the whip.

But instead, Madame yanked my hair and grabbed at my face. She threw me to the floor and ordered me to look up at her. A single ray of sunlight passed through the curtains and touched Madame's face. Her eyes glittered with rage as she said, "This is all your fault, you little *benchod*." Then she threw something wet on my face. At first it was cold, and I assumed it was water. And then, after a moment, the cold turned to heat. Brutal, impossible heat.

My nostrils filled with the smell of something putrid and nauseating. My ears rang with the sounds of my own screams as I writhed on the floor. I lifted my hands to my face, but I was afraid to touch it for fear the burning would spread. The pain moved from burning to throbbing to almost numbing, and then I couldn't move my eyes anymore. That's when everything went black. I'm not sure when I stopped screaming or when Madame left, but I know the smell lingered long enough to haunt me.

Janaki was screaming too. And then I heard footsteps and a young voice cry out in horror. It was Jai, the lassiwala. He must have been preparing his deliveries outside before his early morning rounds.

Janaki wrapped my head with a bed sheet while we waited for the doctor to arrive. When he did, he wrapped my head in bandages and tried to clean my eyes and my forehead with an ointment that stung at each touch. I screamed and didn't stop even after he left. My voice felt raw and new, as if I had morphed into a new person when the acid took my vision.

After I was bandaged and the ointment was applied, Madame came back in. I couldn't open my eyes under the white bandages, but I heard her heavyset body come closer.

"You will never look like your stupid sister again. She has transferred her debt to you, so start working. As for the rest of you," she said, raising her voice to speak to the other girls, "look at her. If you want this to happen to you, try to escape like Amla did."

It hurt so bad that I could not even cry.

• • •

The pain that day was so unbearable I could hardly think of anything except Amla. Maybe I should have listened to her. At least I would have been able to see. Why had I let pride get in my way? On the other hand, she had made a lot of stupid choices in the past.

Now that she was gone, I felt guilty for how I'd reacted when she tried to tell me. Escaping this place didn't necessarily mean she would be better off, but after Madame's attack, I was full of regret. If I had gone with her, we would be together, no matter where we were.

Later that afternoon, Janaki came into my room and sat beside me on the bed. She had gotten information from Jayna the cook.

When the don had arrived early that morning, he said there was a debt owed for Amla's absence. For years, the don had been trying to spend more time alone with Madame. Until now, Madame's brother had managed to convince him to leave her alone. But with the escape, he was no longer able to say no to the don. Madame had to succumb to his advances. Janaki said she saw Madame taking the don into a back room when he arrived.

It was hard to imagine, but it seemed that even Madame was owned. I, too, knew the feeling of being caged with no hope of freedom.

Man power
Stronger than even
The nastiest woman
Alive

CHAPTER 33

There are some moments in life that feel vivid each time you recall them. Scents, sounds, even the way the air felt on your arms. The day when Mummy collapsed. The last time I saw Nani. The day I lost my sister.

We moved to a new building the day after the raid. I tried to feel the dirt beneath my feet as we walked along the road. Tried to smell the places we passed. I counted my steps, wondering how far we would be traveling from the last place Amla had seen me—wondering how many steps it would take to bring us back together . . .

"If she's even alive," Janaki said when I mentioned it to her. She reminded me, as Madame was so fond of doing, that the gundas went out and killed anyone who tried to escape. I knew she wasn't dead, though. I would have felt her die, in my heart, wherever they struck her.

Once, a teacher hit Amla's hand for drawing doodles on her paper. I felt the snap of the ruler on my own fingers. We were classrooms apart since Mummy always said to keep us separate or else we would bother each other in class. Another time, Mummy said that when we were learning to walk, I had fallen and scraped the skin off my knee, causing it to bleed and swell. Amla kept tapping and pointing to her knee for days as mine healed. Mummy told us the story often when we fought. "Always remember, girls, that your hearts and bodies are connected," she'd say.

I was still in bed that evening when Janaki came in. I heard her voice behind me. "You know, Asya, if you don't start seeing customers soon, Madame will have you killed."

"Let her," I said. And I rolled over.

Janaki came back and brought me a lassi from Jai. He was younger than all of us, about eight or nine years old, and for some reason felt an obligation to help heal me. I imagine that the image of my disfigured face would never leave him.

I tried to remove my bandages, but Janaki caught me and told me to leave them. She said it was the only chance to let my eyes heal.

"Will I see again?" I asked her, not really expecting her to know the answer.

She didn't speak, but I heard her breathing, and a small sob escaped her mouth before she muffled it. It was soft. She might not even know I heard it. But I was beginning to listen to cues for how people reacted since I could not see their eyes. I could not see the way they might shift their feet or bite their lips like Amla.

I listened to everything, every sound the floors made, to decipher who was walking. The sounds of doors and voices and animals. The sounds that brought in daylight and evening. It was all I had left in this blackness.

In the village, Amla and I would find comfort in the stillness of night. The white noise of cicadas outside. The sound of Puppa's gentle snore. Water drops falling into the pan Mummy used to wash her face in the dark.

Here, the sounds were different. The sounds of shops closing and cars passing to their homes. The sounds of drunken men singing off-key along with Bollywood songs playing on small radios. The rattling of keys that opened our gate. This was how I knew to be ready for the night.

CHAPTER 34

S everal nights after we moved, a miracle happened. Janaki ran to me that evening and said, "Asya, there is some man here asking for the poetry girl. He says he calls you Tagore?"

I lifted my head from my pillow. Despair and hope warred within me. I would give anything for a friend right now, but what would he say when he saw me?

"Quick, get ready!" Janaki said eagerly. "I will tell him to wait."

My head still felt heavy when I lifted it, but I gathered my strength. I had not eaten in days except for the salty lassi Jai brought me each morning. I told him I had no money, and he said, "It's okay, they are the slightly older ones. If you don't take them, my boss will feed them to the cows." His kindness struck a chord in my heart, one that had not been touched in a long time.

I could tell I had lost weight. My dress hung on my body, and the straps slipped off my shoulders. I couldn't see my face for the rouge on my lips, so I just rinsed out my mouth and walked down to meet him.

I wished I could have seen his face when he saw me. I listened for a gasp, but all I heard was, "You know, it's not polite to make your fans wait, Tagore. What a miracle I found you! I looked one night, then came back twice until some boy selling lassi told me where you were."

Maybe he wasn't that surprised, then. Maybe Jai had told him. He held my hand, and we walked upstairs to my mattress. He shut the curtain and asked me what had happened. He didn't let go of my hand.

I told him the truth. About Amla escaping, and Madame with her acid.

As I spoke, I tried to imagine his face. I remembered what it looked like. His nose, his dark skin.

He put my hand down and was quiet for a moment. I could have filled the silence, but I waited in my darkness for a reply. I thought he might leave, but instead he said, softly, "I feel that I am supposed to help you. If you will have me, I will come each week or more if I can. Tell me what you need when I come."

"What I need?" I asked, confused.

"Where did your bandages come from? Will you need more?"

I said this was kind, but I could not pay him except in the ways I was told to. And I was not sure what my body could even do anymore, I felt so weak.

Before I could finish, his fingers touched my dry lips, telling me to stop. "Tagore, I have come for your poetry. Don't worry about writing and reading them now. I heard Rabindranath Tagore had more poems in his mind than he ever wrote down. I am ready. Tell me now."

The currency of words
Hold value
Far greater than weapons
Of acid attacks
For a girl
Like me

The next time he came a week later, he brought a thick brown paste. "This will speed up the healing, and we can then see if there is any damage to your eyes. Are you doing the exercises?" He had told me to move my eye muscles. He was happy to hear that I could still feel them moving and that the pain was starting to wear off except at night when I lay down.

I lay still, and he cleaned my wounds with water. "Today I am going to apply this paste. It's from a peepal tree. I mixed it with ghee."

As he applied it, he told me that this form of medicine was not the type from the hospitals like Mummy went to. "It is ancient," he said.

The paste felt cool and nourishing.

"Your name," I said.

"Hmm?" he asked. He was methodical in his work. I had caught him off guard.

"You have never told me your name."

I listened to the sound of his breath, his pause.

"Tagore, I am your devoted *prashansak*."

I smiled. My fan.

I am a fan of yours too, I thought.

For the next few weeks, he came as promised, paying for his sessions with me. When I told him I could not repay him for all of this, he told me that his father was a famous Ayurvedic doctor and not to worry about where he got his money.

CHAPTER 35

W e were eating phena bhat one morning when Janaki told me that Madame had bought a new whip. She told me about it in dramatic style, describing Madame strolling through the door, the sun shining on her henna-drenched hair, the whip draped across her shoulder like a snake.

I swallowed the bland porridge and imagined Madame looking for me and shuddered. I hardly slept that afternoon. *Amla, if you are alive, please find me*, I thought hourly.

It had been almost a month since the raid, and while the nights of customers added up again, I looked forward to my favorite customer, who was still coming often—if not every week, sometimes twice in the same week.

"I want to hear the snake one," he said.

I heard a spoon hit the edges of a steel bowl as he made another paste.

Snakes dance
Across the skies
I smell the curl of jasmine smoke
Disappear
As I watch you with my eyes closed

"Hmm, yes," he breathed, as if relaxed by my words. I could tell he was smiling.

I had slowly been able to open my eyes again. Tears still formed at the brightness. He had me rest my head in his lap so he could work over me, applying the paste across my eyes, putting the bandages back on carefully.

"Okay, that's it. Remember we want to wait until they're fully healed to open them all the way," he said and kissed my nose.

I touched his face, this angel of a man.

"Asya," he whispered tenderly. "If I could, I would bring you home with me."

I had told him my real name only after he revealed his name to me: Shiv. I wrote it over and over again in my mind, next to my name.

I let my hand rest on his cheek a bit longer and waited to hear more.

"Your Madame has named a price for you," he told me.

My heart jumped. He had tried to purchase my debt? I hadn't considered it and was caught off guard at his comment.

"I'm afraid it was far more than I could afford," he said sadly. "She says you have acquired your sister's debt, and she knows I am not going to be able to pay for you fully."

"It is all right," I said, unsurprised. "Thank you for trying."

Shiv made a sound of frustration. "When I leave here, the gundas always follow me. Madame has made it clear if I try to take you without paying off your debt, they will find me . . . and hurt me and my family."

Shiv was softhearted—a young man, only twenty-two years old himself—and I knew that he was not the type to fight Madame. He feared for his life.

I found it easier to speak my heart with my eyes always closed now. "We are bound by words and touch. Do not worry. As long as you are here, I can smile again."

He took me into his arms and kissed me gently. I fell into the rhythm of our bodies, and unlike any other time with a man, we made love that night.

• • •

The next morning, Janaki sounded jealous. "I can't believe he stayed. He's going to have to pay for the whole night. Madame is not going to allow this much longer."

I was still tracing the edge of my blouse with my finger as I thought of him kissing my collarbone when I recited the poem about the softness of skin on skin.

"Are you daydreaming?" Janaki asked.

"Daydreaming? I don't know how."

Janaki was waiting for more—I could feel it. But I knew better than to divulge important information to her.

After making love, we had wanted to just lie there and cuddle. He had spent extra time on my bandages, which were thinner now; I could see through them if I let my eyes open slightly. He encouraged me to go easy with my eyes and to practice the exercises. He said eventually he could uncover them fully, and I would be able to keep them open.

It felt miraculous to see anything again, even if my vision was blurry.

He also told me about the new government hospital position he had. "They are trying to merge traditional ancient medicine with Western techniques. It's about time they realized the British didn't have everything right."

I recalled Puppa talking about how things were when he was a young boy and the Raj was in power. I was happy for Shiv, but I knew, even with his new position, our whole night together was a luxury I was not sure would happen again with Janaki on my tail.

Beneath my bandages, I saw Janaki walk into Madame's office, her shoulders stiff with determination. Sajana and Bhima watched from afar as they swept the floor. They exchanged a look before turning their heads to finish their chores.

Sly
Fishing for more
From the one that cannot see
Yet sees
Enough in her heart
To know silence
Is her only power

CHAPTER 36

This was the night, he said, when he could uncover my eyes. He worked slowly, pressing my skin gently as he took off the last of the bandages and took out the drops he had been placing in my eyes each time he wrapped them.

"We will still need to use these drops, but wait before you open. I have something for you."

I heard something rustle, and then he said, "Okay, open."

When I opened my eyes, Shiv was holding a new pencil before my face. "I wanted this to be the first thing you saw after so long." He called it "Tagore's first view."

I slowly let my gaze shift to him, his smile.

"Go on, write something."

I held the pencil and wondered where the stubby old one I had been using went, and where my book was. I reached behind my mattress and felt it there.

I opened to my pages, my words. There were so many poems I had recited to him in my darkness. They felt new, seeing them on paper.

"Can you see?" he asked hopefully.

"Yes," I breathed. "There's so much light." My eyes filled with tears.

I was unsure if they were from the sensitivity or the rush of emotion in my chest. He wiped them nonetheless.

He watched me write and then waited.

I paused before sharing it, but I thought of my sister, what she would tell me at this moment. I imagined her biting her lip and telling me, "Share your heart."

Light fills
The heart's eyes
From the darkness
Emerges
The hands of hope
Holding a pencil
Sharpened with love's grace

When I looked up, our eyes met for the first time in two months.

CHAPTER 37

The autumn rains were heavy that year. We were never busy on those damp days: just the regular clients and some crooked police officers here and there. On those days, after cleaning the brothel, we watched television.

I waited for Shiv. It had been days since he had spent the night. I knew it was hard for him to get there; he only had his scooter, and with the flooding, it was impossible to ride.

My eyes were almost healed. It was a miracle that I could see. He said it was his herbs, but I knew it was his touch, his love. He told me to take it slow.

Nani would tell us when we were ill that she would heal us with love, stroking our foreheads and kissing our noses. I tried to remember the song she sang, but it didn't come to me right away. I often feared I would forget everything that mattered to me and that my moments in the brothel would take over my mind and heart.

The new brothel had a small common area, really just a tiny central room with cushions on the concrete floor. Madame's brother had sent the television for us, saying we could use it when we were good. Madame made sure to tell us, "TV is for girls who listen." I remembered our time at Guhan uncle's home, when we lost ourselves in the stories and sounds of sitcoms about family drama. Now we watched *India's Top Star*, a program where girls and boys our age competed for cash prizes and a movie role. They sang and danced, and acted out scenes from old Hindi films. Since I couldn't spend too much time looking at the TV screen, I mostly listened.

The judges were always praising the talent of these contestants, calling them the new voices of India. I felt so far removed from a world outside that it was hard to visualize my country anymore. I thought of the contestants and their opportunities and felt a pang of jealousy.

A customer once told me that everything was not as it appeared on television. He was one of many assistants for the show and had even met Amitabh Bachan. He had the privilege of collecting and delivering their costumes for each scene. Normally I didn't talk much and always let the men talk, but this time I asked him, "What is Amitabh like?"

He told me how funny he was, and I imagined Amitabh as my father, and my life transformed to that of a girl with no worries except what to pack for holiday trips with my loving Bollywood parents.

He also said everything is rigged in Bollywood. I didn't understand what he meant until we got the television and I could hear the hope in the voices of the contestants. I heard the judges' surprise at their talent. All too often, the poorest children were given accolades, but they never seemed to advance as far as the wealthy ones. Or suddenly someone else won even though the "voting" showed differently.

I was inspired to write a poem about it.

Dreams
Tell lies
To the reality of
A place that swallows
Hope alive

I avoided the mirror. I didn't want to see the monster I saw reflected in people's eyes when they looked at me. Even if I was healed, my fingers could feel the deformity of my skin when I rinsed my face each morning—carefully, as Shiv instructed me to. I trained my eyes on the birthmark on my arm, the only thing that was familiar.

I dreamt of my old face. I was facing the sun and eating pistachio ice cream with Amla, who was smiling by my side as she held her favorite, mango. And then suddenly my face started melting and Amla was screaming. I touched my skin, and it ran through my fingers like slime. My face became monstrous, with bubbles and tight, reptilian skin.

I woke in a sweat and contemplated going to the mirror. Instead I lay there until exhaustion overtook my mental battle and I fell back asleep.

Shiv came the next night with more medicinal drops and said I had to use them every day for at least the week. When I told him that I had not seen myself yet, he asked for my pencil and notebook. I handed it to him, and he found an empty page and told me not to look as he worked. He was studying me and drawing, looking up and down at the page.

"I didn't know you are an artist." I thought of Amla and her beautiful sketches and doodles. My chest ached for her, my heart praying she was all right.

"Are you ready?" he asked.

I nodded, and when he handed me my notebook, I burst into laughter.

His drawing looked like a toddler had done it, an attempt at a face and shading where perhaps my burn was.

"Asya, don't be so serious. If you were that hideous, I wouldn't come here, now would I?" He leaned in to kiss me, but I stopped him.

"Bring me a mirror," I said.

He nodded and went out to find one. I didn't want to walk to our dressing area. I didn't know whom he would ask or where he would go, but he returned with a small makeup compact, which he held open.

I saw the left burn first. It made my eye appear smaller than it was, a long line like a lash across the skin above my eyelid. My right side was worse; my eyebrow was missing hair, and the skin around my eye was ripe pink where it met an outer layer of skin, like I imagined my vagina would look.

The new me.

He took the compact from me and handed me my pencil and book.

Ripe skin
Delicate where the hate fell
Regrows
Against all odds
To a new
Me
Who can see
Clearly
Against all odds.

• • •

I dreamt of Nani that afternoon. Dreams were where my heart opened to speak in the stifling walls of that place. She was wiping my face because I was sweating. "You love this man. You must find a way to tell him."

"Nani, it is not that simple," I replied. "I wish Amla was here."

"And what would Amla do?" Nani asked.

"She would listen to her heart."

Nani smiled at me; the answer was there.

My sheets were wet when I woke up. My coconut oil and damp fears. Bhima approached me and hit my leg. She had a flyer in her hand, and she pointed to it.

Bhima still felt new to us, even after all this time. She was catching Hindi phrases but did not understand much and sometimes tried to answer us in Nepali. She had a look of sadness on her face, but that was also just the way her features were designed. She was the fairest out of all of us, and her black eyes with thick lashes were strikingly bold, yet she never even wore kohl. It was her mouth, shaped like an upside-down heart, that made you feel like she was sad. For this, it was easy to speak softly to her, to feel sorry for her.

I took the flyer into my hand and adjusted my eyes to the light and words. In big red letters it said, FREE CONDOMS AND EXAMS TOMORROW. LEARN ABOUT HIV, DON'T RISK YOUR LIFE.

Madame never passed up free rubbers, but she was weary of anyone checking us so never allowed the doctors who made free rounds into the brothel. I gestured for Bhima to take it to Janaki and took my pencil to circle the words FREE CONDOMS. Since opening my eyes, I had noticed Janaki had lost weight and bore dark circles under her eyes. She looked sicker day by day, and while I knew Madame would never let us be seen, especially me, I hoped Janaki would get checked. I was living proof of Madame's evil nature.

CHAPTER 38

Shiv came to see me later than usual, so I had to see another customer. They sent the man to me because he was on some sort of drug; usually I got the ones who wouldn't mind my scarred face. When he came, he pushed harder into my mouth, telling me to swallow it. I pretended and spat it out as he adjusted his belt buckle, but he saw. I thought he might grab my neck to strangle me, but then Janaki came in, taking me to the side.

"Let's go; time is up," she said to the customer. He had paid less, and the gunda told him he'd have a time constraint.

A short time later, Shiv arrived. He smelled of alcohol, and he was smiling, holding something behind his back.

Sheepishly, he handed me a bag. "Happy New Year." During Diwali, I had mentioned to him how sad I felt at not being with Amla and not even knowing the state of her well-being, and he had said he would bring her to me by the Western New Year to make me smile.

I opened the bag full of beautiful, ripe, yellow amla berries. I hugged him as he took one out and fed a bite to me. "These are the best you have ever tasted."

I left to wash my mouth and shuddered at the thought of the man almost strangling me before Shiv had arrived.

He knew why I left, probably, but he did not ask. He never asked, and I wondered if he ever felt jealous or what it was like for him to love me, if he did, and know I had been with a stranger just minutes before he arrived. When he handed me another of the small, yellow amla fruit, I let the sour notes hit my tongue as hints of sweetness and bitter afternotes filled my palate, washing away traces of the past.

"Bittersweet," I murmured.

He looked at me and smiled. "Yes, it all is."

I loved his ability to read my mind. Without thinking, I said, "I love you, Shiv."

I almost bit my lip like Amla as I waited for him to respond. He was still smiling.

"Tagore, music to my heart. Let's dance."

He lifted me to my feet, bringing me closer so I could feel his heart beating in his chest. I felt his warm breath on my neck as he sang.

Hamari ghazal hai tassavur tumhara
Tumhare bina ab na jeena gawara
Tumhe yoon hi chahenge
Jab tak hai dum

We moved together, dancing to the old film song, listening to the lyrics "My poem is your imagination—I'll keep loving you like this" as I closed my eyes and pretended we were dancing in our own home, in a village where I was free, where my sister had been waiting for me all along, next door in her own home with the love of her life, maybe even Chotu. I was filled with happiness in that dream, away from my miserable reality. Our love could be my ticket out.

CHAPTER 39

"I refused, of course."

I had never seen him so angry. He was lying on his stomach as I massaged his back. It felt good to hear him say he had refused, but what was our fate now?

It was as if he had read my mind. "I told them I am in love with a girl. I didn't say who. I know I can save for your debt. We just need to calculate what you owe for both you and your sister."

I imagined him, working as hard as he did, spending all of his money to see me already. And now he was taking on our debt as well.

I was flattered by his efforts. I knew that you can't ask someone to save you, but each time he stroked my scar on my face, with each kiss, each poem, each smile, I wanted to ask him. I wanted to say, "What if we ran away, our hearts beating against the night winds, following the stars to a new life where we woke up to sip chai in the morning and slept to the pages of poetry each evening?" Hoping was dangerous around here. I knew it would never happen; Shiv made it clear that the gundas had threatened him more than once. But Amla had hoped, and lately I found it easier to imagine her happy somewhere rather than fear something terrible for her—so could I hope too.

I let my fear speak instead.

"Wouldn't it just be easier, Shiv, if you married the girl your parents choose? Who knows if we can even get me out of here? I don't want you risking your life. Plus, look at me. What will your family think?"

He studied me as I spoke.

"Tell me what your heart says," he says.

Cosmic connection
To a man who hears
My words
Over the scars of an unchosen path
For some reason
Forbidden love
Feels right

I waited for him to speak, but instead he pulled me against him. I surrendered to the moment, and as he touched me, with each kiss, I let go of what could go wrong.

CHAPTER 40

I was sweating when I woke up and did not know why. It was hot outside, but that didn't usually bother me much. This was different; I felt unrested, like I had tossed and turned all day. Amla's ghost kept visiting me in my sleep. She said she had put a light in my belly.

When I got out of bed, I dry heaved a few times. Sajana heard through the thin walls and came over to tell me she could give me the pills I needed. "They will clear it out—better to try to do it early," she said. I nodded and pretended I agreed. "Okay, good. Janaki will tell Madame to add the pills to your tab."

"Wait." I remembered Amla's words from my dream: *This is your way out.* "Let me think about it."

Sajana raised an eyebrow. "Asya, do you want that baby to end up like Prachi's?"

Sajana had told us Prachi's story when we were in training, as a cautionary tale for using rubbers. She was a worker who had become pregnant and ended up having a baby girl. As she got older, Sajana said the girl would run around the brothel during the day and would play with her. They loved helping her put on lipstick, seeing her pretend to walk around in heels. Even Madame would smile at her. Prachi died of AIDS when her daughter was only four years old. The girl ended up being bought by someone, and they never saw her again.

The story broke my heart.

"No, no," I said now, "but I want to just think."

Sajana said, "Okay, but don't think too long. It won't work if we don't do it soon. Remember, the procedure is worse. And more expensive."

I knew she spoke from experience. I thought about how Shiv would react that evening. I went on with my chores that afternoon but felt almost seasick most of the time, like I was in a rocking boat on the Ganges. *A baby? What will Shiv think? Will he be excited?* The thought of carrying his baby filled my heart. I no longer wanted to count other men for my debt; would he agree? *Could we escape? Will he tell them he will marry me? Bring me home to his family? Would they accept the child?* My mind wandered through all the possibilities.

I thought I could trust Sajana, but that was wishful thinking. By the end of the day, she had already told Janaki, and news spread from there. When Madame saw me that night, she smirked. I knew she was plotting something. I was afraid she would force the pills on me. I avoided her until I heard her speak behind me. "We could replace Asya with a new girl child. Or even a boy; there is a place for boys too. She is too disfigured anyway."

It took all of me to bite my tongue. Even if I didn't know yet what I wanted, I knew I would never let Madame have my baby. I needed to work out a plan with Shiv. I turned and looked her straight in the eye for a moment and walked away.

Shiv was excited about a new job opportunity that evening. He sat on the mattress. "It's so amazing, Asya, and I don't mind traveling to Howrah all week. I finally feel valued. I won't be in my father's shadow and can save more of my own money for us. And you know, I will be traveling over Rabindra Setu bridge, named after Tagore . . . thinking of my true Tagore every time."

I waited until he was lying down beside me, and when he reached for my blouse, his hand grazed my stomach, and I moved it away without thinking. "What's wrong?"

"We are having a baby." I had practiced telling him the news all day, thinking of clever ways or questions to ask him. Thinking of ways to make it seem magical. And then, when it was time, I was so scared of what his reaction might be that I was a clumsy mess. So much for poetry.

"What? A what?" His expression flitted between a smile and a frown. "How do you know it's, you know, mine?"

I felt ashamed that he needed to ask the question, but of course I understood. "You were the only one without a rubber around that time."

"Asya, does anyone know?"

I nodded. I told him about Sajana and the pills.

"I mean, only take them if you want to."

"Why would I want to? I mean . . . do you want me to?"

We were stumbling with our words, and my heart raced. This was not how I imagined it.

"Asya, I just started this job. I'm only twenty-three, and I don't know how to get you out of here yet. I will do anything for you, but this puts so much pressure on the time. I mean, we would have to get you out of here before he is born."

"He?"

"I mean she; it could be a she. Oh God. What do we do?"

He was a different man than the Shiv who had bandaged me with such careful confidence. Saved my eyesight. Refused a marriage. The tears flooded my eyes. How could I have let my guard down to trust him?

"Oh no, don't cry, okay? Please, we will be fine. I can work double time. I'll stay in Howrah during the weeks, and I'll come see you on weekends or holidays, and we will have enough money before the baby comes. I won't be paying to be here all week that way. We can do this, okay?"

Only then did I realize that I had expected him to scoop me up in his arms and run me out of there. To barge into Madame's office and demand she release the mother of his child. I had expected us to laugh and for him to kiss my belly, stroke my hair, and say, "This was meant for us."

I nodded at his plan and missed my sister as I fought tears. I wanted to believe him, that we could do this like he said.

That night as we lay in each other's arms, I waited until he fell asleep to cry silently.

PART 3

AMLA

DECEMBER 2004

CHAPTER 41

W e were in the back of the Ladki Rights office, where Vishnu kept a small desk and two chairs. Priya shifted in her seat as she jotted something down. We had been in counseling for seven months already since the raid.

"When Asya and I were in the village, we once had a boy get selected to go to IIT. They had created scholarships with a rigorous application process for some lucky village boys to attend the most prestigious technology school in India. Out of thousands of applicants, Shankar got the spot. Everyone gathered around his home the day he was leaving. I remember his smile, the way he looked at everyone as he walked towards his uncle's car. He turned around and smiled. It was a smile I would never forget. Like he had escaped, he was ready to fly, free as a bird. That's supposed to be like me, but all I feel is guilt."

"I see the guilt is still coming up for you. Are you still having the same dream?" She adjusted the black frames on her face.

I nodded. The moment replayed in my mind over and over again and changed: Asya walks over to me during the raid, and time around us stands still. The roof of the brothel opens with ladders that fold down to us. We both look up to see everyone, Janaki and Sajana, even

Jayna, climbing out. Asya and I hold each other's ladders, but when it is my turn to hold hers, the ladder crumbles and she falls, which is when the ground opens up beneath us and swallows just her.

I usually woke up screaming, and Mausi would come running with water.

The first night when Vishnu brought me to his aunt's home, she stayed up with me the whole night, it seemed. Hours after my rescue, I had collapsed on the mattress and succumbed to sleep. I awoke at predawn and rubbed my eyes.

I'll never forget how they felt—like they were on fire. I kept rubbing, but the burning only grew worse. Finally, panicking, I screamed. Mausi reached for her lamp.

"What is it, child?" she asked.

"My eyes!"

Mausi leapt from her bed and ran to me, grabbing a glass of water from the side table. She splashed the water on my eyes and peered down at me, concerned. I stared up at her face, noting the wrinkles beside the crease of her eyes, and her evenly shaped, thick eyebrows. I could see so clearly, and my eyes were fine. Was I dreaming?

Vishnu had mentioned perhaps Asya was crying, calling it twin telepathy; he had heard of it in his medical school training.

"Beti, you are safe now," Mausi had said. "Just rest." I succumbed to her kindness and slept. No one had called me beti in that hellhole.

Priya knew when my mind drifted. "Amla, tell me more about what you feel right now." She often did this. I'd much rather talk about my dreams or answer matter-of-fact questions than share my feelings.

"I feel . . . like I am losing hope."

Before I arrived at my appointment, Vishnu had told me they still had not heard any news from their undercover volunteers on where Madame had relocated the brothel. I had given them all the inside information, such as Janaki being Madame's keeper and Amira's death, as details they could use on the street.

"Do you want to draw about it today?"

I didn't want to, not yet. "No. I can later though. In my journal."

"Okay, I want you to keep drawing in your journal and bring it next time." The phone rang in the front as Priya gathered her things and opened the door.

I heard the young intern at the desk answer the call, "Ladki Rights, how may I help you?"

She was pretty, with small features and wide eyes outlined with kohl. In a flash, I felt tears well, recalling when my sister taught me her kohl trick at the brothel: "Didi, after you apply it, rub the rest that remains on your finger across your eyebrows to smooth them."

As I waited for Vishnu to drive me home, I caught sight of my photo on the wall. When we first came, I wondered whether my picture would be added. I was the last girl they had rescued. After the election, there were new police officers, and departments had changed, making it harder for nongovernment organizations to get inside again. I stared up at those girls' faces. I wondered again, *Will we leave a spot for my sister?* They were all girls like us, some younger and some older. Girls with bright eyes, scarred faces, big lips, small noses. There were so many; it made me sad to think of our world that way.

I tried to recall if I had ever been photographed without my sister besides when Adam came into the brothel. When we were younger, it was mainly the two of us together with Mummy. Puppa never let Mummy touch the camera he borrowed from his coworker a few times, so we had no photos with Puppa except one that Mummy convinced him to let her take. He had been in a good mood that day after getting bonus pay for doing extra hard labor.

Once, Chotu had stolen his father's camera and had me pose by the tree where we met. He made me laugh, and I covered my mouth when he snapped my photo. Days later, he showed me the photo and said he would keep it with him wherever he went. I was wearing a yellow salwar kameez that blended into the rays of sun behind the tree.

My heart tugged at the memory. Sometimes it felt like I was two different girls—one from that life with my family in the village and one from now, a girl who had been in a brothel. *How far away those days in the village are.* The village was like a feeling I could never go back to. An innocence I could never find again.

When they put my photo up on the wall, Vishnu told me, "These are the girls we have helped. We document each case—like yours."

"Why?"

"Why do we document them?"

"No, why do you help them?"

I bit my lip. Did I ask too much? I felt an imaginary poke in my hip, Asya digging her finger in. I recalled how my curiosity often resulted in beatings at the brothel.

But I hadn't known anyone to set out to do such good for others, and Vishnu didn't seem to mind. "Last year, during my senior year in college, I volunteered at a hospital in New York, where I live with my mother. One day, a young girl, maybe eleven years old, came into the emergency room. I followed a resident, my friend Jamal, on rotations there. The girl was scared every time the resident tried to come close to examine her. Her face was cut up, and her lip was bleeding. We asked her what happened, but she pretended not to speak English.

"Jamal took out a triangular gauze pad, and I told Jamal that I was so hungry that all I could think about was a slice of pizza when I saw the gauze. Out of the corner of my eye, I saw that she smiled. I knew she could understand us. A translator came, and she told him that she had fallen and her lip wouldn't stop bleeding, so she came by herself. She said her parents were not here; her uncle had brought her and was in the waiting area. After we bandaged her, Jamal went to get an attending doctor to sign off on her treatment.

"When we were alone, I asked her in English if she liked pizza. She smiled. Then I whispered, 'Did a man do this to you?' She had tears in her eyes and nodded yes. She lifted up her skirt slightly and showed me the bruises on her thighs. I asked her if it was her uncle, and she nodded. Did she need our help? She didn't reply, but the tears fell. So I told her to wait and left to look for the ER physician in charge.

"When I went back to the room, I saw she had been discharged. The nurse told me they needed the room, so she had sent her to the waiting area to wait for me. She wasn't there when I went out. I never saw her again." He paused, touching the crease on his forehead where his eyebrows met, then letting his finger rest in a gentle fist. "You know, my mother was also a survivor of domestic abuse. She left my dad."

I imagined how hard it must have been for his mother. An Indian woman, taking her child and leaving her husband. It was as if Vishnu had read my mind.

"It was hard for my mom. But she had her sister when we came to visit India, and she started volunteering with my mausi and helping other women who were in similar situations. I remember witnessing how healing that was for my mom. It's what inspired me to be where I am today with Ladki Rights."

Today, Vishnu smiled, and I felt like I used to with Chotu. In the past few weeks, we had shared several glances that felt different than they had before.

"Amla, you must be tired. Let's head home so we can see Mausi before she leaves for her kitty party."

Outside, we descended the steps to the parking lot. A small shop sold motorcycle parts on the lower level, and the owner was outside. He said hello and asked how long Vishnu was staying this time. In his struggle for Hindi words, Vishnu said, "For a few hours," which sent the shop owner into belly laughs. I giggled too, and Vishnu smiled like he had been in this situation before.

Slightly red with embarrassment, he said, "Please give me a motorcycle as I need to get to the airport, then." We walked away laughing, and I admired the way Vishnu took his mistake in stride. Most of the men I had met, including my own father, could not laugh when they were embarrassed. Instead they tried to pull others down to make themselves feel better. Sometimes with words, sometimes with fists.

On our scooter ride, I hugged him closely as he weaved beside the moving cars and side roads that led to his aunt's compound.

When we got back to Mausi's, we went into the kitchen and saw that Mausi had cut fresh mango. There was a bowl set in front of a chair at the table. I was surprised at how hungry I was. The sessions with Priya always drained me, but I had started to feel better each time I *released*, as she put it. The cut fruit always felt like such a gift. We had rarely gotten fresh fruit in the brothel. Mostly we ate overcooked rice and bland daal. When I ate food these days, I labeled which tastes were tastes of freedom and which were those of the brothel. It was a game I played. The mango was perfect, in between the yellow and dark orange, at the right sweetness, like the taste the freedom.

"There is more; do not worry," Mausi said as she watched me wolf down the mango as fast as I could shove it in my mouth. She pointed to a basket of mangoes on the counter. "My husband planted that tree years ago, and every year, I would ask him when the fruit would come. After he passed away, they started growing, one by one, and now when it is in season, we get so many I cannot eat them all myself! Vishnu says it is my husband sending us the fruits as love."

Vishnu had retreated to the bedroom to change his clothes.

She waited for me to speak. She was like Vishnu in that way— never pressing, just there. He must have gotten that from his mausi.

"There are still no leads on my sister."

Mausi hesitated. "Tell me more about your sister."

Priya had taught me to reflect on the good as we moved through my emotions over my sister's blame towards me. I told her about the way we looked the same but were so different. The way Asya was always getting me out of trouble and how we got our names. I told her about how I could feel what Asya was thinking sometimes, how we had never been apart. Tears formed in my eyes when I spoke of her this way.

I told Mausi, "Sometimes when we were younger, if someone called for one of us, we would both stand there and see if they could tell us apart. When they said Amla, we both said yes, or Asya, we both said yes, and it drove people mad, but of course we loved it!"

She listened and she smiled.

"You know how my sister and I were just as close before she moved to America with her husband."

I nodded, as she had shared this with me before.

"And so when my husband died, she came and stayed with me for two months, just sleeping in my bed, making me chai, letting me get my strength back. Sisters are strength. We will find your Asya. Ladki Rights is so dedicated to helping and educating underage girls from the brothels."

I knew it as I thought of Bhima, Janaki, and Sajana also.

Mausi's eyes were empathetic, and I felt better after we talked. My freedom made me feel guilty. We would find Asya; we had to. Mausi knew how important it was. She knew what it was to be a sister.

CHAPTER 42

The next week, Priya came to Mausi's home for my counseling session so we would have more privacy. She tried to do this when she could. I think she also must have noticed how safe I felt with Mausi. We held the session in the bedroom, where I sat on the bed and Priya on a chair that Mausi brought in for us. The light coming in from the bedroom window and blinds cast lines across Priya's young face.

I had been having another recurring nightmare where I would walk up to a hospital bed, whispering, "Asya, Asya." There was a human form beneath a sheet, and when I pulled the covers back, it was Mummy, eyes wide open, cold, blue, and dead.

This time Priya brought art supplies for me. The nonprofit had enrolled me in courses they offered that could count towards my secondary school degree. I would need school grades to apply for the university scholarship program, and one of the courses I was looking forward to was a drawing course.

I would start in January, but to prepare, Mausi had given me a drawing pad that I carried with me everywhere. When Priya saw it, she started doing some art therapy with me.

Today, Priya handed me a sketchbook and a neat box of colored oil pastels. She first asked me to draw a house.

I drew the thatched roof of our village home, the strong bamboo and cool mud floors and walls. I drew the nearby well and a sunny sky. Tears formed in my eyes as I drew. I held them at bay. I missed Asya, but I did not cry. From the corner of my eye, I saw Priya jot something down.

When I was done, she asked me to describe the home I drew. I told her it was my home as I described each room. I allowed the memories to flood my heart.

"It's okay to cry." Priya handed me tissues to wipe my nose. She asked if I wanted to draw more. I nodded.

Then she asked me to draw a tree.

"A tree?" That seemed simple enough.

As I drew the tree, it grew wild branches and leaves and started to look like a screaming tree, with angry eyes embedded in its trunk. I felt the heat rise inside, and my pastel colors became darker with each heavy stroke.

"I'm done." I was exhausted. She asked if I wanted to talk about what feelings came up with the tree, but I didn't. I knew it reminded me of Madame.

She said we could talk about it next time and I would do the next drawing at our next visit. As she packed up, I asked her what I would be drawing next time.

She hesitated and then told me. "A person."

"Bring me a small mirror then."

"It does not have to be of yourself. Any person that comes to mind."

"It's not myself I want to draw." There was only one person I could not stop thinking about.

When I went out into the living room, Vishnu was talking to Mausi about the issues with funding. I joined them and sat on the armchair as I leaned into the round silk pillow beside me.

The nonprofit had lost funding. The prime minister had decided to stop allowing nonprofits to receive foreign money in an attempt to control misused funds. One of Ladki Rights' biggest contributors was in New York—a famous artist Vishnu won over through a contact at his medical school.

Earlier in the month, he had shown me a photo of her paintings. One was a long, tall, prickly green plant with dark flowers. I had asked him what kind of plant it was, and he smiled, saying, "Of course you have never seen a cactus." A few days later, he printed out information about the cactus from his computer.

Vishnu was devastated about the funding. Mausi tried to reassure him, telling him there must still be a way. They would speak to her brother-in-law, who served as the Ladki Rights pro-bono accountant. Maybe he would have ideas.

I watched them speak, wondering at their concern for other people. I had my sketch pad nearby, so I began to sketch Vishnu's face. I started with his eyebrows and long nose. His lean face and gentle eyes. I was shading the edges of his chin as he came and peeked over my shoulder.

"Wow, you are pretty good," he said. I smiled and started showing him some of my other sketches.

"Maybe you can sell my sketches here in India for more funds." I was half joking, to lighten his mood, but he jumped up. "Amla, Amla, that's it!" He was next to me, and kissed my forehead. He blushed instantly, as if he hadn't realized what he was doing, and muttered, "Oh, I'm sorry," before running over and lifting Mausi off the ground. I felt sweat forming on my upper lip as heat rose in my cheeks. I was surprised by his affection, but somehow, it felt good. Not scary or wrong. No man in the brothel ever kissed me on my forehead.

Vishnu was telling us about his new idea. "You see, Camilla sells certain paintings in the galleries in New York for our cause. But we can put photos of them on our website. It can broaden who sees her paintings, like those who support us here in India, and provide more funding than the occasional buyer. We can have them pay us from our site and link it to our account to avoid the overseas wire she had to send in the past." He was talking fast, and I felt the energy jumping off his skin. At that moment, I wanted to kiss him back, and I felt ashamed and giddy about it all at once.

CHAPTER 43

Priya helped me apply for a student visa. Vishnu described a program through the nonprofit where I would be able to enroll in an undergraduate program with partner schools, some of which were overseas in the US and London. The program still allowed for a stipend, which I was getting worried about. Even if I wanted to, I couldn't stay with Mausi forever. I ached for my loss, my mother, in the uncertainty of my future. I wanted to bury my face in her sari, ask her what I should do, have her help me navigate the waters I was not used to when it came to money and school and decisions. I knew Asya would be surprised if she had known I actually wanted to study—though I didn't know what.

"We have had success with this visa program to New York, so you can learn more and do what you love. Tell me, Amla, what do you love to do?"

New York? I had never thought of leaving India, nor did I know what I loved to do. "I don't know." I looked at him and bit my lip. Asya had been the one with a clear vision of what she wanted to do. I was always just beside her, throwing rocks through her windows and making everything harder.

Vishnu smiled. "What about art? You are so talented. I am sure Camilla can help you."

I didn't say anything, but nodded as if maybe. I felt comforted in his offer yet also wondered how I could let strangers keep helping me. I felt lost when it came to the application and longed for my sister.

My face must have shown my worry as he said, "That's okay. Don't worry. One day at a time." His smile reassured me. "You can take those classes to help you decide."

The idea of moving on without Asya scared me, and the guilt tugged at my thoughts. But I swallowed and said okay. Taking chances seemed to be second nature for me; plus, I was beginning to like the idea of being in the same place as Vishnu with the New York visa program.

"Good, let's visit the school today. You will meet some of the others, and see where you will stay." The school had worked directly with the Ladki Rights, and he said there were a few other girls from Ladki Rights there already.

Mausi walked into the room with fresh dates. I couldn't hide my fear. Staying in a new place where others were in control made my heart race. What if they did what the brothel did to us? What if Vishnu did not know what was happening there? My head was spinning until I heard Mausi's voice. "Vishnu, Amla is a special case since she still has her sister to search for. Perhaps she can stay with me as she attends her new school. When you leave for the US soon, it will give me good company—and someone to help enjoy my mangoes and dates."

Vishnu looked back and forth between us. "Would you like that, Amla?"

I smiled.

"Amla, yaar, we can work with the program to finish so you can start at the next admissions cycle. It can take almost six months to a whole year. They work with other nonprofits too. It will give us time to get paperwork in order. Do you still want to try that New York pizza?"

I nodded. He was always trying. A year would certainly give us enough time to find Asya despite the obstacles, like the crooked cops.

He said he had the best volunteers going undercover to locate her. Months out of the brothel, and I was still adjusting to being outside its walls and trying to trust my decisions and the world around me.

CHAPTER 44

While I knew the day would come, I was still nervous about visiting the school to register. I was turning eighteen soon, which was old to be finishing secondary school, but I had lost time, and the university Vishnu spoke of in New York required a diploma. As we drove through the city, I thought about Asya and how she always got lost in the scenes of cities, probably thinking up poems. I thought about Madame and what she must be doing to her. I wondered if anyone would wish Asya a happy birthday when she turned eighteen—if anyone even knew. If we would find her by then.

When we had first arrived at the brothel, it was Janaki's birthday, and I drew her a cake. They had marveled at the way I shaded the picture; even Asya was impressed. After a time, we started to hold tight to those moments as girls and keep them to ourselves. It seemed like it made them more special, our secret birthday milestones.

Vishnu and the driver were chatting about the roads opening up, with winter rainfall clearing out as the season ended. When the flood was at its peak, there was no way to get around. I noticed the decal of the trio of goddesses fading on the plastic door of the driver's glove compartment and thought of Mausi. She would hum sometimes, the *aarti* for Saraswati, the goddess she prayed to. Her humming in the kitchen reminded me of Mummy.

I spent car rides like this dreaming about Asya. In my moments with Mausi at home, she sensed it, I knew. When I wiped the tears before anyone could see, I would hear her call me to help her. Silently, we would cut the unripe mango to be dried and prepare the spices for the achar she made.

Would I be like her one day? Would I ever be someone's mausi or even mummy? Have a family on my own, hum my children songs in a kitchen? Probably not. Having a family usually meant having a man, and the idea of being with a man forever made my stomach turn. Although Vishnu seemed okay . . .

I felt my face turn red from thinking about him again.

We parked in front of a small brick building with a long, open path. A woman with a sari emerged. For a moment I thought she was the aunt who brought us here on the train, disguised. Reflexively, I closed my eyes and screamed. Vishnu led me back to the car and said, "Breathe, breathe," until my head stopped spinning.

My ears were ringing. When I could finally speak, I told him about the morning after our sixteenth birthday. I told him about the rain on the car window and the way the air smelled. I told him when we pulled up to the school, it felt the same, and suddenly I didn't know who and what to trust anymore. I told him I just wanted to be with my sister, my safe place, curled up side by side and holding each other. I told him I didn't know what I would do without her.

When the words stopped, he watched me for a long moment. Then he opened the door, calling for the driver.

"Amla, what if we took a trip to your village today? For something familiar? We have to schedule your home visit anyway. We can call the office to book a flight."

Priya had said this might help, but only when I was ready. I still wasn't sure if I could face my grandparents and admit what had happened. Then I thought of Nani stroking my forehead and kissing my nose to heal anything with love. About our home and memories of a life that felt so far away but was all I knew as love. Ladki Rights assessed homes for all the girls they helped, to see if they were safe to return to. I nodded, and Vishnu briefed the driver on our new plan. He sat beside me, balanced and calm, like his name.

CHAPTER 45

The flight was not even the length of a whole movie, but I took in every detail to try to remember to tell Asya when we were reunited one day. I thought of all the times we imitated planes and dreamt of going places. The Mumbai airport was crowded, full of business travelers, families, and foreign tourists, and I followed Vishnu's lead.

Ladki Rights arranged a driver for us after the flight. I watched the shanty huts around the airport disappear from my car window. As we departed from the city noise and traffic, my window landscape was replaced with dense trees, and I found myself dozing off from fatigue. When we got closer to the village, we passed the bus station on the outskirts of town, the last place Asya and I had been before leaving. It felt like so long ago. Back then my worries were about sneaking kisses in with Chotu, and now . . .

I shook my head to get rid of the thoughts of the men, and women, who had harmed me. I wanted to be here, in the place I had only known with my sister. Yet I wasn't sure what to expect. Would Dadi and Dada reject me? At least I had Mausi.

I directed them towards the closest place we could bring the car to Nani's compound. It was like time had stood still. The buckets lining the side of the dirt road remained the same, as if no one had used them all this time, even though I knew every family lined up to take turns with them every morning.

But something had changed. I felt it as we walked towards my nani's home. When we got there, a young boy emerged from the home. He looked up at Vishnu and then ran back inside. I almost followed him before a woman poked her head out from behind the curtain.

"I am Amla. Is my nani here? Her name is Seva ben."

My heart beat faster as I searched the woman's eyes. I knew before she said a word.

"Beti, she passed a few months back. Our family was given the compound recently. I heard she was a very nice woman. I'm sorry, I don't know much."

My regret for leaving, for not coming sooner, flooded me. Tears had already formed in my eyes when I felt Vishnu's hand upon my shoulder.

"Amla, I'm sorry."

She was the last I had left of my mother.

We walked back towards the car in silence. I swallowed my sadness, my disappointment, and my regret for leaving. I should have come right after I was saved. Then I would have seen her, could maybe have even been with her in her final moments. I wondered whether she'd died alone, and who had found her.

"Asya, Amla? Beti?"

Hearing our names together brought me back to my childhood, when people often called us by both names, unable to distinguish between us.

I turned to see a familiar face. "Karan-ji," I said. He was a kind neighbor; he often carried Nani's water pail or vegetable basket inside. He lived with his wife and their disabled son, who Nani apparently sang to each evening when he was a baby to help calm his colic.

"Beti, oh, everyone was so worried. Where is your sister?"

I hesitated on what and how to say what had happened. I shoved the word *brothel* away as I looked down to avoid seeing what he would think.

"We were taken," I said, my voice sounding thin to my own ears. I pointed at Vishnu. "This man helped me, but Asya is still there with the bad people."

"Is he the police?" Karan-ji asked.

Vishnu explained about his organization, and how it helped girls. His Hindi was still awkward, so Uncle understood right away that Vishnu was an NRI.

Karan-ji looked Vishnu up and down a few times. He was skeptical, I could tell, but he told me about Nani. How she had a fall, and her hip was broken; then she got sick with a terrible cough before she passed. I shuddered at the thought of her suffering alone.

Karan-ji seemed to read my mind. "She was not alone, Amla; do not worry. She had us, and even your dadi and dada were so kind. Your nani, she left some things for you and your sister. Before her brother cleared the home and went back to his village, he left it with your dadi to give to you whenever you returned. She always said you both would come back."

I couldn't imagine their friendship, what with all their bickering before we had left.

"Where are Dadi and Dada?" I asked.

"Yes, they are in their home. You must see them. They will be happy you girls are safe."

"Thank you, Karan-ji. We will go." I didn't have the heart to remind him that Asya was far from safe.

I told Vishnu we could walk. It would be nice to show him the village. Part of me also wanted to pass Chotu's compound. After all this time, I wondered if he had gotten married.

The village ground felt familiar to the soles of my feet. The sights and sounds, they were my home. The temple's bell and loud music from the chaiwala. I cringed, thinking about what we had done, leaving behind the familiarity of all we had known. We had been trying to escape marrying men we didn't know, and ended up with strange men anyway.

"Did your sister and you fetch water like that?" Vishnu asked quietly, gesturing towards two young girls at the well.

The last time I had fetched water was when Mummy collapsed. I nodded and he was quiet. I wanted to say more, but the words stuck in my throat. My feet were stuck again, like that day. What would Dadi say? We approached our compound, though I told Vishnu our home probably had been sold as my grandparents had wanted to do before Asya and I left; I was unsure if Puppa ever came back. We had long assumed him dead, but he might not be.

"Are you ready?" Vishnu asked me with kindness in his voice as we arrived at Dadi and Dada's home.

I could smell the oil tadka simmering for lunch. My stomach churned. I swallowed the hesitation. Now or never. "My dadi makes the best subzi; let's go see what's for lunch."

Vishnu smiled as we headed onward, and I called from the open door.

We heard a wooden belan drop; she must have been rolling roti.

Dadi had aged, softer at her mouth yet with more wrinkles by her eyes. I ran to her, and she embraced me. "Beti, beti," she sobbed. Even Dada was holding me.

When we released our embrace, I introduced them to Vishnu.

"He rescued me. Asya and I went to Mumbai for Mummy and we were taken." I didn't say where we were taken to. I saw the look in Dadi and Dada's eyes, a mix of fear and relief. They took Vishnu's hands and thanked him. Vishnu was humble.

"Amla is the brave one. That is how it really happened."

Dadi asked, "Asya?" And I shook my head as she put her hands over her mouth.

Dada took my hands. "Oh, beti, we just made your favorite, mooli paratha. It is perfect you are here."

For the first time since we had arrived, I had an appetite. I ate plate after plate of the spiced radishes in the layered bread, letting the ghee cover my fingers with each bite. I noticed Dada had not eaten. He was smiling at me. I was relieved they hadn't asked about where I had been. Why we left. I was afraid that if I told them what the men did to me,

I would be cast as unmarriageable, and for any girl in our village, that was the lowest of places to be.

I asked if they knew what had happened to Puppa.

Dadi and Dada glanced at each other. After a long silence, Dadi cleared her throat.

"Yes, beti."

Dadi went on to explain his condition. A few weeks after Asya and I had left, he returned to the village. After learning that we ran away, he became mute. He wouldn't talk.

Puppa was alive?

I stopped eating and looked outside. I could see our compound. They had not sold it. I stood and felt Vishnu behind me immediately. I turned and told him it was okay, but I needed to go see him.

He nodded. We walked across the village in silence. I felt Vishnu's support as I opened the door to our quiet home.

It was dirty. There was dust everywhere, and some of the furniture was gone. I saw his back in a chair. It was this chair my sister and I would climb into as young girls to sit side by side.

"Puppa?"

His head lifted, and he turned to me. We walked towards each other, and he was sobbing as I let him hold me, let him stroke my face and kiss my forehead. As distant as I had felt, as angry as I once was, the love from my parent felt good. In the brothel, ideas about ways we could leave came and went. An earthquake would crumble the building, and we all would run; our old teachers would storm in and demand Asya and I be let back into our village's school—anything that allowed me to escape into my imagination for even a minute. I closed my eyes and thought of the one time I had hoped my puppa would walk in to save us from the brothel. I had told Asya about it as she fixed up a bruise a customer had left on her face. She scoffed, saying Puppa was dead to her. The anger about Mummy, I still had that too. Could I forgive him now?

He looked behind me for Asya, and I shook my head. "We still have to find her." I told him I wanted to introduce him to someone, and he looked confused.

I led him outside to Vishnu, who smiled and waved at my puppa.

"That is Vishnu. He works for an organization that helps girls who are kidnapped and sold. Guhan uncle sold us when we went to look for Mummy." My jaw tightened. I didn't realize how fast my heart would race when I told Puppa what had happened.

"Guhan? He did not return my phone calls." His voice drifted. He was in disbelief. "I am so sorry, my beti. We will find her. We can ask Vishnu to go back . . ."

I heard Puppa's promises. But as I listened to his plan, something inside of me hardened the joy my heart wanted to feel. My father would not come to find her? Shouldn't he want to be the one to find his daughter? He said he loved us, but had he even looked for us? I was underwhelmed by his words; he disappointed me like always.

The sun was strong where we stood, and we naturally headed back to Dadi and Dada's home.

As Dadi hugged him, her son, I saw the love of mother to child. This was like my mother I had lost, who we could not save. I suddenly missed my mother so deeply that tears filled my eyes.

Dadi was talking, saying how wonderful it was to hear her son's voice. Now that I was back, she said, I could stay and take care of Puppa, and he would be himself again.

The room started to feel hot, and I felt myself shrinking, melting away from her words. Without warning, everything went dark.

· · ·

"She's been through a lot. This might have been too much," Vishnu was saying above me.

I was lying down on their mattress pad. Vishnu was there, and Dadi was holding a rag she must have had on my head.

When my eyes opened, Vishnu said, "Okay, slow and steady." He spoke in English this time, and I smiled to hear him speak comfortably.

"You fainted, Amla. I think you need to rest a bit more," he said in his awkward Hindi this time and got me to giggle.

He smiled and said, "What's so funny?" which sent me into more laughter.

I saw Dadi watch us curiously from the corner of her eye before she told me to have a drink of water.

"I spoke to your family about everything, Amla. And I think I may just have some more of your dadi's delicious food; then I can head back tomorrow. I will alert the driver if I can call and book an earlier flight. I'll cancel your return leg, if you would like, so you can spend more time with your family."

My stomach sank. Why did he say "I," not "we"? Was he planning to leave me here?

"I come." Even though he had spoken in Hindi, I answered in English.

I waited for him to tell me it would be better if I stayed here, with Puppa. I waited for him to tell me that I should wait for Asya here and be with my family. But he only nodded and said, "Okay."

"Okay, tomorrow, let's talk about it," Puppa interrupted.

I listened as they all decided on sleeping arrangements. Vishnu would stay with Puppa. Dadi wanted to watch over me and be sure I was okay, so I would stay with her. Dada would sleep in the common room on the sofa.

As Vishnu went to the compound with Puppa, my stomach felt a familiar warmth, like when I would see Chotu in the village. Could it be?

I ignored it and went to help Dadi in the kitchen.

I dreamt of Asya all night. I kept hearing her whispering to me like when we were girls. In my dreams, we were running together in the dark night, but she kept disappearing, leaving me panting and running to find her.

Dadi covered me with a rag, saying I was sweating in my sleep.

• • •

As we prepared breakfast the next morning, Dadi turned to watch me strain the ground assam leaves and ginger pieces out of the chai.

"You want to go with that man instead of staying here with your puppa."

I looked up. She wasn't asking but telling me, and I wasn't sure how to answer, but it sounded right to my heart.

I couldn't imagine being in the village without Asya and having to bear the stigma of coming from the brothel, plus taking care of my puppa, who I had not forgiven. The thought of staying had not even crossed my mind when we got here; it was to be just a visit.

"Yes, Dadi, I want to study and go back. I can always visit again. I know you had or have your own ideas about what I should do, but—"

"Then you must go." She placed the chapati in the metal tin and didn't turn around. I let her continue. "When you both left, before your nani passed away, we understood something together. I became close to your nani as we prayed for you girls every day together. We were the women of this family, and only we understood your desire to leave. I know you did not want to marry those men, but I did not know what else to do. I should have tried harder. I should have talked to you both. And your nani was right. I regret we didn't let your mother go back to school. The money was always so tight, and then it was too late. When we lost you, I vowed to myself that if you ever came back, I would never hold you back again."

Her voice was shaking with emotion as she spoke, and as I poured her the first cup of chai, I handed it to her and kissed her cheek. "Thank you, Dadi," I whispered. I might not be able to forgive Puppa, but at least I could release the anger I held for Dadi, especially since it had been my choice to leave with Asya. That was something.

Puppa and Vishnu joined us for breakfast. I noticed Vishnu watching me when I laughed at one of Dada's jokes. I wasn't sure, but for that brief moment, I felt a connection between us.

When we finished eating, I told them I wanted to go see my old school, and Vishnu asked if he could join me.

As we walked, I told him about Asya. I had been thinking about her all morning after my dream. I talked about her all the time, of course, but I realized he only knew about the Asya from the brothel who secretly wrote poems, not the Asya from the village. Not the true Asya. So I told him about her crush on our yoga teacher and how nervous she would get, always falling out of balance and crashing to the ground. He laughed as I imitated her in vrksasana. The ease with which I spoke to him started to feel like I had my own crush on him. How could I fall for him, though? How would that even work with the organization and him in America?

"What about you? Who was your crush?" he asked, interrupting my thoughts.

I blushed at the thought of saying "You."

"There was a boy. My friend Chotu. He helped Asya and me escape. I would like to see him if we have time after walking by the school. Can you wait for me?"

He looked at me for a moment and then smiled. "Sure, if your dadi can make more of that chai while I wait."

"I think she would be pleased to make it for you," I replied.

When we walked by Chotu's compound, I didn't see him working on his bike in front, like I had hoped. I noticed a small car, though, covered in marriage flowers. Vishnu saw my face change.

"Why don't we stay another night?" he said. "The flights have not been confirmed yet, but there is a late-afternoon flight we can catch so we can just head out after breakfast and make it back before dark tomorrow if you'd like. It would be nice to spend the morning with your family before we go."

This thoughtful understanding—this was what it was about Vishnu that I knew would capture my heart.

CHAPTER 46

After we returned from the village, Vishnu and I spent New Year's Eve at Mausi's.

Early in the afternoon, one of the volunteers working undercover in Sonagachi to develop a new raid plan had met an older prostitute who claimed to know Asya when they saw my photo. When she told him to wait, he sent a text message to Vishnu, who ran to tell me. I was helping Mausi trim her jasmine flowers in the garden as he ran out.

Mausi made more chai, and we all sat in the kitchen, just waiting. The whole time we waited, my heart was racing. I knew it. I knew she would come back to me by the New Year.

Over an hour later, Vishnu's phone rang. He answered on the first ring. I watched his face for clues, for an answer. He looked down and ran his fingers through his hair. When he hung up, he explained that the prostitute had returned with her pimp, who demanded money for talking to her. They started chasing the volunteer for his watch, his phone, and any belongings. He threw it all at them. Luckily he had teamed up with another volunteer, who was waiting in the car.

She had conned him. Mausi rubbed my back gently.

"I can stay home, beti." Mausi had New Year's plans, and while I was disappointed, I did not want her missing her time with her friends. Mausi was going to a kitty party with her girlfriends, a few aunties who made it a ritual after she lost her husband. I looked over at the bowl of fresh kheer she had made to bring over as Vishnu answered.

"No, Mausi, don't worry. You go. I can show Amla the ball drop, and we will order fire pizza—not like New York, but it will do."

We saw Mausi out and hugged her. Then Vishnu plopped down on the couch, and I followed. "We are in the future here in India because of the time change, so we can watch it tomorrow on New Year's Day." He showed me a video from a previous year, of him and his friends shivering outside and counting down, surrounded by what seemed like a million people.

I could tell it made him happy to see his friends. He was leaving for New York soon to return to medical school. I was to continue with my studies and would help Ladki Rights search for Asya. Asya and I had never had many friends; we only had one another. There were a few girls when we were young, but Mummy always said we preferred one another.

I thought of my friendship with Amira and how jealous Asya had been. Was I insensitive back then? I thought I was drawn to Amira for her guidance, but was it that or because she was so liked? Or was it because it bothered Asya so much? Would I be able to make friends in university?

"Hello? Earth to Amla?"

Vishnu had tried to show me another video.

"I'm sorry, I was lost in thought."

"What are these thoughts?" He sat closer to me and waited. If Mausi had been there, I would have moved away from him out of propriety, but lately, I capitalized on these moments when she was not around. I would lean my head closer to his while we looked at something; or when I rode behind him on his scooter, I hugged him a bit more.

I shook my head and smiled.

He was looking at me, and I felt my body tingle as he brought his face closer.

When we kissed, I let my lips melt into his.

"Are you okay?"

I leaned in and kissed him back. I had fantasized about our kiss. Yes, I was okay. I was safe. I was happy. I wanted to be with him. I felt so alone without Asya, especially after leaving the village, as if it was behind me once again.

I was surprised when I felt him move away.

"Amla, I think if you come to New York, it will not only help you but . . . also I like you . . . very much." I watched his face, the softness of his eyes. How he always thought before he spoke. "Our organization has a policy which I cannot break. If you agree, I can talk to the board for permission. For us to be together."

"To be married?" My heart was beating.

"Yes, if that is what the decision is."

There was so much to admire about Vishnu, and I knew the feeling in my heart for him was more than friendship. I nodded as he playfully tugged at my hair and showed me the second video of his New Year's. I half-heartedly watched, letting myself daydream of being with him.

CHAPTER 47

We returned to the office right after New Year's Day. That afternoon after my session, Priya gave me the okay to go with Vishnu to look for Asya. She said I was emotionally ready, and Vishnu understood I needed to go with the team after our hope was crushed on New Year's Eve. Vishnu had scheduled a meeting with the board as well for the next morning.

The evening we went back to the brothel, I waited in the car with a green scarf around my face, just allowing my eyes to peek through, like a Muslim girl. Mausi handed me the scarf, and when the tears came, I told her it reminded me of my mummy. She said, "Then you should keep it with you."

I had promised Vishnu I wouldn't get out of the car, but it was a lie. If I saw Asya myself, I was ready to rush to her side and not let her go, no matter what happened afterwards.

Vishnu was driving, and a new man, Ryan, a volunteer from Australia, sat beside him. He had the same kind blue eyes Adam had. His English was funny sounding the way Vishnu's Hindi sounded.

"You know we aren't conducting a raid today. We just have to let her know if we see her, like we let you know, okay? I can't promise anything," Vishnu said as he started the car.

I knew he was trying to protect me, but my hope was deeper than anything I could describe to him. I needed to be part of it. I handed Ryan the note saying, DIDI, IT'S SAFE. Asya would know my handwriting.

Ryan stepped out of the car a few blocks from the brothel.

While we waited, Vishnu told me he wanted to play a game.

"Okay, I will say a word, and you have to tell me your favorite of whatever it is, and then you say a word, and I'll tell you my favorite. Ready? Color, go."

"Purple. Your turn, food."

"Oh, this is hard," he said. "Pizza from New York." I knew he would say that. On New Year's night, he described it as "a big naan topped with red sauce, like a tomato chutney, and then cheese, paneer, all melted on top," as he made a wide wreath with his hands. It was delicious.

He smiled, and said, "Sport."

I must have frowned in confusion because he said, "Come on, pick a sport!"

"Okay, cricket. Now you tell me color."

"Green, like your scarf."

Someone knocked on the window. I was alarmed and ducked in my seat, my mind leaping to the fear that it was a crooked police officer. But it was a small child, begging. We had always ignored these children when riding with Puppa. Most people I saw when we drove ignored them also. But Vishnu reached into his pockets, looking for rupees to give. He found a few coins and a crumpled bill as he rolled his window down and said, "*Kahna*, go eat."

We went back to our game. I felt myself softening even more to this kindhearted man as I waited for Ryan to return with news of my sister.

Ryan was gone for a long time. We played our game until we ran out of ideas, and then lapsed into silence. I saw Vishnu close his eyes as the sunset faded on the car windows. I followed suit, and I must have fallen asleep, soothed by his quiet breathing.

When Ryan opened the car door, I jumped slightly in my seat. He was sweating and his face was bright red. "Even at night, it's so hot!" he complained.

I imagined what this must be like for him, the heat of my country—not only the sun, but also the chilies that made heat rise in your stomach. So very different from his own home. I had only heard tidbits about America from Chaya and Nisha at Guhan uncle's. How clean and sterile places were, the way the cold could seep into your bones in the winter.

"I couldn't find her," Ryan said. "I searched first for her as a customer, but then I even asked everyone I saw. I asked the owners, the workers—heck, even the little kids. Whoever spoke English didn't know, and whoever didn't speak it didn't seem like they knew."

Vishnu translated it all for me, and when he was done, I told him I had to be the one to go. I knew who to ask. I knew the inside people.

Vishnu shook his head. "It's too risky. But let's come up with a plan before I leave for New York. Tell me more details."

Tell him more? I had already told them everything. "What do you mean?" I asked.

"I mean even who you guys bought your Thums Up from."

Without warning, I burst into tears. Vishnu reached over and pressed his thumbs to my cheeks, dashing away my tears. "Do you like Thums Up?" he asked gently.

And that was all I heard before I lost it even more; I just cried into his hands.

He held me until I stopped crying. Ryan stayed silent. When I slowed down, Vishnu let go of me. I started wiping my face with a green scarf. I had an impulse and grabbed the handle of the car door, shaking it to open, and when it did, I jumped out of the car.

But Ryan was strong and fast, and I felt his hands on my back, around my waist, lifting me up as I kicked. He pushed me back inside and closed the door.

Vishnu locked the doors, and they started driving. I looked out the window and didn't speak.

"Do you really want to go back to that life?" Vishnu asked me in a calm voice I couldn't ignore.

That life? To be stripped of my autonomy and be treated as less than human? Of course not. But I wanted Asya out of that life too.

"I want my sister."

"Amla, she is not at that brothel anymore, and we still don't know where she is. If we go in without planning, we are bound to fail. With you, we had a lot of planning and research. We wanted to save more than one, but we had not planned for everything, and we were lucky we even got you. Now we know some more of what we're up against. I know we can find your sister, but you have to promise me that we are on the same team. I know it's hard, after everything that has happened to you, but I promise, we are doing everything." He held my hands as he spoke.

I studied him. I thought of his story about the girl and her uncle. About his tenderness the other night. In the brothel, I learned that you can see what men are about when they don't speak. What their temperament is like, if they are hiding something, what they fear and what they want.

He was kind, and after all this time, I believed him.

"Okay, I am on your team."

He smiled and said, "Ryan, she says she's on our team. I think we need to get her some ninja gear considering the way she jumped out of the car, right?"

Ryan snorted but didn't reply.

I stared out the window, watching the city go by. Vishnu stayed next to me, his hand holding my knee with love. *Asya, don't worry. We are coming for you,* I thought.

CHAPTER 48

I read the formal report, and the decision was clear: we would need to be married if we wanted to pursue each other. Priya had weighed in that I would need to continue counseling, although she was pleased with my progress.

"Is it what you want?" I was scared of him being forced into marrying me.

"Amla, yes. It is."

I let Vishnu tell Mausi and telephone his mother alone while I went to meet Priya.

Vishnu didn't have much time in India; he needed to return to the US for medical school. Mausi hugged me and started discussing the arrangements right away. Vishnu said his mother could not wait to meet me. I admired how they let Vishnu make his own choices. Mausi had arranged for a pundit to attend a small ceremony at the home with the staff from the office and a few families. With the stigma of my past, Mausi left the rest of the families out of it.

It was hard to believe that Vishnu was going back and it would be months before I saw him again. After the ceremony was booked, we had spent his last weeks sneaking around Mausi, telling her we had to go back to the office or going to the movies and not really watching the film at all.

It was intoxicating. I longed to tell Asya about it, even if she frowned on us the way she had done with Chotu. It was different with Vishnu than with Chotu. I was seen with Vishnu; he understood me and heard me.

Mausi had been eyeing us—when we went out, when we ate together, when Vishnu would tease me. I heard him tell her one morning, "Mausi, don't worry. We are just getting close before we tie the knot. She's like my best friend."

The morning of our ceremony, he and I took a walk. He had finished his packing, and Mausi was making a special lunch and shooed us out of the kitchen despite my offer to help. I reveled in the normalcy, enjoying his company.

Mausi had a tailor stitch a new blouse and let me wear her wedding sari. When we returned from our stroll, I ran my fingers over the delicate silk pattern and the velvet border filled with small pearls. Unthinkingly I murmured, "It's like a dream come true."

Priya came over to fix the golden tikka at my forehead. "You are strong and smart. It is why he cares for you. You deserve this."

It was like a fairy tale, but at the same time, the guilt filled me for leaving Asya.

Golden marigolds surrounded Mausi's living room. She balanced their strong fragrance with the Laxmi dhoop sticks she placed in a few houseplants. We went outside to the small firepit the pundit had set up. Everyone sat on the ground behind us as we circled and said the seven verses, the vows that would join our souls for seven lifetimes, as the pundit's Sanskrit words joined the rhythm we chose to pace our circles by. I passed the mango tree symbolizing Mausi's husband and the roots they'd planted, an example of love passed onto Vishnu. I glanced around, and most of the nonprofit volunteers and board members were present, smiling and enjoying the salty lassi Mausi had prepared. There were only two who had vehemently disagreed with Vishnu's request at first, whom

I had never met and who in the end, Vishnu explained, agreed.

On my request, we all ate pineapple cake together afterwards. There was joy around me, and I longed for my sister, for Mummy. Slowly, guests began to leave, wishing us luck and love as they headed out. Mausi had made plans to stay with her friend that evening. When she left, I took Vishnu's hands into mine as we walked to his bedroom. He looked at me and touched my hair, the nape of my neck. I gazed at him, and our eyes trusted one another. When he kissed me, and as we undressed, I allowed his tender touch, I accepted the feeling of desire. I was not afraid like I had been before. And as he pressed his body inside of me, I felt love flow through me for the first time ever.

As we lay beside each other then, I asked him to tell me something I did not know yet.

His father and mother had gone to the US as a young couple; Vishnu was only a year old when they arrived. He said it was not easy for immigrants back then. His father was there on a student visa. He was studying to be an engineer, but they had little money. All of Vishnu's memories of his father involved anger and stress. He would yell or throw things. Typical man.

But then he started to hit Vishnu's mother. That was when Vishnu said his hatred towards his father began to grow. And the day he laid a hand on Vishnu, his mother escaped with him to a shelter she had heard about from a woman at her temple. That was the beauty of New York; she barely knew English but got help from the women there.

There was a woman from Japan who had a son the same age as Vishnu. She shared her tea with his mother. "One day I will introduce you to her," Vishnu told me as he turned his body to face mine and moved the hair away from my eye. "She is like my second mother."

I asked about the woman's son, if they were still friends. Vishnu looked sad. He said that the boy went to search for his father and never returned. I saw then, for a moment, a deeper understanding of his reluctance to let me search for Asya. He worried it would drive me away. Possibly lead to my own disappearance again.

"Will you forget me?"

He put his hand on my chest. "Forget you? It was fate that I found you."

As my tears started forming, he added, "Besides, you have to come try that New York pizza, right?"

I smiled, and I let my heart become wide open once again.

CHAPTER 49

A few weeks after Vishnu left, I woke up nauseous. I had been going to the office, where the volunteers had developed a map of the brothels they were researching and trying to visit to find Asya. I was going through it with them but said I needed to go home early. I thought it was the sugar cane juice from the day before. It had been an unusually hot day, stagnant with thick air, and even my underwear was damp. The cold juice was just what I was craving. The machine had looked quite rusty, but I drank it anyway.

Priya offered to take me home and said she would call the school and let the teacher know I would miss class that afternoon, to allow me to get rest.

When we got to Mausi's home, Mausi was hanging the laundry as Priya told her I was nauseous. I felt them eyeing me as I went to the bedroom and lay down.

I heard some whispers.

When Priya left, Mausi came in and put her hand to my forehead. I was not feverish; good news, she said.

She put her hand gently on my back. I did want to tell her that I missed Vishnu. That I couldn't concentrate and that between my new classes, him, and Asya, the thoughts made my head spin. That I was not sure it was possible for me to be pregnant after just one time with him, but if it was, how would I tell Vishnu? What about the schooling everyone was helping me secure and work towards?

"I just need rest, Mausi."

She nodded and left the room.

I woke up that evening to the sound of Mausi's prayers and sat next to her as she chanted and rang the bell. I was feeling rested but had counted the days since my last time of the month, and I knew.

As Mausi stood, she asked me if I was hungry.

"Mausi, I need to talk to Vishnu." I touched my belly and continued, "But I am scared."

What about his school? How did he feel about me now that he was back in New York? She looked over at me and put down the small bell.

"We can tell him together. But first, we must get you some food."

I gazed at her alter as she walked to the kitchen, and I thanked the small idol of Saraswati for Mausi's presence in my life.

I searched the goddess of knowledge for answers in my silence. I tried to listen. The breath of my heart reminded me of where my answers were. I was breathing, like I had done to center myself at school, letting the sound fill me like Sandeep bhai had taught us to.

As I let the breath carry me, I realized I wasn't sure about God anymore. I hadn't questioned any of what had happened to me, but why would God allow young girls to suffer?

And if I was to be a mother, would I pray like Mausi? Would that make me a better mother? Was it Mummy who led me to safety with Vishnu and Mausi? Why didn't Asya come, then? Why did Mummy leave her there, alone? Was Mummy reincarnated inside of Mausi or Vishnu? Who would I turn to for answers the way Mummy turned to Nani?

I focused and let the questions go as I imagined the baby inside of me until my eyes opened to more clarity than I had before. Sure, I was scared about becoming a mother and bringing a child into this world. Would I need to stop my dream for college like my own Mummy did?

As a student himself, could Vishnu sustain us financially? But I saw Vishnu was striving to make this world better, a better life for our baby. Maybe it would be easier together.

Mausi was putting the last roti on a small plate to bring to the table for us to eat.

"Beti, do you want to keep this baby?" she asked. "It is your choice."

Choice? What a strange thought. While in the brothel, we were given the choice, but only because our bodies were being used for Madame's gain. Here, Mausi was telling me this huge decision was up to me and no one else. I had never really been given the ability to make true choices. But even as anxiety almost overwhelmed me, I pictured Vishnu: his sweet smile, his bright laugh, and his kind heart. I remembered that a new life was inside of me—a life that would bring more kindness into this world. I nodded. *Yes, I want to keep this baby.*

But I was unsure of how this would work logistically. The future was unclear, but I could not share all of this with Mausi. I was still trying to make sense of it myself. I longed for Asya to pour it all out to, the way she held space for me to process my thoughts.

"When my husband and I learned we could not have children, we often thought about adoption. In a country of so many poor children, it would have been easy. Then when my sister had Vishnu, we were overjoyed. He brought so much love to our home when he was here. We were sad, of course, when they moved to New York, but Vishnu used to tell me that when he had kids of his own, they would have two grandmothers, and he would point to his mother and me.

"And it is true, beti, but of course we need to be sure you all are settled. You both are so young. But this nonprofit, it became my child, and all the girls we have helped. I knew you were special, Amla."

She smiled at me from her heart, the way Mummy always did. Yet even in her optimistic encouragement, I feared what Vishnu's reaction would be. I knew how men could be when thrown into situations they were not prepared for.

PART 4

ASYA

FEBRUARY 2005

CHAPTER 50

Those first days after Shiv left for his new job, I felt alone. I wrote poetry, looking forward to when I could share each poem with him.

But months later, I stopped. What was the point? I hadn't heard from him, and I was forced to continue to work. Would my baby and I survive this?

Jai knew something was wrong. He started bringing me day-old lassi again. I wasn't eating, but Sajana said I had to for the baby. The pills would not work anymore.

"Do you want the procedure?" she asked almost every day now. "It's risky. It's not with a doctor." But every day I shook my head. I wouldn't risk my life, even though it felt like it was already over.

I was growing life inside of me. I felt it and couldn't imagine stopping this life, one that was worthy of love, of a life outside of here.

He said he would send letters. When we woke up the last morning I saw him, he said, "Don't worry. I will go and make so much money that we will be fine in the end. I will get you out of here, you and our baby."

"So we will not see each other?" I asked.

"I know it will be hard. You have to stay strong for our baby. I will send letters, then you send me your poems."

Now, with us moving buildings, I did not know how and where he planned to send these letters to me.

I still hadn't heard from Madame about my request either. When I was about six months along, I asked her if I could be relieved of duties until the baby came. It was too hard to give blow jobs without gagging more than normal, and it hurt when men rested on top of me. I would take on all the other girls' chores. She had looked at me and squinted before saying she would let me know.

The week after my request, Madame had a meeting for all the girls. The last meeting we'd had was months ago, when Janaki was ill, sweating, and fatigued. At the time, Madame mentioned we would talk about HIV. Talking about it meant she threw some extra rubbers from the free workshop at us without addressing that her favorite girl might die. Janaki had up and down days but never stopped working. She was getting thinner, and her eyes were more and more sunken.

This time, we filled the common area, sweating from the day's heat. The fan was broken, and even the TV was damp from humidity.

She was wearing Mummy's earrings. I couldn't take my eyes off of her. When our belongings went missing after we had arrived, Amla and I often wondered about the earrings. We assumed they were sold off, but Madame had kept them all this time. Had she put them on after my acid attack? My heart raced as she started with the usual.

"It seems you girls have gotten lazy. I have noticed the floor is collecting dust sooner, obviously your fault. I should beat you all for the way you have ignored your duties here."

I looked down and ran my toe over the floor to feel the dust. Then she spoke about the changes.

"I am going to have some health procedures for my lungs. Since I am responsible for all of your degenerate lives, we need to increase revenue, so I have a plan. We will be designating each of you to different customer requests. This will make things easier for the gundas and encourage customers to pay more if they want to see their favorites." She looked at each of us and continued.

"We have raised our prices for customers who wish to keep one of you to themselves," she said, and this time she looked straight at me. I imagined cutting her eyes out of her head. Ripping the earrings off her ears. "If someone wants one of you, but you are on a different duty, they need to pay double. Think of this as good; it helps with your tabs. We will rotate each week. It will be fun."

She laughed, wickedly. As a young girl, Amla and I had read stories of the *Mahabharata* and the demon Putana who tried to breastfeed Krishna poisoned milk. Her face was scary and wild, full of evil motives. Even though Krishna defeated her, I had nightmares from the photo my mother showed me in the storybook, and I remember wondering how anyone could be so evil.

Madame Mina was that woman.

She listed our names and our new sexual duties. My ears grew hot from the way she talked about us. As if we were nothing. It was her way of saying she had denied my request and made it worse. I hated her. "Asya, with your situation you can do all the blow jobs."

I hated all of the jobs in the brothel, but especially that. I wanted to vomit just thinking about it. Life felt like it was over.

I pictured Shiv, smiling, so hopeful, and now gone. He could never have been able to pay off both our debts. So it was up to me. Could I defeat this demon? I held my stomach and knew I had to.

CHAPTER 51

After Madame's big announcement, Bhima was the first to feel the wrath of Madame's new whip. She had been caught hoarding money. Janaki revealed the empty ghee container that she had stolen from Jayna to keep the extra rupees in. Apparently, Bhima had been giving men extra services for half price, then asking the men for the money behind closed curtains to keep for herself.

We heard the lashings and screams through the thin walls when we were supposed to be doing chores. Sajana and I were folding laundry.

I kept my eyes focused on my hands, noticing how they had aged and felt rougher than when Amla and I had left the village. At each cry and slap of flesh I heard, I kept my focus on the clothes and imagined Shiv running in that evening, holding his special ointments and herbs, instructing me how to apply them on Bhima to help her.

I pictured his voice, his smile, and the tears fell one by one as I kept my eyes on my hands.

"At least it is not you, Asya, for the baby's sake." Sajana spoke low, and while I sensed her compassion, I couldn't bring myself to look at her. I was afraid to meet eyes with anyone ever again. Trusting his eyes was what got me to fall for Shiv, who I now knew was never coming back.

That night, Bhima still had to see customers. We heard her scream when men touched her back, which was still raw with lash marks.

Janaki gave her ghee to spread on each injury in between.

That morning, we fell asleep to Bhima's muffled cries of pain.

When we awoke, Janaki found her in the bathroom. Bhima had taken her own life with a cracked mirror she used to slit her wrists.

Bhima's Hindi had never improved much, and since she didn't know Bengali either, she struggled to communicate with anyone. We had learned little about Bhima, except how much she loved pomegranate, that her favorite color was orange, and how much she liked to dance. We only found out she was Nepalese from the TV. Sometimes we watched the news prior to *India's Top Star*. There was a segment on the border dispute between Nepal and India. When they zoomed in on an area and we saw Nepalese soldiers, she ran to the TV, saying, "*Makan!*"—the word she had learned in Hindi as "home." Janaki had said she came from the mountains, and I realized how little Janaki knew of the world, having never gone to proper school.

I had always wondered how she withstood the isolation and the horror of this place. Now I realized: she didn't. She was so far from anything she knew, more than any of us; she had nothing to remind her of a happier time. She had none of the things that kept us going.

Madame had Bhima's body removed silently by the gundas. We never knew where they took her. I thought of the evil stories Madame had told us of the customers who said they would save you but instead sold your organs. The only person I could picture doing anything that horrendous was Madame.

I mourned Bhima by myself that day, chanting the prayers of Rama that my mother had etched in my mind as our lineage. I wanted to give Bhima's soul a chance to live again, somewhere far from here and closer to her people. The life growing in me kicked as I chanted, and I held my belly with a promise to protect it with all of my heart. How? I didn't know yet, but knew I had to do everything and anything to try.

CHAPTER 52

"Didi, Didi." It was Jai, standing right in front of me.

"Eh, how did you get in here?"

My vision was blurred, so I blinked until it cleared. Jai was looking down at me anxiously. I was on the floor for some reason. Confused, I examined my body to make sure I was fully dressed. How long had I been on the floor like this? Was it day or night?

My head hurt, and when I touched my eyebrow, I found a cut and some dried blood. I grabbed my belly and sighed with relief. It was intact. Did Madame do something to me? I panicked; I felt my face. My scars and eyes were still there.

What happened?

Lately, my sense of smell had been so strong that everything made me feel nauseous. A vague memory surfaced: a man coming at me, bloodshot eyes and a sweaty mustache.

He had such a horrible stench that I pushed him away when he unzipped his pants.

Madame was getting sicker, and the brothel had suffered. She couldn't afford to keep us in our last brothel. I noticed that she no longer wore Mummy's earrings. We had to move, and this time we found an old building with square, sectioned-off units. Each of us stayed in a tiny room that felt more like a prison cell, with just one small opening in the concrete walls to exit and enter a long corridor.

I was not producing much revenue; no one wanted to see me. My belly was swollen at this point, and Madame had started searching for a new girl, young and fresh. "Stop caring for Asya," she told Janaki one morning, unaware I was right outside the door. "She can rot for all I care, but if the baby survives, it's ours."

Jai's voice brought me back to the present.

"Didi, drink this, please." He stuck the straw to my lips. I was expecting lassi, but instead it tasted like Thums Up. I started giggling, the taste reminding me of happier days.

"Amla, Amla, I will save some for you," I said through my laughter and my tears. Was I delirious?

I was screaming it now, and laughing uncontrollably.

"Didi, please drink."

My eyes opened more. The sugar rush felt quick, like I wanted to jump up but my body was still trying to figure out how to move.

"Didi, I thought you were dead." He looked at my belly, concerned.

I covered my mouth and put one hand to my stomach, closing my eyes. What if my baby was no longer? I waited on the cold concrete floor, breathless, for a sign of life. I looked at the dried blood on the ground. Janaki or Sajana—no one had come?

Jai was looking at my poetry book. "Didi, what is this?"

"Wasted words." I got up slowly as he put it down and helped me.

"Can I have this one?"

He pointed to a poem I had written about Amla. I was surprised he could read.

"Sure, it's the least I can give you for always helping me." I looked over at the lassi he left me. I wondered if I could force myself to drink it.

"I have no one too," Jai said quietly. "I like poetry. I always bring my lassi bottles to the university—you know, the big buildings in College Square near Muhammad Ali Park? There is a group of girls;

they love when I come, always buying. Sometimes there is a teacher there. Everyone makes a big deal out of him. They say he has written many books, and he recites poetry, like yours."

My baby started to stir. I opened my eyes to him. "Jai, I have an idea."

Dreams of her
Beating heart
My soul has died
When I see her face
In my broken eye
I have no one in this hellish place
Without
The sister of
My heart

CHAPTER 53

"The teacher man, he took your poem and read it. He said it was brilliant, that you needed to be published. He wanted me to bring you, but I told him I couldn't because of the gundas, the debt, and your baby. He says to me, 'Okay, bring me more of her poems. Bring me ten. The truth is a fire in the world that will blaze her freedom.'

"The students that were listening to him started clapping and putting money into a hat to give to you. I don't know if you can trust him, but you have to publish the poems, right, Didi?"

My eyes opened to see a fist full of crumpled rupees. He handed them to me, and my wrists twitched to write more for the first time since I can't remember when. This was more than I expected, support from the professor but also other students. I dug up my poems—I had hoarded the ones I wrote for Shiv in the pile of my undergarments—and handed them to Jai.

"Also bring me food?" I asked him and gave him some of the crumpled rupees back. His eyes brightened at my words, and he scurried out of my cell.

The following week, the professor told Jai that he wanted ten poems a week. In exchange, he would send paper, food, and water with Jai. As I wrote, his words echoed in my mind: "We will free her and she will be an author." Jai told me that I was becoming a symbol at the university. Many students were starting to organize and say they wanted to break me out of here. The teacher told Jai to tell me that they would come protest to save me. I found this gesture sweet and also realized how uninformed the students were on the gundas' power. Madame could have me killed. It would have to be planned.

. . .

The week after Jai picked up my poems, he brought me puchka. The baby kept craving the crunchy puri shell, salted potatoes, the sweetness of tamarind chutney and water full of black salt and masala.

As I ate, he sat across from me and told me the story of how he lost his family. They had been on a train platform because his father got a new farming job further away. I imagined the platform like the one Amla and I had been on, with all the pushing and shoving. He said his family—his mother, father, and older brother—boarded the train. He had been holding his father's hand, but someone pushed him so hard that he fell. There were so many people he couldn't get up, and he heard his father screaming his name, but the train started, and the platform was too full for his father to get out. Jai tried to run alongside the train, but it went too fast, and before long it was gone, disappearing down the tracks.

He waited at that station for what felt like days. The police eventually picked him up because he fainted on the platform. He hadn't had any water. They brought him to the station, and he overheard them saying they were going to bring him to an orphanage.

"I told them I wanted to go back to wait for my father. I was so young I only knew his first name. I still only know *Mukesh*. I knew how to spell; my father taught me to read. 'M-u-k-e-s.' They laughed and said they needed an errand boy. They asked me if I wanted to be an errand boy if they helped me find my father. I agreed.

"But the older policeman told me one day that the main officer was involved in selling kids to a man who ran a beggar scheme. Sometimes he hurt the beggar kids to get more sympathy and money from pedestrians that he stole from each day. He told me to run away to another station and gave me the address. So one night when they left the station, I ran away, but before I could get there, the gundas found me. They started having me get them Thums Up, lassi, whatever they needed. I told them I had a home, but really when I left every night I went to hide and sleep. I worked fast. The owner of the store where I got the lassi told me he could give me two rupees per lassi I sold and that I could sleep on his stand's floor when he locked it. It was safer than finding new spots every day."

And that's how he became lassiwala, which was what most people called him.

But he had told me his real name, etched in his heart. Jai. Like my own mother's name, Jaya, rooted in the honest victory. I imagined Jai's mother with the same sweet, dimpled smile he had, his father with the same caring eyes he bore, both choosing his name.

"Jai," I told him when he finished his story, "I will not let anyone think I need to be saved. I do not want to belong to the hands of anyone else anymore. I have a plan. And wherever I go, I'll take you with me."

Jai smiled like he understood. The next day he took ten more poems back to the professor.

Words are what free
Women whose currency
Is a stolen body
That wouldn't burn
Or rot
Words
Are what give
Her life

CHAPTER 54

Alone in my cell, I began to fear that the professor would never publish me. That my plan, to delay the protest until Madame's surgery date, would not work. In my mind, I pictured them raiding the brothel, demanding I be freed. I had heard Madame make plans to put Janaki in charge, which would make things tricky, but Jai was sure we could manage it. When I touched my belly, I missed my sister, our innocent childhood. I was still angry about Shiv and his choice to abandon his child and me. I was even angrier that I had fallen for his words. I started to dream of the time when Amla and I were separated for a week by Madame. It was punishment for my sister slicing the red-eyed man's face.

Usually I could smell him before he entered the brothel—musky, like he had been sweating for hours. The betel nut he chewed had turned his teeth a shade of red that matched the sclera of his eyes.

It didn't matter how many times he came to me; my body always tensed up with him. But I had learned in those months of acclimation that it didn't matter what my body felt. I didn't matter anymore. He took turns with the two of us. By then, Amla had stopped crying before each time. Even my stubborn sister didn't want to get beat anymore.

One night the red-eyed man was angry when he arrived. The gundas still let him in. He started hitting me. I ducked and tried to escape, but eventually I was backed into a corner and couldn't move as I felt the strikes against my back over and over. I wasn't sure how long I had been under attack when I heard him suddenly scream and stop. Amla stood above him. There was a red gash on the side of his face.

Madame ran over and slapped us, sending my head to the ground, the taste of blood overwhelming anything that made sense as a gunda grabbed him and kicked him out.

She separated us to different cots the next day after Amla cleaned up my wounds. In between our uninvited visitors, the men who claimed our bodies, we lay there in the daytime to rest. While apart, we would share distant memories about our village. I'd start with a few words and she would finish. It drove Bhima, Sajana, and Janaki mad as they lay between us, but we always ended up in fits of giggles and deflected the pain.

"We chased the kite so far that—"

"We ended up in cow dung!"

Now, I dreamt of our laughter, afraid I would soon forget the way it sounded. As I fell asleep, missing when my sister's feet met mine, the tears slid down my face, and I swallowed what was left of my memories into my large belly.

The next morning, my mummy's birthday, Jai told me the professor had sent the manuscript to his publisher and that I would be free soon.

On that same night, my contractions started. The baby was arriving earlier than she should have, but I had no choice. It was time.

I birthed her in a back room on an old mattress as Janaki was with a customer in the next room. Between my pushes, I could hear his loud moans. It took a while for me to finally drown it out, staring at an old blue-and-red Thums Up soda calendar against the chipped gray walls next to the bed. Eventually my hips thrust open, and I was breathing but didn't feel it anymore—and not like the way I blocked out men on top of me. It was different, like light was entering my body and ripping me apart inside, taking away all the darkness this place made me swallow and opening my heart and vagina wide and raw to let her emerge. Sajana was there helping me, like the love in her name, bright and encouraging.

"Asya, you can do it, you can do it," she said.

You can do it. I tried to remember the last time I had told myself that and truly believed it. I couldn't think of a single moment until I felt her.

I felt my darling child descend, and I was filled with the surprise of hope. I felt her saving me when I thought I was unable to be saved. I was crying, crying when it was over because here she was, her pure screams, and as my mind raced through all the ways I would need to protect her, I held her bloody body to my bosom while she searched for my nipple. It was my mother's birthday. Now it would be my child's as well. Sajana had me push more, the placenta emerging as she put it aside in a rag cloth she would later discard. In my village, families waited nine days after birth for the puja ceremony where the placenta was buried. Here, there was no time or place for anything sacred.

As I nourished her, I realized I would do anything for her. She was my reason to find a way out of the hell that surrounded us. But in the moment, in that very moment I looked into her eyes and gave her life, as I sustained her with milk, I muttered, "Amla." It had been my first word as a baby. It was the name of my heartbeat partner before I exited my own mother's womb.

Amla. This would be my baby's name.

CHAPTER 55

One month after I gave birth, I sat on the floor, waiting for my plan to happen. I had pictured it over and over, willing it into action. I heard the banging first. It sounded like an earthquake. I started crying for my baby: "*Mera bachcha.*"

By pure grace, Madame had taken Janaki with her that morning. She had to go early for testing before her lung surgery and had found a free HIV clinic near her appointment, but even in her sick way of loving Janaki, she said she'd add the medications to Janaki's tab.

Sajana arrived in my doorway, clutching my naked baby in her arms. She handed her to me. She had witnessed the power of my birth, had seen what a mother is capable of. She had once longed for such protection herself. I motioned for her to come with us. We locked eyes, but she just walked away to her room.

I understood. Sometimes it's hard to leave behind what you know.

Jai dashed in. That was my cue to hurry down the stairs.

It felt surreal, how we walked out. The students standing there, almost one hundred of them, set my baby and me free. The large signs in their hands: Free Asya; Let Her Go; Poetry Is Power; Babies Don't Belong in Brothels. The two gundas on duty stepped aside.

Later, when Jai imitated the gundas' expressions of shock, it sent us all into giggles.

I'll never forget what it felt like, to hold my baby to my chest and walk away forever from the place that had covered me in blood and rags. I felt the energy of the group of students surrounding me in protection as the other mob marched on. One girl wrapped her dupatta around me, and another gave me her scarf for my baby. My plan had actually worked.

As we got into the car the professor walked me to, he said, "I am finally meeting our Tagore."

His words reminded me of Shiv's. The tears started to flow, and I smiled. I was free. Jai was my angel.

The boy
Angel from above
Late mother to
Bring her daughter
The soma of humanity

• • •

When we arrived at the university, I learned the students had raised funds for me and volunteered to help with the baby, meals, and to give me a place to stay until I could get on my feet. They arranged for me to meet with a nonprofit counseling group as well.

I stayed with a friendly student named Neela. I confided in her, telling her that I wanted to find my sister, and she started researching right away.

Neela reminded me of Amla. She was graceful and kind, sure of herself, and smart. She was studying accounting, but her passion was journalism. "My father says I need to study accounting, but whatever, yaar; I still write for the paper," she said with a grin.

The students wrote about my story in their newspaper. It was a miracle, they said. They interviewed Jai and called him my brother. I didn't mind: he was. The freedom felt miraculous to me, and I drank in every minute of it. I took in the sounds of students laughing, cars honking, and got used to sleeping at night. Being outside in sunlight. The normalcy of life that I had missed.

Neela helped me read the news and tried to trace stories back to when Amla left the brothel or when Shiv didn't return.

"What if she wasn't rescued? What if someone took her somewhere more horrible?" I would ask Neela these questions at night, and she'd say we would find the answers, to just sleep on it. I'd nurse my baby, and we would all fall asleep that way, in one bed.

"Do you want to find Shiv?" she asked me one night.

We were eating masala fries on her floor as she studied for her next exam. By this time, baby Amla was lifting her head up and smiling at us.

"I want to forget Shiv," I replied. The only family I wanted was my sister and my daughter. *Jai, too,* I mentally added. He was family now. He had started putting all his earnings in a tiffin box on the kitchen counter. "This is for our home," he'd say.

Neela's parents were diplomats. They sent her money routinely for things like groceries and school supplies. When Neela asked for more funds, they didn't question her, and she put it towards my baby's diaper cloths so we could stay with her. "Don't worry," she said when I protested. "They won't notice."

My poetry book had sold well, but there were many fees, the professor told me. Fees required to print and distribute the book from the university publisher. There was money left, but it was not enough to find my own home yet. I kept writing more to enter poetry contests so I could contribute to Neela, who always refused, yet I told her it felt good to contribute to my own freedom that way.

I was reciting a poem to the baby one evening, and when she fell asleep, Neela looked up from her textbook and whispered, "Your voice is mesmerizing, Asya." I thought of how Shiv had said the same thing.

After the article in the college paper, my book received more attention, and the college bookstore started getting more traffic. Neela and I walked to the bookstore the next morning, and I met the owner, Rajiv, a small man who seemed to be always smiling.

"Namaste," he greeted us with his hands together. He agreed to host a book reading and signing. I needed to let my voice be heard, and if I sold more copies, I could save more for my own place.

"Asya, beti, you will be famous, like Tagore," he said.

CHAPTER 56

For the event, Neela lent me her most beautiful salwar kameez. It was white with green stripes—and a green dupatta. "I love it," I told her. "I read the one about the green scarf," she said.

There were so many students there for the reading that people were even waiting outside for my book and to see me.

After the reading, I walked over to my book-signing table and scanned the crowd. I saw a pale-faced man, and my heart skipped a beat. Was it the man who had come for Amla? It felt so long ago that I couldn't remember his face.

I nudged Neela; we had to talk to him. Neela said every white man might not know Amla, but she agreed, and I watched her hand him a copy to bring to my table.

When he walked over, Neela joined and he said, "*Namaste, pyar keso ho?*"

We started laughing at his word confusion, and he smiled and admitted that his Hindi was "just so-so."

He told us that his name was David, to which I said, "More like Devi," and he smiled and said, "Yes, like the goddess, except for me and my people it means a musician shepherd turned king."

Neela translated the book cover and the poem I had read, and he looked at the book, carefully running his fingers over it. He wore a ring with a gold star.

He told Neela he was from France, just visiting, but had heard about the university's architecture. He happened to walk by and wanted to see what the commotion was about. "A book like this would change the hearts of so many people," he said. "I've worked on international women's rights research for over a decade." He waved the book in the air. "This is what matters; this is what we should read." As Neela translated to me, I looked over at the professor, who was counting sales with the bookstore owner. I had learned that the professor was taking a cut, because he had "discovered" my talent.

I told Neela, "Let's keep this Devi man to ourselves."

Neela nodded and gave David her apartment's phone number. She said we could talk again later. He nodded as the next student approached my table, and Neela motioned for him to call as she picked up my baby, who was getting fussy, from Rajiv's wife.

After the store emptied out, the professor told me how many sales we had made and what my cut was after we paid Rajiv. In a county of hustlers, I realized I was not as free as I had thought. I too had to hustle on my own.

● ● ●

That evening, David called. Neela answered the phone and translated between us. Before he could ask me about my book, I asked him about his ring. I had seen him fidget with it. I noticed that about men who came to the brothel: they sometimes held on to important necklaces or rings when they were unsure of something. He said it was a family heirloom. He asked me if I was interested in having the book published outside of India. Of course, yes, that would be a dream.

"I can help you," he said as Neela waited with the receiver. I paused, trying to find trust in another stranger, a man, again. I told Neela I wanted collateral, something that could assure me he wouldn't scam me, betray me, or use me as I had been.

She told him I would agree to work with him if he lent me the ring until we finished working together. He refused. We hung up.

The next morning, as Neela prepared tea and I changed the baby, he called again.

Neela answered and translated for me. "Why did you ask about the ring?" I told her to tell him this book was my only possession. My only freedom. It was my daughter's heirloom now. The ring was a symbol that meant we could trust each other. If he followed my terms, I would return it.

I wasn't sure if he would agree, and I knew I was playing with fire. I thought of the true goddess Devi and her Agni, the fire that blazed her power. What if he refused and I lost my chance? I thought about it, but I kept coming back to the same conclusion: this was the only way I knew and could be sure that he wouldn't betray me.

He had a friend in the publishing industry. A woman he said he had dated. *Dated.* I didn't know this word. As he spoke, I put my hand over the phone and mouthed to Neela, "What is dated?" She smiled, telling me I had so much to learn, to just listen.

When he finally agreed, my stomach fluttered.

The next afternoon, we met at the university courtyard, and I had Neela write me a contract with the French man. David mentioned he would speak with his contact and work on a real contract. But I still needed assurance. Our arrangement was simple. It just said all the earnings would be in my name; he would not receive a cut like the professor had. The book was mine and no one else's.

A week later, we heard from David. He said his friend would have my book translated to French and English. Was I okay with this? I was okay with as many people knowing my story as possible, yes. To stop it from happening to others—and so that my daughter would know I used my voice to speak up for girls like her. So that perhaps if Amla was somewhere out there, she could find it.

I would have Neela read the translation to assure my poems were still my poems.

The day he sent an advance copy of my new book, it was a hardcover, unlike the soft one the professor had arranged. It had my name in gold letters. The cover was plain green.

Inscribed on the first page when opening it were the words FOR AMLA.

PART 5

AMLA

JUNE 2005

CHAPTER 57

"How do you have so many things to pack?"

I was folding the last of my clothes, but most of what I packed were baby items gifted to us from all the volunteers and Mausi's friends. Vishnu had bought me a new green scarf with a matching baby hat during a short visit back when I told him I was pregnant. While I finished my studies in India and secured my paperwork with the help of Ladki Rights, I was able to gain a full scholarship admission to an art program with the City College of New York to begin right after the New Year. It was perfect timing with my birth date.

I was eighteen years old, but it was hard to believe I was four years younger than him. My life experiences made me feel much older.

"I need to pack everything that reminds me of my India," I explained.

He smiled at the reference. When I had started my studies, I told him I could not leave my country behind. He knew it had to do with Asya too, and he had dedicated almost all of the volunteer staff at Ladki Rights to work on finding her whenever they could be spared from their other projects. It was a battle I still faced, leaving my sister behind, but as I touched my belly, I knew it was the right decision.

"We could go see your puppa again, you know, before we go."

I had stayed in touch with Dadi and Dada since we reunited. Vishnu had purchased a prepaid cell phone for them to use. They often called to see if we had any updates on finding Asya. But they also called to ask for money.

Not long after our visit, Puppa stopped working and started drinking again. I remembered how it was when Mummy was sick and told Vishnu not to send them anything. I told him to turn off their phone. He was surprised, told me to think about it. He had grown up without a father, and he likely thought I was throwing away a chance at a relationship with him. I understood his sensitivity to that. But I was done with him, and with Dada and Dadi enabling his actions. The only family I wanted was my sister.

Vishnu never looked for his own father and said he never would. He often said, "I will never be the father my father was to our baby." My experience had taught me that men were always a problem; their anger, their embarrassment, their desires all ended in my own pain. But when I looked into Vishnu's eyes, the conviction I saw there made me believe him.

That was why I trusted his plan to have the baby in the US, wait six months, then return to India when we could. Everyone in the NGO would still be searching. It would be good for the baby to be born as a US citizen, for me to start my program. I could always go part-time later, he said. The uncertain future scared me, and not knowing if I would find Asya saddened me, but I trusted myself to trust him; it was all I could do.

CHAPTER 58

I felt Vishnu relax into his seat when the plane took off and wondered if he too felt the excitement that had started to manifest in my stomach, creeping up through my chest. I had never been on a plane before, and I took in the sound of clicking seat belts around us and the cold air blowing at my temples. I listened intently to the airline hostess describe in Hindi what to do in the event of an emergency. When she switched to English, I tried to listen for the phrases I knew, but she spoke so quickly that I soon gave up. I leaned back and imagined all the differences awaiting me in a new land.

I had packed the letter Nani wrote to us before passing, the one with her bangles, one for each of us. NEVER LEAVE EACH OTHER'S SIDES, it said. I cried for hours when I first read it. Now I kept it close to remind myself I would return. It was comforting, in a way, but I still felt that I was betraying Asya by leaving India. Searching for her was all I had done for over a year, but we hadn't come close to finding her. What if she thought I had forgotten her? Was she even still alive?

I looked around us at the English signs I recognized—No SMOKING, EXIT, EMERGENCY—and thought of all the new words I would need to learn to navigate my new city.

A woman in the row behind us was discussing her wedding plans. She spoke of the flowers, saying that they were "simply gorgeous." She placed emphasis on the first syllable of *gorgeous*, which I practiced saying silently to myself.

I thought of the marigold and rose-petal garlands used in the weddings I had seen at home, with our whole village flooding the streets. I thought of how different Asya's and my life would be had we accepted the marriage proposals Dadi had planned to arrange. Would it have been better to stay? At least then we would be together.

I could not sleep, so, like the young child in front of me, I stared out the window as we moved swiftly past the patterns of night clouds. I wondered about the family in front of us, whose dialect I could not understand. Possibly South Indian. I heard the sounds of Telugu when the boy pointed out the window and asked his mother something. Through the seats I saw the boy holding on to her shawl, curling his fingers at the fringed ends as I touched my belly. This would be me soon. A mother.

I closed my eyes as I felt the plane descend. When the wheels touched the ground, I waited for my heart to finally stop pounding. We were here. In the terminal, everyone moved fast, like in Mumbai, and so we kept our pace but stayed close. At immigration and customs, the officials asked us questions and inspected our passports and visas, looking down at our photos and then to our faces. I was smiling slightly in my passport photo. Vishnu had made me laugh when it was taken, both of us overjoyed to finally get through the process, which had been difficult without proper documents. When we passed the baggage area, I took a deep breath in and released. I was here.

CHAPTER 59

The plan was for me to stay with Vishnu's mother in the apartment he has secured for her near the hospital. Vishnu would return to his graduate-school housing—small apartments by the university—until his roommate could transition out of the apartment and he could bring me there. "Don't worry. She lives right near your school. I will show you," he said when we spoke about it before our flight.

I found all of this intriguing. Why didn't he live with his mother? He said it was the way things were in America. "Once you go off to study, you move into your own home."

"Who makes you warm milk when you are studying?"

He started to laugh. "Amla, seriously? Who likes warm milk?"

I giggled, but my heart ached as I thought of Mummy bringing us milk mixed with turmeric, cardamom, and honey as we studied for exams.

Riding in the taxi now, I was surprised by the sense of orderliness outside. The garbage cans at each street corner, the herds of people waiting patiently for lights to change before speeding forward, the ways cars stayed in their lanes.

"What do you think?"

Every time I looked out my car window, it felt as if I might miss something on the other side. There was an energy, a beat to the whole city that rushed through my body. I thought of the first time Asya and I went to Mumbai with Puppa, how we couldn't believe how many cars there were, but New York had even more. It was like nothing I could have imagined.

Vishnu had shown me videos on his phone of the buildings and people walking on the streets, but he hadn't described the music of his city. In Mumbai, when Asya and I were in bed with Chaya and Nisha, we would fall asleep to the sounds of rickshaws and bells from evening carts closing. In our village, we dozed off to the sounds of birds and insects singing in the night. In the brothel, we heard other noises, yelling or thumping on a wall.

When I rolled down the cab window, I heard the sounds of car horns and music in a tongue I was just getting used to. But the smell made me roll the window back up. Vishnu laughed, and the cab driver looked through his rearview, not amused.

"You vant music?" he asked in an accent Vishnu later told me was Turkish.

The cab driver turned on the radio, and soon enough he and Vishnu were talking about jazz. I closed my eyes, imagining how Asya would react if she were here beside me, happy, holding my arm and looking out the window with us, my baby and me.

"Amla, look!"

I opened my eyes and almost cried.

"This is Times Square," Vishnu said.

The buildings looked like they went up to the heavens. They reminded me of Mumbai, but seeing them all together in their vastness was beyond anything I had ever witnessed. Dancers performed and artists drew faces of people on the sidewalk. In India people tended to look the same. Here I saw all types of skin colors, hair colors, and clothing. Even some with almost no clothing. Vishnu laughed when I pointed at a man in tight underwear and a wide-brimmed hat. He told me that was the naked cowboy. Almost no one stopped or blinked an eye at him. And the ones who did stop took photos as they pleased. Everyone seemed so free.

He squeezed my hand. "This is our new home."

For a little while, I thought, squeezing his hand back.

CHAPTER 60

We arrived at Vishnu's mother's apartment while she was making us afternoon tea. I had craved fresh chai the whole plane ride, the bland Lipton tea bags lacking the masala and ginger of a good brew. Vishnu's mother had kind eyes like her son. She put her hand on my stomach and said, "I had a dream about this," and then she came and hugged us both. I melted into her arms. I had been fluctuating between emotions with the baby growing inside of me in a new world, and I wanted to be held so badly.

Her apartment felt like Mausi's home, the way she kept photos up and small accents around the place, like the carved Ganesha statue at the entrance and embroidered pillows on her couch. Vishnu helped me bring my things into the guest room.

"I'll see you tomorrow right after work," he whispered and placed his hand on the curve of my back, kissing me gently. When we went back out, I went into the kitchen to help, but his mother had already set the plates of warm paratha and steaming cups of chai as she waited for us.

"Come, beti." When I realized she was speaking to me, not Vishnu, I softened at her motherly tone and sat beside her.

I was exhausted at nightfall. Vishnu was too. He left after dinner, and I barely had the energy to brush my teeth.

Even so, I heard his mother moaning from what sounded like pain. I lay in my bed, unsure of what to do until she stopped and I fell asleep.

Eleven days later, I knew his mother's secret. Vishnu's mother was dying. I recognized the sounds that preceded my own mother's collapse on the day that changed our lives.

I could hear not only her moans at night but her gagging in the bathroom in the morning. She excused herself often enough for me to know it was not just a troubled bladder. Her eyes drifted like she was not getting enough sleep.

She was sick, and Vishnu did not know. Vishnu, who was overexcited about the baby, didn't seem to notice anything different about his mother when he came over.

The jet lag had worn off, and Vishnu returned to school and to work at the hospital. He came for dinner each evening, after which we would take a walk. By then, I was into my second trimester, and the walks felt good. Our court marriage was scheduled for the end of the month, and Vishnu had started to prep his graduate-housing apartment. His roommate had agreed to move in with another friend.

Two weeks after moving in with her, when his mother and I were alone after Vishnu left one evening, I asked her, "Auntie, are you all right?"

"Beti, call me Mummy. I am not all right, but I will be soon." I could not call her Mummy, but maybe I would be able to in time . . . if we had it. I could not hear the word *mummy* without a stab to my heart. I wondered when that would subside, and if Asya felt it too.

She went into her bedroom and gently closed the door.

We fell into a silent routine of grating ginger for chai and afternoon naps as we nursed our bodies, me for new life and her for the end of life. I knew what Vishnu meant when he said his mother was the strongest woman he knew.

I touched my belly and wondered if there was some sort of switch when women gave birth. The switch that said,

You are now shakti; the divinity has been granted.

You are no longer worthless and meant to be used and abused.

You will not be sold anymore, and as a mother, if you give birth to a girl, you will have to do everything in your power to protect her from enduring the injustices of the curse girls are given in this world, so . . . you better be strong.

I made note to talk to Priya about it when we had our virtual counsel session.

Exactly one month after we arrived, Vishnu's mother spoke her truth. He came for dinner after finishing his hospital rounds early. His mother spoke slowly as we picked at the basmati rice and curried kidney beans on our plates.

"When you were in India, I had a test done. I had started to forget things—first where my keys were, but then it was things like my computer password and even our zip code."

"Mom, that happens in old age. I know—"

She put her hand up, and he looked down in retreat.

"They found a tumor on my brain. The chemo is over, and yet they say it would be better to operate. But because of the location, they cannot operate on it. We will wait and see. I hope I will see your lovely baby born . . ."

Vishnu started bawling uncontrollably, but I didn't shed any tears. I don't know if it was because I already knew, had already seen his mother sick, had already lost my own mother, or because I had lost my sister perhaps for good. I felt a tightness, a ball in my chest, but I also knew that this was what the world was, this suffering.

I hugged Vishnu, then his mother. When they embraced each other, I silently stepped out and went to the window in the family room. There was a photo of Vishnu smiling in a graduation cap and gown, holding a paper in his hand, his eyes gleaming. It was the only photo besides an idol of Ganesha on the whole shelf. His mother was Vishnu's world; he was her world. Vishnu was the type of person who saved people. Where was the karma in his mother dying in this terrible way? Where was the Ganesha who protects the families, the Ganesha his mother prayed to every day? *Where is the person who will save this kind, generous woman? A woman who named her son after a god who was meant to preserve and protect the universe?*

I let the tears fall silently and wondered what kind of world I was bringing our baby into. Why had this child chosen me? I didn't belong here. I wanted to go back to India. But even there, where did I belong? Without my sister, I felt lost. It was my choice to leave her, and now here I was. I was free but trapped in my guilt.

Vishnu and his mother came and found me there, the three of us embracing for the first and last time like that.

CHAPTER 61

"Feels like India, right?" Vishnu said as we strolled down 125th Street while his mother napped.

I smiled. India had this heat, but without the dampness that comes after Holi, it didn't feel the same to me. I thought about Holi a lot in the summer heat, the day when everyone comes together and forgets what caste, what religion they are. The colors that filled the streets would last for weeks into the monsoon, and sometimes you could see the bright hues bleed in the flooded streets. I missed Asya's hand on my cheek.

We passed a group of tourists snapping photos of the Apollo.

Vishnu didn't understand why I wouldn't let him hire a hospice aid for his mother.

"You are pregnant. You just started shadowing courses. My insurance for Mom through the hospital will cover most of it. You need your rest; you can't stay up with her and tend to her every need. And with my crazy studying and hospital hours, it will help us."

I pictured my nani, who sat with my own mother during our births, and what my mother did for her and my dadi when they were ill.

"You wouldn't understand."

We were still set to move in together when our court marriage was completed, but I didn't admit to him that I enjoyed the time apart.

One day, when I visited the school to sit in on a photography course before I started, the professor noticed me touching an old camera in the lecture room after class and said, "We have this here for the studio, but since we don't have anything scheduled until the winter for it, we won't be using it. Why don't you borrow it until you start here and see what you think?"

The professor was kind to me. He was an immigrant himself, from the Dominican Republic and saw it was hard for me to connect with the other youthful students. None of them were expectant immigrant mothers like I was.

My new expression through photography started with a photo of Vishnu's mother drinking her chai. Through the lens, I saw the emotion in her eyes, like her actions were speaking silently to me the way I saw the world when I drew.

When I took the camera to my professor the next day, I asked him how I could develop the photo. He showed me the small insert and chip and told me to go to the Duane Reade, where I often went to pick up Vishnu's mother's medicines. Vishnu had given me a credit card, which I could still not fathom was true currency. I plugged in the little blue chip card and selected the photos to print. The worker told me it would take an hour, but I didn't mind waiting. It was thrilling to see my photos, my art, come to life. I took more photos on my way home, snapping at the moments people took for granted: smiling at a shop owner they've known for years; looking up in awe at the sky.

I left early for class the next morning, spending time clicking on the camera. When I came home late that day, I told his mother that I had stopped to watch a music performance and then cooled off in a store as I walked home.

But his mother did not respond. She was humming a mantra.

She had begun doing this, humming or reciting mantras daily. The Sanskrit words were familiar to me: words of light and transcendence mostly, but sometimes words that were deeply sad; at those times, she sounded dark and fierce.

It was like she had been possessed by different goddesses.

Vishnu called a colleague, who spoke about some neural pathways, but I knew his mother was speaking to a place beyond anything we knew. She had tapped inside of herself to a wisdom that was letting her pull away from us. Whoever she was, I photographed her raw beauty—wild hair, hand to heart, and eyes looking up at the sky; and her head softened to the ground during her prayers as if she would melt right there. I photographed her and whispered, "Mummy" one day, watching tears roll down her face when she chanted prayers as Vishnu wiped her forehead.

I photographed her the next morning when we found her without a heartbeat and with peace settled on her face. I had captured more than the woman I had been living with—I saw the stories of the woman Vishnu told me about, strong, bold, loving. One smile, one set of eyes, told a lifetime. One single photograph could say so much. His mother's struggles, sadness, pain. I thought of all the stories I had been through, the stories I had witnessed of the young women in the brothel, and as I stared at the photograph, I knew what it was that I wanted to concentrate on and do.

CHAPTER 62

After his mother died, Vishnu took a week off to grieve. It was hard for him to leave school for that long, but his dean wouldn't hear of him coming back any sooner.

We spent the first day arranging the logistics of the wake, including finding a pundit for the puja at the apartment. In the village, the pundit came to the home first, and then the person was carried to be cremated. Here, his mummy had left the home, and her body was lying in a cold center where the wake would be performed. So much emphasis was placed outside of the home.

I also learned that they didn't have just one pundit for their community here. Vishnu had to call five different Hindu temples in Queens to see who was available to come to Manhattan. I watched him effortlessly take control, and when I saw the creases on his forehead and his worn eyes as he phoned funeral centers that performed cremation, I would rub his back silently. I hoped my hand would remind him that he was loved. I began to feel the importance of my strength in our relationship and my ability to hold space for him as a wife, and to realize what would serve me as a mother.

Mausi arrived the next day, wearing a white sari. When he saw her, Vishnu cried.

Vishnu had lent me his mother's white sari and his white T-shirts
to wear for the next thirteen days, as I didn't own anything white to
wear with my belly growing. I hesitated taking the sari and suggested
we go get a new one for the funeral, but he insisted. I ran my fingers
over it that night. So much love rested in its pleats.

Mausi was in mourning, her eyes red and puffy, but she kept
fussing over me, saying the baby needed food. She placed the turmeric
for her sister's forehead in a bowl and had a family friend bring me rava
kesari since she could not cook it herself.

"The fire in the house is not lit until the fire in the cremation has
gone out," I recalled my mother saying as she cooked food for our
neighbors every day when her friend's father-in-law passed just a year
before Mummy did. At first, I ate the sweet ghee and flour porridge for
Mausi's sake; despite being pregnant, I did not have an appetite with
all the heaviness in the air. Yet at that first bite, my baby reminded me
of how hungry I was, and I ate the whole bowl.

The small apartment felt full with Vishnu and his mother's friends.
Vishnu's old roommate had helped move the sofa out of the living
room, and we all sat on the floor. Auntie Keiko, the Japanese woman
who helped Vishnu's mother when he was a boy, came over to set the
blankets to sit on and placed flowers in vases. His friend Camilla came
with her girlfriend and hugged us both.

When the pundit arrived, we sat somberly in the living room. The
pundit had Vishnu channel the god of his name's power with darbha
grass he tied, saying it had purifying properties and was a channel of
Lord Vishnu's power.

"Naarayana . . . Naarayana . . . Naarayana."

I thought of Amira, how we had never allowed her soul to leave
peacefully. I thought of Mummy, of how our visit to the cremation
grounds hadn't been enough. Putting a hand on my belly to feel my
baby's kicks, the vibration of our chanting voices settled a peace over
me for the ones I had loved and lost, a closure I needed so badly.

CHAPTER 63

A month after officially being married, Vishnu and I took a drive. It had only been two months since Mausi left us to return to India. She planned to come back to help in my postpartum.

After his mother died, we had our court marriage with Keiko as our witness on Asya's and my birthday. Another date could not be had for a few months, and Vishnu insisted his mother would want us to celebrate our official legal union. To celebrate my birthday. That night I cried for Asya, and he cried for his mother.

I had of course pictured our move differently. I imagined us putting marigold garlands from our wedding at the front door, cheerfully opening boxes and unpacking dishes together. We had spent a somber weekend packing his mother's apartment and then another weekend unpacking into his. Camilla insisted we keep the apartment all month, but Vishnu refused. "I can't keep coming back here," he said.

I was uncomfortable in the heat of New York with my huge belly. He suggested riding to Long Island with the air-conditioning on and stopping at one of his favorite spots. But as we set out on our drive, it began to rain.

"Summer rain," he hummed. I watched the rain hit the roofs of the sparse cars around us, listened to the hum of the wipers.

We drove past trees and cars, hills and signs. I felt the freedom that came from the solitude of this country.

It felt like we were invisible, driving in the privacy of our little world.

If we had been in India in monsoon season, I imagined we would see babies strapped to mothers' backs and groups of ladies taking turns holding each other's loads. I pictured the shopkeepers swimming baskets of goods to their neighbors across streets full of heavy rain. Vendors, extended family, and neighbors all helped each other in our village and constantly spoke to us. Even in the brothel, we stuck together; we were all we had. Here, I noticed even with countless people out and about, everyone was alone. Alone in the coffee shop, walking to work alone, or waiting at the register alone. And even amongst friends, a privacy existed, to do as one pleased, something I had never felt before. While a lack of responsibility to a tribe felt like freedom, I wondered then, who looked out for you? I always had Asya. And now, where was she?

I couldn't imagine growing up without a sibling. Would Vishnu and I have more children? He was an only child, and I wasn't sure he understood my deep connection to my sister.

I watched him drive, tapping the steering wheel to his favorite Beatles album. Where did his mind go on these silent drives?

He reached for my hand. "Are you happy?" He asked me this every few days.

I put my hand on my belly. "Yes, of course I am happy."

I answered in ways I knew would make him smile. The brothel rules hadn't left me. *Always be pleasing; every man that leaves your curtain should be smiling. It is your duty here.*

I shook my head free of the thought. My memories of the brothel were infrequent but unpleasant.

I should have been happy, and most days I was. When we met our friends for dinner, Vishnu's grief would recede, and he would come alive, telling us stories, talking about things that mattered to him. He picked out paint for the baby's room. He spent the whole week putting together furniture and setting it all up. "You have only one job," he said. "Pick the paint and leave the rest up to me."

I ached to feel his joy, but instead I just ached. I felt lost in the newness of the city, in the customs I was still trying to understand, and guilty for being safe while Asya was not. I felt ashamed, saddened, and torn for feeling the way I did. In the end, he chose the paint color himself: a light, warm yellow.

We drove until we reached the shore. When we got out of the car, he chased me slowly as I hugged my large belly and the rain drenched us.

"It looks like when Asya and I were in Mumbai at Juhu Beach."

He wrapped his arms around me from behind. "I promise we will go back after the baby is born."

I nodded and tried to believe that we would.

When the contractions started on Mummy's birthday, Vishnu stood by me, rubbing my back. "Amla, you can do it," he said.

He was encouraging, but I longed for Asya. I longed for the way she made me laugh, her voice filling me as the pain radiated down my leg, my lower back feeling the brunt of it at each tug and movement, at each stretch of skin. I was crying uncontrollably, and he held me, saying, "Don't worry, we can have them offer you an epidural."

"No, no, no, that's not it."

"Okay, I just want you to be comfortable."

I was thinking of my sister, who was still somewhere, I hoped, when she should have been by my side.

I started shaking from the crying, and the doctor recommended the epidural, so I took it and let my legs go numb. Eventually the shaking stopped and I felt more relaxed. I let my eyes close.

"She should sleep. She's been at it for twenty-two hours already," I heard someone say. "Once she's fully dilated, we can wake her."

There was light coming from the tunnel as I saw her shadow. *Asya, Asya.* I chased her but started to feel pain in my belly.

Asya, I'm having a baby, Asya, please! But she was running away. Her dark shadow started to disappear. *No, don't go! Asya, please!*

"Okay, it's time. Let's get ready for some big pushes, okay?"

Where was my doctor? An older man with small blue eyes and thick white hair stood at the end of the bed. Where was my sweet, petite, female doctor?

"Amla, this is Dr. Dupont," Vishnu said. "Since you labored through Dr. Saks's shift, he's on call and here to deliver you." Vishnu's words were so far away, like Asya's shadow, and I was immobile. A strange man was looking at my vagina, and I began to panic. I couldn't do that again.

A loud beeping sound started by my ear, and nurses raced into the room. "The baby's heart rate is dropping. We need her to push now!" someone said.

"Save her. Save Asya," I pleaded.

And then suddenly, my body knew what to do. I was pushing, my baby was emerging, hips feeling wide, cracking, tissues tearing, the blood, and like a divine moment of pain and happiness . . . there she was. Precious, saved. Vishnu kissed me as they cleaned her up, then handed her to me.

My child, saved.

"Asya."

"Yes, yes, we can name her Asya, for your sister; whatever you want. She's so perfect. Thank you." Vishnu was overjoyed.

For my sister.

My baby girl, saved. Alive, well, loved.

I let him kiss me and kiss her as I locked eyes with my darling girl.

CHAPTER 64

I was still crying at times after Mausi left. I just missed her so much. I missed the fenugreek tea and dates she smothered with ghee that she'd place next to me when I nursed. I missed the way she held our baby girl and sang songs that filled me with memories of our India. I missed the way she felt like Mummy. Even with Vishnu's phone calls during the day and help at night, I was lonely. I longed for Asya and our sisterhood.

Vishnu's schedule had become intense, so as the days grew colder and we left the apartment less, he called Keiko to come over every few days to check on us.

One day, as she burped the baby, she asked, "Amla, do you still take your photos?" I was folding the receiving blankets strewn on the couch.

Vishnu had bought a gorgeous multislotted frame with fairies etched in the corners for the baby's room. He said I could fill it with my photographs of her. We had decided together to delay my full-time enrollment to the fall, though I would take a small course load in the spring. It would give me time with the baby, but it delayed everything, even our trip to find my sister. Vishnu had bought a new camera to lift my spirits, but in the three months since baby Asya had been born, and I only snapped a few. The frame remained empty.

"I should do it more. I just am not sure when, with all the feedings and diapering and everything."

It was a lie. I knew Keiko was studying me. The truth was, I had lost motivation, and I felt lonely. I had read the pamphlet on signs of postpartum depression at the doctor's office, but I thought of how much I loved the baby. How could I be depressed?

"Now that she is fed and will nap soon, why don't you put a coat on and take a walk? You know, my friend Seth owns a bookstore on 123rd and Broadway. It's called the Rare Read. He has some photography and art on the walls I think you would like. It's not that long of a walk if you want to stop over. And bring some of your prints; he loves displaying local artists."

My doubt on leaving dissolved at seeing her sing and rock baby Asya to sleep. I imagined all mothers felt this when leaving their babies.

The air was brisk, and I wished I had packed a scarf. How swiftly the season had changed from the damp heat of summer to the chill of autumn. I pulled the hat over my ears and kept walking. My nipples had finally healed, and as I walked I was no longer bothered by the brush of fabric against them. I had been looking at myself in the mirror each morning. The way my body had changed. This vessel that the world had taken so much of. I wondered if my experience as a mother was different than others'. Did they feel isolated when home all day? Did they feel scared if they were doing any of it right or wrong?

I still continued my therapy with Priya over the phone. The other night, she had asked me, "What do you feel has changed for you besides the changes in your body?"

For almost two years in the brothel, I had felt worthless. But my child valued me beyond measure. Most days, it brought me to tears. Yet even so, I felt a sense of loss. I could not explain it to anyone. My sister was the only one who might understand.

Today, my soul filled with gratitude for Keiko. I was missing sisterhood, the way women knew what other women needed. The way my sister always knew.

The store was easy to spot. Though small, it was filled with books in the store window—not even on display, just stacked to the ceiling in neat piles. I was surprised that I had never noticed it on my walks when I was pregnant.

When I walked in, the bells above the door rang. "Shut the door! Keep the cold out, please!" said a gruff voice behind a shelf.

Keiko's friend was nothing like I had pictured. He was very old and at first very serious. I was holding my bag with a few of my prints in an envelope. "You must be Amla. Keiko told me that you may stop in. I am Seth Roth. I hear you like photography."

"Yes, thank you, I am . . . pleased to meet you." I hadn't spoken to a stranger in so long that I stumbled on my words and bit my lip.

He started showing me the areas where he kept photographs and small paintings. They had price tags and were all over the store above the bookshelves. Wherever there was wall space, he filled it. Would he even have room for mine?

I stopped at a photograph of two women, one looking down and laughing and the other smiling at her friend. Or sister. It was full of joy, and I didn't realize I was smiling until Seth said, "That one always makes me smile too. Keiko tells me you are studying photography?"

"Yes. Well, I am enrolled in art school, but I started taking photographs recently."

When I showed him my prints, he said, "Oh, I can see these going right over there."

There was a small space next to a carved wooden sign that read, PHOTOGRAPHY. I suddenly had the urge to ask him, "When can I start?"

"Start? Do you mean display your prints?"

He looked surprised at my eagerness. I felt surprised at myself too. Yet it was exactly what I needed, and I felt if I didn't ask, I would lose the chance to. I wondered if the urgency came from losing my chance to be with Asya, wherever she ended up. Or her losing the chance to be with me, here and free. I didn't want to lose any more chances when it came to what I loved.

"Okay, let me think." He tapped his chin and asked, "Can you come here next Tuesday evening to display some of your prints? We can feature you that day. I do an artist or author hour every Tuesday to introduce someone new to the shop. My last author just caught the flu. She was going to be . . ."

He went on, but I didn't hear him as my heart sang yes. I felt life flow back into me. To have that creative expression back and involve myself in something outside of the baby felt like just what I needed. Next Tuesday was Vishnu's only night off from his new rotations, but I still said yes. I would need to break the news to him.

When I got home, the baby was crying. She was hungry again. I took her into my arms and nursed her on the couch as Keiko prepared tea for us.

I was humming when Keiko walked over.

I told her thank you and explained that Mr. Roth would be displaying my photographs.

"Amla, it will be good for you, trust me. You need to focus on something besides the baby. I will come help you watch the baby on Tuesday and whenever you need."

"Speaking of next week, Vishnu will be alone when I go. I'll need to tell him."

She handed me a small teacup.

"Hibiscus—it's good for you. And don't worry; Vishnu will understand. He has been hoping you would find something to make you smile these days." She smiled at me as she took a sip, and I silently thanked Mummy for sending me these angels.

CHAPTER 65

The baby was teething. I had tried to soothe her, nursing her all night, but she was relentless, and I felt frustration in my very bones. It was the night before my debut at Rare Reads. When I finally got her to sleep, I went to the kitchen for water. Even the inside of my nose felt dry.

Vishnu was on call and came back at 3 a.m. to find me crying in the kitchen, my head in my hands as I leaned over the counter. I had found a clear spot next to the pile of dishes and mail. Our whole place was a mess. He started putting the dishes in the sink as he asked me what happened.

"Why are you putting those stupid dishes away?" I yelled and heard the baby cry again as I pushed a dirty glass bowl at him, which he caught before it could fly off the counter. My head was pounding. I bit my lip.

He came over and embraced me. I fell into him and let the tightness in my chest melt into his warmth for the first time since we got to New York. His quiet embrace held my exhaustion, my fear of never finding my sister, my grief of losing my old life and feeling lost in this new one. He carried me to the bed and kissed my forehead. I lay there, listening to him coo at baby Asya and rock her. I was still awake when he went to the kitchen and did the dishes before coming into our bed. As I dozed off, he whispered, "I can help you, my love. Postpartum is hard, and I know I haven't been here. You're doing amazing . . ."

I closed my eyes and let his words gently blanket the wounds of my heart.

CHAPTER 66

Ms. Sue was a regular at Mr. Roth's store, a short, stocky woman with radiant, deep-brown skin. I envied her confidence and mimicked her expressions in the mirror when I went home.

She had come to see me at Artist Hour every week that month since that first Tuesday. Most of Mr. Roth's devoted customers were his age, and they all seemed to know one another.

As I wrapped up my last photo, I thought about the baby. Being apart from her felt nice, but the guilt always stayed with me, and I missed her smell and soft skin.

Ms. Sue came and sat beside me. "What was this one inspired by?" She pointed to the photo of a small girl looking up at a subway platform. The girl was holding a smaller girl's hand, her sister, who wore a green scarf. They both looked scared but excited all at once.

I smiled sadly. "This girl's expression reminded me of my own story. I was just a girl when my sister and I were taken. The last time we still had our innocence was at a train station. I had a green scarf just like it that my mother owned."

Ms. Sue's eyes widened. She stood to the side, silent, as I answered another guest's question. I could almost feel her mind working, her emotions soaring. It was strange; I wondered what I had said. I knew my story was alarming to many. Maybe she lingered out of sympathy. Women often did that, telling me how brave I was. I didn't mind it, but it also didn't make me feel any better about the past.

"Amla, have you read the book *Poems by an Indian Girl in a Brothel*?"

When I shook my head, she jumped to her feet, pulling me by the arm. "I can't believe Seth didn't make the connection," she said, talking fast. "He just got this in, and I've been reading it. The story is so close to yours, but I imagine many girls have terrible stories from the brothels. But then you talked about your mother's green scarf. That green scarf—that's such a specific detail. I wonder . . ." She handed me the book and watched me open it.

The cover was a shiny green color, just like Mummy's scarf. And there beneath the title was Asya's name, written in bright-gold letters. My hands trembled as I opened the book to the first page and read the inscription: FOR AMLA.

I didn't wait for Sue to speak. I hugged her, crying, and Mr. Roth came out, asking what the ruckus was about. As they phoned Vishnu, I was so joyous I could hardly speak through the tears. It was like everything that was stuck inside of me was breaking free. Even Mr. Roth took off his glasses and cried with me. He mentioned there were only a few bookstores he knew that carried European publications like he did. "This is divinity," he said.

That evening, Vishnu came home early. We phoned Ladki Rights. They phoned the bookstore and the university and found out that for a long time, the book had only been available in a select college bookstore in India. Now, though, it had become popular all over Europe.

Adam said, "I have her address. I am on my way there now. I will tell your sister. You found her, Amla."

It was like a dream.

Vishnu was ecstatic. He swirled our baby girl around and frantically searched for airline flights. When he started booking, I saw that he had planned it roundtrip. "Vishnu, we have to book it as one way."

He looked up at me. "Okay, we can change it later. It's better to have something reserved, and then she can book a flight home with us."

"My home is with her," I said.

He pressed his lips together as he often did when something worried him and changed my flight to one way, his eyes turning soft with tears.

CHAPTER 67

ASYA

The day Shiv called me, I didn't need him to speak to know who was on the line. He was humming the song he had sung to me the day I said I loved him. I waited for him to finish, and when he spoke, he said, "Asya, I went to an ashram. I had to find myself, and in the meantime, you found freedom."

The sound of his breathing melted me. I let myself remember his breath by my ear, my neck.

I recited a poem. With courage in my heart, I began,

"Waiting
While sounds of doom fill the air
I visit us
When time stood still
For words and breath
To touch my empty heart."

"I am still your biggest fan, my Tagore. Your book is so beautiful. I met someone here, but I want to—"

I hung up. He never called again, but when the phone rang one day not long after, I almost thought it was him.

"Hello, is this Asya?"

"Yes, who is this?" By the Western accent, I was hoping it wasn't a fan who had gotten my phone number. I searched the room for Jai; he was playing peek-a-boo with the baby.

"This is Adam from Ladki Rights. We are the organization that saved your sister, Amla. She is going to call you to coordinate. We are all so glad to reunite you both—"

I dropped the phone. "Amla!" I screamed.

Jai ran over, his eyes wide. "She is okay, Asya; she is right here, Didi," he soothed me, holding up the baby.

I nodded and reached a shaking hand down to pick up the dropped phone.

"Hello?"

"Yes, okay, so she will be calling you from the US now, once we hang up."

"Yes, of course, thank you, thank you." In my mind, I thanked this Adam and thanked God over and over as he explained what had happened to Amla. The God that I had given up on, the magic that I wasn't sure of anymore, the voice inside of me that I questioned until each time I looked at the moon and knew we were watching the same one. I thanked him that, in the end, we had found our gifts, my poetry and her photography, to break free from all that held us down, past the darkest moments and back to each other. My sister.

When the phone rang, I snatched it up before the first ring had finished.

"Asya?"

EPILOGUE

TWO YEARS LATER

AMLA

We were celebrating our birthdays. Both our girls were running around; Jaya chased Seva, and then they started again when she caught her.

I smiled at how apt their names were for their personalities. Seva was just like Nani, with her giving heart and hugs that could melt the world, and Asya's daughter, Jaya, was just like our mummy, winning us over with her sweet songs.

It was Asya's idea to change their names when we finally found each other, to make it less confusing. We laughed at the stars when we told each other. What were the odds that we would both have daughters and decide to name them Amla and Asya? Back then, they were only babies, so it was easy.

Jai came back with the chocolate cake. "Didi, this is all I could find, and it was so costly!" Asya was always telling him not to worry about the expense, but he made sure to find the best one from the bakery that was not overpriced. "That hotel was charging double, and they did not even bake it fresh!" he told us with outrage.

My phone buzzed. I looked down to see Vishnu's name: I TRIED TO SKYPE, he texted. ARE YOU GIRLS ON? I WANT TO SING TOO!

I smiled and pictured him waiting by the phone in his pajamas.

Five more minutes. We just got the cake, I texted back.

We had decided it was best this way—a few months in India and a few months in New York at a time. That way Vishnu could work in New York, and I could finish school part-time and continue my work as head photographer with Ladki Rights, too. After giving birth, photography was what kept me going. It was how I found my sister.

"Cake time!"

Seva was screaming now, and I reached for my phone. "Okay, yes, one more minute until cake time! Let's call Puppa as we wait for Neela auntie to come up."

The sun was bright. We had to find a spot where he could see us on video. The view of Juhu Beach was marvelous from Asya's flat. Asya came over to me and said, "Remember when we looked up at this as girls?"

It's funny the way even sisters see things differently. At that time, I was so fixated on Guhan uncle that I hadn't even looked up at the buildings.

After Neela arrived, we all sang. Our chosen family. Jai was smiling, Neela clapping. Vishnu sang loudly from the screen.

I smiled at the photograph I held to give Asya. It was of our daughters, holding hands in their sleep, the way Asya and I did as girls. Asya had a poem she wanted to share with me.

Waves crashed
And train platforms took us
To distant places
Until
We followed
What our souls knew to do
Leading us right back
To where we always belonged

We both were wearing Nani's bangles as we exchanged our gifts. We had had them engraved on the inside with three words: For My Sister.

AUTHOR'S NOTE

I had not planned on writing this book. I generally write short stories. Many of these stories have been related to my experience in a first-generation immigrant family.

When I visited India as a young woman, I witnessed beautiful parts of the culture I had inherited from my ancestors—the introspective musings of Vedic knowledge, the rich and vibrant colors of holidays, the meaning behind everything. Every spice in our flavorful dishes had a healing purpose; every sound in a song had a vibrational meaning. When I returned to the US from these visits, I wanted to dance like the Bollywood stars, to wear saris like my mother, and to buy vegetables from street markets like my father did as a child.

Yet, I questioned what did not seem right—the adapted rituals that excluded the girl child, the customs that devalued her existence. The ways women were subordinate.

I longed to understand where the depth of this gender bias came from. So, in my college days, I explored gender issues in women's studies courses with Dr. Marsha J. Tyson Darling, professor of history and interdisciplinary studies who taught Women in International Development at Adelphi University, New York. Dr. Darling's guidance on my research on global femicide opened my eyes to the cultural practices that harm girls and women to preserve male honor. Is the second-class status and unequal treatment of being a girl inescapable?

I took this question with me everywhere. In graduate school at Tufts University, I focused grant research on exploring the impact of oral health on domestic violence victims. During my public health career, I spent volunteer days in Uganda with the Just Like My Child Foundation and the Girl Power Project, where I witnessed the ways empowering girls with education can empower a village.

When I started writing the story of Asya and Amla years ago, it became clear to me that it was more than just a short story. I wanted to share the voice of the underrepresented girls in India and echo the voice of trapped female voices everywhere. Doing the research that accompanied this fictional narrative, I came to see and feel the pain and anguish two girls experienced because they were abandoned and betrayed. I learned how connected and concerned I was about the plight of these two girls.

I imagined my own mother's childhood and what would have happened had her parents not valued education for her. Growing up, she had even said to me, "I love my India, but life is not fair for girls there. I am glad you are able to be who you are in the US." My Indian family has always supported and respected me, but what if they hadn't?

As a mother myself now, I worry for all girls. Girls throbbing with ideas and joy. Girls who love to read and play sports. Girls who are like my own little girl.

Having finished writing Asya and Amla's story, I reached out to Dr. Darling after almost two decades. As the professor who had made the biggest impact on my journey, she and I discussed the current state of girls and women around the world. And through our discussions, I learned the ways women used their voices to break down barriers. How without the power of voice, girls and women can be sold against their will . . . not only in India, but everywhere.

Dr. Darling: Your most important contribution in writing this novel is that you have given voice and visibility to the voiceless, who are often held morally responsible for their own degradation. Trafficked girls and women are marginalized and lack the agency to represent themselves, which if given an opportunity, they would address their own oppression in ways that make it clear to the rest of us that they have been betrayed and compromised. What is your hope for what your book will accomplish?

Puja: I hope that as people read this story, they will connect to the story of girls who could be anyone they know. I believe one of our greatest human qualities is our ability to feel and connect with one another. People have been using the power of sharing stories since ancient times. Stories bring people together and can inspire us. This story is meant to do exactly that as well as honor the girls who this happens to every day.

Dr. Darling: In your account of Amla and Asya's life, you present them as human and not "a thing." Why is that a centerpiece of your novel?

Puja: The sad reality is that in India and many parts of the world, women are denied and culturally deemed as second class. Why has prenatal sex determination been used so adversely against female fetuses that the Indian government was forced to ban it? Why are many Indian girls still denied education? I understood that their gender was a cyclical burden being passed down generation after generation. When a girl is born and regarded as a "curse," they are dehumanized and cast as "other." It was important for me to present Amla and Asya's thoughts and feelings and give them true agency throughout the novel. I wanted to use my own voice to carry theirs.

Dr. Darling: How would you respond to the concern that you are tearing into cultural practices?

Puja: Turning inward from the deep reverence for Eastern meditation I developed through the years of my yoga and meditation journey, I started to understand how important it was to see what is relevant to humanity, to shine a light on both the shadows and the light of my cultural heritage. It is easy to turn the other away when a conversation or topic gets difficult. I am grateful that after having gained more insight about a troublesome social issue, I am motivated by compassion to do something about it.

Dr. Darling: What about Karma and caste? How do you respond to the idea or belief that Amla and Asya are living out their Karma and no one should intervene?

Puja: No one deserves a lesser version of life. So often we think about Karma as a fixed destiny. However, when we act in accordance with our inner guides and connection to Nature and Source, we are in flow with the Universe. These tools, like looking to the stars or understanding our present actions, are simply there for us to learn from and to guide us to the best versions of ourselves. The misconception of a fixed version of evolution leads us away from our truest nature, which is compassion.

Even caste was created. The argument exists that it was further enforced and formalized as a systemic method of control and classification during British rule of India.[1] As something created, I believe it can change. Let's engage in transformation.

Dr. Darling: Obviously, you hope the story of Asya and Amla stirs thinking and a call to intervene in the trafficking of

1   Riser-Kositsky, Sasha (2009) "The Political Intensification of Caste: India Under the Raj," Penn History Review: Vol. 17 : Iss. 1 , Article 3.

girls and women around the world. What is your hope for interventions that sustain meaningful change?

Puja: The primary objective of my novel is awareness. With increased awareness, we can talk more. We can share with others who do not know the many stories of missing girls everywhere. My hope is that the reader will be inspired to learn more on this topic, and to act on behalf of the advocacy efforts for prevention and awareness on the trafficking of girls and women.

The following provides information on existing efforts to help eradicate human trafficking.

The International Labor Organization estimates that there are 40.3 million victims of human trafficking globally.[2] The United Nations reports that female victims continue to be the primary targets, and one in every three victims is a child.[3]

While I am not a trafficking expert, there are many organizations on the ground every day, working to end this modern-day slavery. If you are looking for ways to help this cause, here are just a few nonprofit organizations that I came across during this novel's research that inspired me:

1. Oasis, India: https://www.oasisindia.org/
2. Child Rights and You (CRY): https://www.cry.org/
3. Operation Underground Railroad (OUR): https://www.ourrescue.org/
4. Deliver Fund: https://deliverfund.org/

---

2   https://www.ilo.org/global/publications/books/WCMS_575479/lang--en/index.htm

3   https://www.unodc.org/unodc/en/human-trafficking/faqs.html

ACKNOWLEDGMENTS

My first novel. I am grateful for many people who have been on this book's journey with me. First, I acknowledge the brave girls and women who continue to share their true stories and also those who cannot. This is for all sisters. To you, the reader, I truly appreciate you for supporting my work. To all my meditation teachers from courses to books, without the gift of self-reflection, I would not have found my voice.

Thank you to Just Like My Child Foundation, Girl Power Project, and my friend Vivian Glyck. I am grateful for those months of overseas volunteer work that inspired me to write a story about girls whose voices are not heard. To our friend Lidia Domagalska for always supporting us. To Kids for Peace where I learned so much from the years I served as a board member. To Manav Sadhna whose mission I truly admire and love my visits to The Gandhi Ashram when in India. To Unity SME, my powerhouse friend Sapna Patel, for working together. For the nonprofit that guided me upon my research for this novel, Oasis India, thank you to Mangneo Lhungdim, Sulekha Thapa, and Vishwas Udgirkar for being so open during my many questions. Along with the organizations listed earlier, my hope is that others see the work you do for change.

Alicia Brav and Trish Martinez, co-chairs of San Diego Regional Advisory Council on Human Trafficking & Commercial Sexual Exploitation of Children (CSEC), Community subcommittee, thank you for your collaboration and dedication to the work you do. To Dr. Barbara Klein, thank you for your wisdom on twin psychology. Dr. Marsha J. Tyson Darling, it was the universe that brought us together; thank you for your wisdom and guidance from then to now.

To my publisher team at Koehler Books: John Koehler, thank you for taking a leap and believing in me. Miranda Dillon, I'll never forget how nervous I was at our first meeting and how good it felt to hear how you connected with my story. Hannah Woodlan, thank you for all the markup that went into the grueling process of editing for this to come out on the other side. Lauren Sheldon, thank you for the best book cover I could ask for.

Plus, thank you to my early editors, from my draft days of tweaking and encouragement with Amy Maranville to the later iterations of more editing to get it refined with Ronit Wagman. To our Deep Origins team, especially Omar Michael, thank you for not only your marketing expertise but your unique ability to truly organize my creative energy, i.e., make sense of poetic voice notes. Thank you to Akira Chan and Renee Airya Chan of Rare Media for the most perfect book trailer.

To the authors who helped me during the query process, all the questions I had as a first-time author and for those who spent time reviewing my novel to provide the notes of praise adorning this book, your words were like wind to my new author wings.

To my first beta readers, my extended family and OG friends from youth, for the years of stories and poems I shared, my girls Neha Desai and Nikki Chokshi for reading the early version that this novel once was. To my book club girls, thank you for knowing exactly what I needed to read when I came up for air during this book process. To my Chai Mommas for sharing my voice on social media and being there in friendship. And to my closest friends from all walks of life, for being my cheerleaders in true sisterhood.

To my late grandmother Lila, my nani, who passed away at this novel's inception. She is a reminder of the change women have seen in the near century she graced this earth with her courage, love, and faith. Her smile will always stay with me. For my late grandfather Krishna Dada, who made me fall in love with the art of storytelling. To my father-in-law, Pradyumna, and mother-in-law, Kalpana, your love and blessings have always felt so supportive. To my sister-in-law, Jigna Bhalla, for our many conversations on how we can make this a world that is worthy for our girls. To my encouraging parents, Jitendra and Devila, my real-life giving tree, who taught me to believe in miracles the minute they held me. Dad, there was nothing you wouldn't do for us, and Mom, there was nothing you couldn't handle. I am here because of your sacrifices. To my sister and brother, Mili and Anuj, this book is about the undying bond a sister can carry, and I owe every ounce of knowing that to the both of you. Thank you for your true-to-the-bone love. Mili, for reading this and reminding me that you have always been waiting. Anuj, for being my soundboard and keeping me going with your calm positivity.

To my husband, Amish, my forever soul mate, I am grateful for your everything, the hugs, kisses, prayers, love, guidance, and countless moments of support in making this dream come true and guiding me to trust that all my dreams can come true. To our dog Roxy, for the unconditional love in our home that every writer needs by her side. Lastly, thank you to my beloved children, Laila and Ayan. It was after I became a mother that I was able to rise into my truth and become an author. You both are the essence of my becoming.

GLOSSARY OF TERMS

Asana: Sanskrit, yoga or meditation body posture

Aa jao: Hindi, "Come in"

Ayurvedic: relating to Ayurveda, the ancient medicine system of India. In Sanskrit, *Ayur* means "life" and *Veda* means "knowledge or science"

Bahut accha: Hindi, "very good" or "nice"

Basant Panchami: kite festival in India to welcome spring

Benchod: Hindi, slang curse word, "sisterfucker"

Beti: Hindi, also Beta, endearing term for children, translates to "dear"

Bhabu: Hindi and Bengali, a term of respect for men, slang word for "pimp"

Bhai: Hindi, "brother"

Bharatanatyam: a major form of Indian classical dance

Biryani: an Indian dish of highly seasoned rice with either meat or vegetables

Chai: Hindi, short for masala chai, black tea made with milk and spices such as cinnamon, cardamom and ginger

Chaiwala: street seller of tea

Chakra: Sanskrit, "wheel" or "cycle"; energy centers, known as seven main chakras situated along the spine, from the base of your spine to the crown of your head

Chana masala: an Indian dish of spiced chickpeas in gravy

Chalo: Gujarati, "Let's go"

Dada: Hindi, father's father

Dadi: Hindi, father's mother

Dalit: in the traditional Indian caste system, a member of the lowest caste, known as untouchable

Dupatta: Hindi, a length of material worn as a scarf or head covering in India

Ghanta: Sanskrit, ritual bell used in Hindu religious practices

Ghee: Hindi, clarified butter

Gujarati: language of the state of Gujarat in India

Gundas: Hindi, "gangsters," usually a group of violent criminals

Hijra: Hindi, a person whose gender identity is neither male or female; transgender and generally a person assigned as male at birth but who expresses themselves as female in India

Holi: a joyous Hindu festival that welcomes spring, also known as the festival of colors; signifies good over evil

Jain: ancient Indian religion

Jalebi: a popular Indian sweet of maida flour deep fried in a circular or pretzel shape, then soaked in sugar syrup

Jharu: Hindi, a long-handled and fanned broom used to sweep the floor

Kesar pista kulfi: traditional Indian saffron and pistachio-flavored ice cream treat

Ladki: Hindi, "girl"

Lassi: Hindi, yogurt drink, flavors such as mango or salty

Lehenga: Hindi, Indian dress often consisting of an ankle-length skirt

Mahabharata: one of the major Sanskrit epics of ancient India, known as the longest poem ever written

Marathi: language predominantly spoken by Marathi people in the Indian state of Maharashtra

Masala: Hindi, any of a number of spice mixtures ground into a paste or powder for use in Indian cooking

Mausi: Hindi, also spelled *Masi*; mother's sister

Motee ladki: Hindi, "big woman"

Muladhara chakra: Sanskrit, root chakra at the base of the spine

Mummy: Hindi, informal term for "mother"

Naan: Hindi, leavened, oven-baked or tawa-fried flatbread eaten in India

Nana: Hindi, mother's father

Nani: Hindi, mother's mother

Paan: Hindi, an Indian after-dinner treat folded into a triangle or rolled that consists of a betel leaf filled with chopped betel (areca) nut, slaked lime, and other ingredients

Paneer tikka masala: Hindi, an Indian dish of marinated paneer cheese served in a spiced gravy

Panjabi: a native or inhabitant of the region of Punjab, India

Parsi: Parsis or Parsees are an ethnoreligious group of the Indian subcontinent whose ancestors migrated to India from Sassanid Iran to avoid persecution

Pashmina: a fine-quality shawl made from wool

Pav bhaji: a fast food Indian dish consisting of a thick vegetable curry served with a soft bread roll

Peepal: a tree native to India where every part of the tree has several medicinal benefits discovered in ancient times in the science of Ayurveda

Phena bhat: starchy rice gruel or porridge, popular Bengali dish known in Kolkata

Prana: Sanskrit, "breath," considered as a life-giving force

Prashansak: Hindi, "fan"

Pulao: Hindi, an Indian rice dish, cooked in seasoned broth and an array of spices, including coriander seeds, cumin, cardamom, cloves, and others

Puppa: Hindi, informal term for "father"

Roti: Hindi, a type of unleavened bread made from wheat flour

Saab/Sahib: a form of address or title placed after a man's name or designation, used as a mark of respect in some areas of India

Salwar kameez: Hindi, a long tunic worn over a pair of baggy trousers, usually worn by women in India and Pakistan

Sari: Hindi, a garment consisting of a length of cotton or silk elaborately draped around the body, traditionally worn by women in South Asia

Shabash: Hindi, an expression meaning "Well done"

Shakti: Sanskrit, female power

Sravana: the fifth month of the Hindu solar calendar and known for the arrival of south-west monsoons

Subzi: in Indian cuisine, a vegetable cooked in gravy

Surya namaskar: Sanskrit, a specific sequence of twelve yoga asana, otherwise known as a "sun salutation"

Thali: Hindi, "plate"

Theek hai: Hindi, "It's okay" or "That's fine"

Tiffin: Hindi, light meal, packed

Topi: Hindi, cap for head

Vaishya: the third of the four Hindu castes

Yaar: Hindi, slang for "buddy"

CPSIA information can be obtained
at www.ICGtesting.com
Printed in the USA
JSHW030919081222
34406JS00004B/23

9 781646 637966